Published by Acoustical Books, LLC

KenLozito.com

Cover design by Jeff Brown

IF YOU WOULD LIKE TO BE NOTIFIED WHEN MY NEXT BOOK IS RELEASED VISIT

WWW.KENLOZITO.COM

ISBN: 978-1-945223-48-8

IMPULSE

KEN LOZITO

ACOUSTICAL BOOKS LLC

PROLOGUE

AN EXCERPT from the colonial archives: The First Generation of the Colony:

The *Ark* program was Earth's most ambitious effort to establish an interstellar colony in a star system twenty-five light-years away. The *Ark* was comprised of one massive ship and over a hundred automated support ships. To survive the long journey, all colonists were put into stasis and were monitored by the *Ark's* computer systems.

Communications with Earth were maintained through the deep space buoy network, which bolstered data transmissions to the *Ark*. As the *Ark* traveled through interstellar space, auto-factories built comms buoys designed to send and receive data communications from Earth.

Unbeknown to the colonists, the *Ark* received a massive update to its computer systems which overrode the core mission parameters. This included a new destination much farther away along with protocols for the automated ships to continue to gather resources on the long journey. What started out as an eighty-five-year journey, took over two hundred years to complete. The colonists woke to a star system approximately sixty light-years from Earth.

Due to limitations of the *Ark's* computer systems, detailed data received from Earth was expunged, leaving the colonists with limited insight as to what happened. Communications were limited to the speed of light, so the colonists could expect to wait a hundred and twenty years for a response from Earth. However, the *Ark's* powerful sensors monitored Earth's star system throughout its long journey. Analysis of the data revealed that some kind of calamity had befallen the Earth and the entire solar system.

Fragmented data received from Earth referred to a virus outbreak that lead to a massive war between Earth and local colonies. The virus, known as the Vemus, altered human physiology and all mammalian life on Earth. The data received from Earth included references to a massive fleet of ships. Analysis of the deep space buoy network revealed that the buoys had gone offline sequentially, beginning with those closest to Earth. It was theorized that what had happened to Earth was now in route to the colony. It was later determined that the deep space buoy network was destroyed by the Vemus fleet.

Vemus Wars: Detailed references to the Vemus Wars can be found in the colonial archives under the *Nemesis* volumes.

Colonial Defense Force: Commonly referred to as CDF, is the colonial military established to protect the colony. There were many colonists involved with the creation of the CDF, but the most influential colonist regarding its origins is General Connor Gates.

New Earth: Three hundred thousand colonists were brought out of stasis and began exploring the planet that would ultimately be named New Earth. The first generation of colonists created a home on a planet teeming with life. There was also archeological evidence of an advanced civilization similar to humans. However, since the colonist hadn't found any intelligent species currently inhabiting the planet, it was widely believed that whoever had built the cities abandoned the planet, or had wiped themselves out through multiple global wars.

Post Vemus War exploration lead to the discovery that the intelligent species, now known as Ovarrow, had not left the planet, but had gone into stasis in underground bunkers found across the main continent. Detailed references to these discoveries can be found under the *We're Not Alone: Discovery* volumes in these archives.

Ovarrow stasis technology is inferior to those used by humans. This lead to severe illness and rapid aging experienced by some Ovarrow when brought out of stasis. Colonial scientists helped the Ovarrow overcome many of these issues, but the effects of inferior stasis technology still significantly impacts their species.

It is impossible to reference the Ovarrow without also referencing a species known as the Krake. The Krake are a technologically advanced civilization who discovered the use of gateway technology that allowed them to explore the multiverse. Through the use of Spacegates and Arch Gateways (On planets), the Krake were able to explore different versions of their star system across multiple universes. The Krake discovered multiple versions of 'New Earth' where Ovarrow had evolved to various states of technological advancement. However, the Krake were unable to find any other universe in which where their own civilization existed. This lead to a fundamental shift in the Krake society as they sought to understand why an inferior species like the Ovarrow thrived, yet their own species hadn't evolved at all. The Krake became a society obsessed with perfecting their predictive capabilities and its effects on all conflicts as they pertain to individuals, groups, and societies as a whole. The Krake studied and exploited Ovarrow across multiple universes, including the universe with New Earth.

Krake War: There is a significant portion of this archive dedicated to the Krake War. There have been multiple volumes written about the Krake War, but a detailed accounting of it is beyond the goal of this brief.

Multiverse Reference: The CDF conducted many operations into the multiverse to first learn about the Krake, but also to find allies. Analysis of Krake data repositories revealed that they had a limited understanding of the multiverse. For example, the Krake explored the multiverse for centuries and learned that there were limits to how many universes they had access to. Human physicists throughout time have theorized about the existence of infinite universes. However, since the Krake had successfully pierced the veil or bubble that separates universes, they concluded that their access to the multiverse was limited. Furthermore, over time the Krake were unable to access universes that they'd once visited. Like the Krake, colonial scientists do not understand why, but further study is required.

Post Krake War: Two dominant factions of Ovarrow were discovered through colonial exploration of New Earth, the Mekaal and the Konus.

The Mekaal were a faction that resided in stasis until colonial scientists brought them out. The computer systems that controlled their stasis pods had failed, leaving many to die while never coming out of stasis. The colonial government established a program to assist the Mekaal, and they remain allies of the colony. There are ongoing efforts to fully integrate the Mekaal into colonial society.

Konus - Easily the most dominant faction of Ovarrow on

New Earth. Their population had been estimated to over a million before the Krake Wars, but their population has decreased from war with the Krake and a conflict with the CDF. The Konus successfully came out of stasis decades before the colonists arrived on New Earth. The Konus fearing a Krake invasion, kept their presence a secret while they brought other Ovarrow out of stasis to become part of their society.

Through years of war and hardship, the Ovarrow of New Earth became a militaristic society that employed brutal governance tactics. The Mekaal, through their association with the colonists, abandoned the stricter societal practices choosing instead to embrace a more individualist approach similar to the laws of the colony.

The colony strives to maintain a peaceful coexistence with all Ovarrow factions on New Earth, but as the colony grows, so do some divisions that believe the colony should limit its interactions with any Ovarrow, whether they be the Mekaal or the Konus. There are factions among the Ovarrow who promote the idea that the colonists are invaders and have no right to live on the planet.

General Connor Gates, a founding member of the CDF, was instrumental in defeating the Vemus and the Krake, and has proven to be tough but fair in his dealings with Ovarrow. His actions throughout the colony's brief history are still studied by future officers in the Colonial Defense Force as well as various universities that study interspecies diplomacy.

1

"THIS DOESN'T LOOK GOOD," Sergeant Bravos muttered.

"Lieutenant Raines," Diaz said.

"Yes, Captain?"

"What is my rule about alarmists in my reserve company?"

"Put up or shut up, Captain."

"That's right," Diaz said. "The enemy is out there, waiting to lure us out."

Lightning flickered across the night sky, followed by the distant booming of a retreating thunderstorm.

Hiding in a thick tree high above the CDF reserves, Connor watched as Diaz shook his head at his troops. They wouldn't expect a CDF general to be doing stealth recon.

Connor wore a multipurpose protection suit, or MPS, in stealth mode, which allowed him to sneak past the defenses Diaz had deployed in the area. He didn't need to exert much strength to hold his position because the MPS took the burden off of him by locking into place. Even though it wasn't as versatile as a

Nexstar combat suit, the MPS was second to none when it came to stealth recon.

"New orders have just come in, Captain," Lieutenant Raines said. "We're to initiate rescue operations of Delta Platoon."

Several of the soldiers nearby swore.

"The Mekaal let themselves get captured again?" Diaz asked.

"Looks that way. They're carrying critical intel that requires retrieval," Raines answered.

"This is bullshit," Sergeant Bravos said. "This is the seventh time this week they've been captured. If they couldn't get it right the other times, why do they keep getting picked for retrieval missions, sir?"

"Doesn't matter, and knowing wouldn't change anything," Diaz said. "Mekaal soldiers are here to learn."

"I never want them guarding my back. It's no wonder the Krake nearly wiped them out," Bravos said.

"And if it wasn't for us, they would have. Right, Sergeant Bravos?" Diaz asked.

"Exactly, Captain. So, why are we on rescue duty?"

"I get it. It's been a long week, and I'm ready to get back to Sanctuary, too—eat some good food and sleep in my own bed with much better company than you animals. We all are. But since the Mekaal have stepped in it again, it'll be up to us to show them how it's done," Diaz said.

Connor decided it was time the complaining troops were taught a lesson and sent a signal to the rest of his squad hidden away among the trees. Twenty Mekaal soldiers in stealth MPSs dropped down, taking the reservists completely by surprise. Several CDF soldiers tried to bring their weapons up but were shot for their trouble. They sank to the ground as the practice shots commanded their combat suits to go into a wounded cycle.

Diaz spun around and found himself staring down the barrel of an AR-74.

"Looks like you could use someone to watch your back."

"Connor?" Diaz said in disbelief. "I mean… General Gates. I didn't think you left the mobile command center anymore."

Connor grinned. "I wanted to get some fresh air."

Diaz nodded and glanced at the soldiers who were with Connor.

"Mekaal commandos," Connor said.

The Mekaal were a race of beings known as Ovarrow, the indigenous species that had evolved on New Earth. They were bipedal, with a range of skin tones that encompassed brown, tan, and yellow. Their skin appeared pebbled like that of a reptile. Pointy protrusions stemmed from their shoulders and elbows. They had long arms and hands large enough to grip a man's head, and their severe brow lines stretched to the backs of their wedge-shaped heads. They were lean and strong, but they had a bit of a stoop that made their heads bob when they moved.

A nearby Mekaal strode over to them. The Ovarrow translators randomly assigned slightly modulated human accents to the speakers in order to convey more meaningful communication between the two species. For this particular exchange, the translator had assigned an Aussie accent.

"Captain, I'm First Fist Urret. We found some gaps in your defenses. Perhaps you could have benefited from a few Mekaal watching your backs this evening."

Diaz gave Urret a long look. "Perhaps you can go fu—" he stopped and looked at Connor. "What's going on here, General?"

Connor and Diaz had been friends for twenty-two years and were among the early risers when the *Ark* had arrived at New Earth. Although Diaz was no longer an active member of the Colonial Defense Force, he was still in the reserves, and he reverted back to standard military decorum when in the field. Wounded pride aside, Diaz was not a fan of any Ovarrow.

"I figured your soldiers were tired of sitting out here in the rain," Connor replied.

Diaz glanced at his men. "You've got that right. What do you need us to do?"

Connor smiled. "That's the man I know," he said and gestured for the other soldiers to gather around while a medic visited the "wounded soldiers" to reverse the mock injuries. "I'm not going to beat around the bush. You reacted to the news of Delta Platoon's capture exactly the way we expected you to."

Diaz grunted and bobbed his head to the side. "A ruse. They were just pretending to be incompetent the entire week. What for?"

"To get them into position. Major Harris believes he's in a good position to hold his location at the compound and ride out the clock. The games end, and he and his company win," Connor replied.

Diaz glanced at Urret. The Mekaal officer simply regarded him, and Diaz looked back at Connor. "Harris has Mekaal under his command?"

"That he does. There are mixed squads of CDF and Mekaal soldiers guarding the compound."

"So how do you propose we get inside?" Diaz asked.

"Orchestrated chaos."

"Isn't that cheating, General?"

"You're assuming I know the entire operation for these war games. I don't, but I've put enough of them together to notice the patterns, so I thought I'd introduce something new. We need to deploy. I'll give you your assignments on the way," Connor said.

A quiet muttering could be heard among the reservists as

word quickly spread that Connor was with them. No one would have been expecting the CDF general to take the field with such a small force, which amused Connor because that was exactly what he would expect someone like himself to do. He had a reputation for turning standard tactics on their proverbial heads.

Major Harris was a good officer and would use every means at his disposal to protect the compound. However, Connor was counting on a pattern of thinking he'd observed among the CDF in recent years. They'd survived two major wars since colonizing New Earth. Their enemies had been extremely powerful in their own ways, and both had brought overwhelming forces to the battlefield, but the CDF had managed to defeat them. In the eight years since the Krake had been defeated, leaving their homeworld in ruins, they hadn't returned. There was speculation that factions of Krake survivors would one day rise up, but the colonists weren't aware of any such activity.

After eight years of relative peace, Connor needed to keep the CDF ready to defend the colony should the need arise. But as the years had gone by, he'd noticed a certain amount of complacency settle into the CDF and the colony as a whole. He hadn't anticipated the challenge of maintaining a certain level of readiness without losing the skills they'd gained over the years. These mock battles were the closest they'd come to fighting a real battle, but Connor knew they couldn't replace the real thing. Nothing could replace the experience gained in combat, but there were no more unifying enemies to fight. This sometimes made him anxious, and the best way to keep a solid state of readiness was through training. These war games were an expansion of what regular CDF soldiers went through. Connor had included CDF reserves, Colonial Field Ops and Security, civilian volunteers, and even invited the Mekaal to participate. The number of civilian volunteers had also increased over the years, and Field Ops had taken the lead in organizing them into support roles. Most colonists understood the need to be ready for the unexpected. Fighting wars among their own homes had taught them that lesson, but eventually, those memories would fade. When they were gone altogether, it would be the CDF who must maintain vigilance against whatever threatened the colony.

Connor finished bringing Diaz up to speed.

"This is devious, even for you."

Connor shrugged a little. "You know the saying: If you're not cheating, then you're doing it wrong."

"You're the boss, sir," Diaz said and gave a sideways glance at the soldier walking next to them. "Something you want to ask, Lieutenant Raines?"

"Just looking forward to some payback, Captain," Raines replied.

Diaz nodded and looked at Connor. "We had to defend against Charlie Company at the beginning of the week. Supply-run duty."

"I heard. Do you think I chose this outfit by chance?" Connor asked.

Diaz grinned. "For someone who wasn't involved, you're awfully well informed, sir."

Connor leaned toward his friend. "It would be more fun if we had even fewer men."

"They already outnumber us five to one."

Connor sighed. "I know. Not much of a challenge."

Raines sputtered a surprised cough, and Diaz looked at him.

"General Gates loves to challenge his soldiers. I've had to deal with this since before there *was* a CDF," Diaz said and looked at Connor. "So, do we get any air support?"

"Now where's the fun in that?"

"Understood, General. Lieutenant Raines, we'll need a

couple of squads to disable their troop carriers—actually, no. Cancel that. Let's *use* their troop carriers," Diaz said.

Connor tilted his head to the side in an acknowledging nod.

"General, I still don't understand why you wanted Delta Platoon to get captured," Lieutenant Raines said.

"That's easy," Sergeant Bravos said.

Raines looked at Bravos, eyebrows raised.

"Go on, Sergeant," Connor urged.

"It gives us soldiers on the inside. They'll be disarmed, sure, but their weapons will be stored inside the compound. And it's not a permanent encampment, so the security won't be as tight as it would be somewhere else," Sergeant Bravos said.

"What's that give us?" Lieutenant Raines asked.

"Delta is both a diversionary and reserve force. It's easy to hide small, short-range systems' disruptor devices. You could put them on a timer for when help arrives. Their power signatures are hard to detect."

"Good work, Sergeant Bravos," Connor said.

"Assuming that Charlie Company disarmed Delta Platoon and brought their weapons back to the compound. They could just as easily have disposed of them," Diaz said.

Connor nodded. "It's a risk, but there are other ways to sneak tech inside a compound. We'll find out what made it through when we get closer."

The reservist company wasn't at full strength, but Connor knew they were all veterans. Some of them might be a little out of practice, but they'd had all week to sharpen old skills. He'd led a couple of smaller squads on purely stealth reconnaissance missions to observe all the different groups; however, this was the first direct engagement he'd be participating in. Diaz was right. He'd gotten tired of watching from the sidelines.

They split into three groups when they were within five

hundred meters of the compound, set up in an abandoned Ovarrow town that had been augmented with defensive barricades and towers. Recon drones patrolled the area and were monitored by the watch-standers on duty.

The forest covered most of their approach until they came to the outskirts of the town. Connor glanced at the time on his internal HUD. They had to give the other teams time to get into position. He could have used a couple of snipers, but there were none assigned to this group. Reserve companies were mostly comprised of former infantry, a few medics, and some cyber warfare specialists. The Mekaal soldiers were mainly a fighting force with similar skillsets. Connor had selected Urret because he'd shown a proclivity for sneaking around.

Connor activated the tactical comlink channel. "Deploy our decoys, Lieutenant Raines."

"Yes, General, deploying decoys."

Fist-sized communication drones flew into the area. They'd been deployed several kilometers away and flew close to the ground to avoid detection. Their flight patterns would mimic swarmer attack drones that would lead the compound's defense drones away.

The towers came alive with bright lights, bathing the surrounding area. Weapons fire flashed into the night, and Connor watched as the soldiers in the watchtowers began scrambling under the mock attack.

They crawled forward.

"Contact, they've detected us," Lieutenant Raines said. He was leading the second group.

"Engage and keep their attention," Diaz said.

Connor checked the comlink channel, looking for Urret's status update, but he hadn't received confirmation yet.

Urret and his two squads of Mekaal soldiers were heading toward the opposite side of the compound.

"They probably got caught. Harris is too good to fall for this," Diaz said.

"Too soon to tell."

"The Mekaal aren't cut out for this kind of engagement."

"You're wrong. They've had a lot more practice at it than we've had."

"Yeah, maybe before they spent two hundred years in faulty stasis pods hidden in underground bunkers," Diaz replied.

Connor looked at him. "Who's a grumpy bastard tonight?"

"Damn it, I know. I just don't trust them. The Ovarrow are your crusade, not mine."

Sirens blared from the compound as the CDF soldiers inside came to full battle readiness. Suddenly, the power generators went offline, and the compound was plunged into darkness.

That was Urett's signal. Connor and the other soldiers ran toward the compound, quickly closing the distance. They'd only have a dozen seconds before power was restored. The CDF soldiers began firing on them, and tracer rounds blazed a red path through the night. Connor and the others returned fire in controlled bursts as they continued toward the corner of an old building and took cover inside. The drones provided them with accurate mapping of the area. Although their drones were small and difficult to shoot down, Major Harris had deployed his own attack drones that would eventually take out the ones Connor was using.

The floodlights came back on, but only about half were working. Connor heard screaming under the din of the weapons fire. The doors to the compound burst open and then dislodged from the frames.

"How did you manage that?" Diaz asked.

"Delta Company was captured hours ago, long enough for key systems to be compromised," Connor replied.

"How did they miss it? It should have been detected."

"It was detected. Right now."

"It should have been detected before."

"Security systems only alert when an exploit protocol is detected. With the hacking devices hidden in the enemy weapons, it was only a matter of time before low-level systems communications were compromised."

Diaz nodded. "And the only thing it can do is throw out an alert right before the exploit protocol does what it wants."

"Now we'll see how Harris deals with the chaos inside a compound that's been compromised," Connor replied.

As it turned out, the CDF regulars gave a good accounting of themselves despite the mayhem Connor had set loose, but they'd lost control of the prisoners. Urret was able to free the Deltas, which caught the defenders in the middle of multiple attack forces. Clusters of soldiers had been able to regroup, but Connor had managed to pin down Major Harris, compromising the entire compound, and the surviving Mekaal had escaped with critical intel captured from the compound's computer systems.

The war games ended and full functionality was restored to the "slain" soldiers. Major Macovy Harris had the look of a man who'd just been knocked on his posterior. He blinked several times and then looked at Connor.

"Take a few moments if you need, Major Harris."

Harris sighed and shook his head. "You handed our asses to us, General. I never anticipated using the prisoners as a diversionary tactic, or that their equipment could compromise our systems like they did."

"What would you change?"

"There were serious gaps in our defenses. Protocols weren't

followed for the safe handling of enemy weapons. We were too reliant on recon drones. You exploited all our weaknesses. Death by a thousand cuts. I'd like time to do a proper evaluation and write up a proposal on how we could improve our chances."

"I'd expect nothing less from you. These games are meant to challenge us. Going through the motions isn't good enough to defend the colony," Connor said.

"Understood, General. There won't be a next time."

"Dismissed."

Harris turned to leave but stopped. "General, I just want to say that if I was going to get my ass kicked by anyone out here, I'm glad it was you."

Connor grinned. "Make sure you return the favor to anyone else you come across, in training or otherwise."

"Yes, General," Harris said and left the area.

Diaz had watched the exchange and shook his head once they were alone.

"Comments?" Connor asked.

"I guess I've had my ass handed to me by you so many times that it's not quite the surprise it is for other people." Diaz frowned and then chuckled. "You, Kasey, Samson… God, that guy was relentless. And Wil." He exhaled forcefully. "Reisman could run circles around the best of them."

Remembering deceased friends was something they didn't shy away from. "With them, you either learned fast or you gave up. Samson loved seeing what people were made of," Connor said.

"I gave him a run for his money a few times, but that man was a fighter."

"Still think we could have won without the Mekaal?"

Diaz compressed his lips. "The Mekaal can fight. They just can't be trusted."

"Geez, Juan, they're not going anywhere. We have to work with them."

"I know that, Connor. We'd just be better off without them."

That was it. Once Diaz made up his mind, there was very little Connor could do to change it. It wasn't worth belaboring the point.

"Let's get going, or Victoria will call out a search party for you. I promised her I'd bring you back without injury," Connor said.

Diaz made a show of checking his arms. "I'm a little bruised."

"I'm sure she'll take care of you."

"My shoulders are kinda tight. Do you think you can massage them for me?"

"I'll get right on that. In fact, why don't you wait here, and I'll send someone to carry you."

Diaz grinned, and they both headed toward the nearby troop carrier.

2

A FINAL ASSEMBLY was scheduled to celebrate the conclusion of the fourth annual multi-divisional war games. The CDF base at Sanctuary was hosting this year's event, which pushed the limits of the colonial city's capacity for accommodating visitors. No longer a frontier city, Sanctuary had grown enough in population to be on equal footing with the other colonial cities.

The war games had started out as a purely military exercise but had expanded in scope to include non-military personnel, as well as Mekaal soldiers and a cadre of civilian observers. Connor knew there'd been more than a few wagers placed on the outcomes of the engagements, but the stunning upset was the loss of the compound.

Reports of Connor's involvement in the field had quickly spread. Speeches were made and assessments given, along with feedback on tactics that could be improved, as well as the tactics that had been demonstrated to be most effective.

In the early afternoon, Connor sat in his office at the CDF. His workplace had come a long way from the secondary command center he'd had when he'd been reinstated into the CDF. There were a couple of couches and armchairs, along with a pair of display cases that exhibited various achievements he'd attained, but what drew his gaze were the photos that cycled through a designated display area between the two cases. These were the photos he'd accumulated throughout his time on New Earth. Having been a last-minute addition to the *Ark,* and an unknown one at that, he hadn't been able to bring anything with him. He had nothing from his life before the colony.

The photos cycled through a randomized order, and sometimes he wouldn't see an image repeat for months. Some of the images were of major events from the colony and others were more personal. He stood up and walked around the desk, peering at the grouping the computer was currently displaying. A recent family picture showed Lenora with her hands resting on Ethan's shoulders and their daughter Lauren standing in front of Connor. The portrait had been taken near the edge of a cliff, and the sun was setting behind them.

Diaz had been right. The kids had grown up fast. His eleven-year-old daughter was almost as tall as his wife. Her hair was long and full like his wife's and just as beautiful. God help any boys who looked in her direction over the next few years. He smiled.

The image dissolved and another appeared in its place, displaying the face of a young man staring back at him. He had short dark hair with dark brown eyes and a strong jawline like Connor's. The image had been taken from a two-hundred-year-old video message to Connor from the son he'd unwittingly left behind on Earth. The edges of his son's lips had lifted into a partial smile, but his gaze was as hard as steel, and his smile contained the bitter resolve of a person who knew they were about to die. Connor inhaled deeply and sighed. The sensors on the wall knew he was looking at these images and wouldn't change them until he looked away. He didn't. He'd added this image to his collection himself. He owed his firstborn son that much, at least. He would be remembered.

A faint pang squeezed the back of his throat, and though it didn't carry the anguish he'd once felt, it would never be completely gone. He'd made his peace with it. He had a new family, and the promise to himself he'd kept was not to repeat the mistakes he'd made in the past. He was a good father to his family, which was how he made up for the things he'd never had a chance to do in his old life. One day, Ethan and Lauren would learn about their long-lost half-brother. They'd soon notice the candle Lenora lit every year on his son's birthday. He and Lenora did it together, sharing a few moments of silence before going on with their days.

His office door chimed and Connor looked away from the photos. "Yeah," he said, his voice sounding a little strained.

"General Gates, sir, General Hayes is here to see you," Cadet Oliver Hayes said with a bit of amusement in his voice.

Connor snorted. "Tell your father I'm not taking any visitors at the moment. He'll have to come back tomorrow."

"Understood, General," Cadet Hayes replied.

The door to Connor's office opened and Nathan Hayes walked in. He was lean, with tawny-colored hair and a neatly trimmed beard. He carried a bottle of bourbon with him and held it up when he saw Connor.

"I see you steamrolled right over my man out there," Connor quipped.

Nathan laughed. "You'll have to forgive me, Connor. Oliver was mine before he ever was yours."

Oliver Hayes was sixteen years old and was assisting Connor's staff at base.

Nathan glanced at the wall behind Connor with a slight frown, and then his eyebrows raised.

"That's my son, Sean."

Nathan came to stand next to him. "I had no idea you had this. God, he looks so much like you," he said, looking at the photograph and then at Connor.

"Yeah," Connor replied. They both stared at the image for a few moments. Then Connor gestured toward the nearby couch. "I figured you'd be stopping by."

"Savanah and I will be having dinner with Oliver when he gets off duty, but I had to see you before returning to Sierra," Nathan said and sat down.

Connor grabbed a couple of glasses and Nathan poured them two fingers' worth of bourbon.

Nathan raised his glass and Connor did the same. "What should we drink to?"

Connor shrugged. "No one got seriously injured during the games."

Nathan grinned. "I'll drink to that."

They drained their glasses, and the amber liquid warmed Connor's chest.

"One of these days you're going to have to tell me how you make this," Connor said.

"If I ever take on any partners, you'll be the first to know," Nathan said as he poured them some more.

They sipped their drinks in companionable silence, and then Nathan set his glass down on the table. He leaned back and scratched his beard.

"Did you see the latest population counts?" Nathan asked.

"I did. Over one point four million people in this colony now."

"Quite an achievement in twenty-two years with a starting point of three hundred thousand souls."

"Tobias Quinn would have been pleased."

Nathan nodded. "Did you know he interviewed me for the Ark Program?"

"I'm not surprised. He liked to be personally involved in just about everything," Connor said and took another sip of bourbon, holding it in his mouth for a few seconds before swallowing. "You should tell me why you came before we lose a few hours reminiscing about absent friends."

Nathan grinned. "It would be time well spent, but I hear you. This visit isn't only for the purpose of a few drinks, but before I get to that, I heard a rumor of a certain clandestine operation on the last day of the games."

Connor chuckled. "For you, my friend, I can confirm it."

Nathan's eyes gleamed. "It *was* you. So that's why you didn't want to know about the deployments."

Connor recounted his role in the games.

"It's not a bad idea to have a few stealth units out there to observe and whatnot."

"It was fun. I haven't done anything like that for a while."

They were both quiet for a few moments.

"We need to talk about the future of the CDF," Nathan said.

"What about it?"

"The security council would like us to consider reducing our numbers and maybe shuffle some things around," Nathan replied.

"I can't say I'm surprised to hear it. The colonial charter for the CDF hasn't changed much since its inception."

"You and Tobias were quite thorough with it."

Connor chuckled. "We didn't write it from scratch. I worked with a few people, and we drew from the NA Alliance of Old

Earth for the framework. We adapted it to suit the colony, but we don't need to change it all that much to reduce our numbers."

Nathan nodded. "We've been operating on a wartime basis for a long time now, and that's going to change."

"The challenge comes with defining what a peacetime CDF should look like. What would our plans be if we suddenly needed to increase our numbers because of a threat like the Krake?"

"I'm reluctant to ask for input outside the CDF without having something in place to guide the conversation. I don't want to give any opportunist much to work with," Nathan said.

"I can get behind that," Connor agreed.

"Good," Nathan said. "We also need to consider continuity planning. Who steps up to take the reins if and when either of us retires?"

"Is there something you're not telling me?"

Nathan shook his head. "I'm not going anywhere anytime soon, but we need to start grooming leaders for the future. And besides, maybe we don't need to wear quite as many hats as we do to run the CDF."

"What's Savanah's take on this?" Connor asked.

"She doesn't want to run it."

Connor pursed his lips a little. "I'm surprised."

"So am I, but if my wife is anything, it's decisive. We have a couple of colonels who I could see stepping up into a brigadier general's role."

"We do a good job of cross-training in respective fields, but there aren't many who have competency in most of them."

Nathan regarded him for a few moments. "They can't all be Sean Quinn."

Connor dipped his head once. "He's held command posts in the infantry, spec ops, logistics and support, fleet engagement, intelligence, and research and development. But there's just one thing."

"He's young. He'll only be forty this year."

"Hell, I was just a few years older than he is when I got here," Connor replied.

Nathan considered it for a few moments. "He's a strong candidate, but I don't know if he'd be interested in the job. He's a lot like you. He'd rather be out in the field doing something than running things."

"True, but he could do it, and I know I'd sleep better if he were running things after our tenure is over." Connor frowned for a second and shook his head.

"What?"

"I just had a thought. It's stupid."

Nathan finished his bourbon and set his glass down. "If there's a time for stupid, it might as well be now."

"There was a running joke about certain types of people. They were to be stored in a glass container with a sign that reads, 'Break glass in times of war.' It just popped into my head."

"I see you've figured it out. That's the other thing the Security Council wanted me to discuss with you."

"Good luck with that."

Nathan grinned. "Sean is definitely among the top tier of candidates, but something else we should consider is whether the candidates need exposure to all facets of the CDF in order to be a general. Sean's exposure to them is rather unique because of his proximity to you."

Connor inhaled deeply and held his breath for a few moments. "I understand what you're saying, but we need to clearly define the qualifications so it'll be easy for the Security Council to approve the candidates."

"I'll put together some thoughts on it, and between the two of us, we can get it pushed through a review process."

Connor regarded Nathan for a few seconds. "Are you sure you're not going to retire?"

"No. Maybe someday. What would you do if you retired?"

"I already retired once. It didn't take," Connor replied.

The average human lifespan was two hundred years, so there was plenty of time to have multiple careers. He'd joined the military on his eighteenth birthday and never looked back. It had always been part of who he was. It wasn't until he got with Lenora that he'd even considered doing something else.

He shrugged. "I did enjoy exploring New Earth... Lenora's influence."

"Understood. Savanah and I were talking about it the other day. We could take on different roles in the CDF. That's almost like having multiple careers."

"Yeah, but you're right. We need to expand the leadership so the CDF remains in good hands."

"We'll need to consider our roles in the CDF, too, so we don't put ourselves out of a job," Nathan said.

"As long as we don't get swept to the side and forgotten."

Connor, along with a lot of other good people, had created the Colonial Defense Force, though he was often credited as the founder. But in any event, the force had done its job, and it seemed as if the colony was finally being allowed to catch its breath and embrace a future without war.

3

ISAAC HASTENED UP the broad steps to the Biological Research Building at the Colonial Research Institute's West Campus, and his shoulders brushed against the automatic doors with an embarrassing boom. He clenched his teeth, but the atrium was mostly clear. All remnants of the morning rush were gone but for the people loitering in the interior, waiting for later classes to begin.

Stomach quailing, he hastened across the atrium, heading toward the security checkpoint for the professional laboratory wing. When he reached the security desk, no one was sitting there, and he peered through the window. There was an unlocked holoscreen and a chair that was swiveled toward the rear door. Whoever had been on duty must have just stepped out.

Isaac leaned to the side, looking for someone in the offices beyond. "Hello," he said, tapping on the security glass. "I need to get through. Hello!"

Nothing. No reply. No stirring from beyond. Silence.

He rolled his eyes and pounded on the glass. "Hello! I'm running late, and I need to get through. Is anyone there?"

He glanced toward the turnstile, realizing he could just hop across. No one would know. He peered down the corridor that led to the elevators, gave one last furtive glance at the empty security desk, and sighed explosively. Moving purposefully toward the turnstile, he then quickly backstepped.

"No," he said, shoulders slumping a little. He was already late, and if he didn't follow the security protocols, he'd be in even more trouble.

He brought up his personal holoscreen and checked the schedule to see who he'd be assisting today. After briefly navigating the overly helpful interface, he swore.

"Uh oh, looks like someone's running late again," a voice taunted from behind him.

Isaac spun around and saw Curtis Palmer's smug grin, his wicked gaze gleefully soaking in Isaac's distress. A small group of students flanked him. Isaac ignored them and looked back at the security desk. He couldn't afford to screw this up.

"Late again. Townsend is not gonna like this," Curtis said and glanced at his friends. "Remember the last lab assistant? They didn't make it past three months."

"Come on, man. This isn't his fault. There's no one working the desk."

"Jordan, Jordan. There was someone here fifteen minutes ago," Curtis replied.

Jordan rolled her eyes and looked at Isaac. "Don't worry about it."

Isaac kept peering through the security glass, hoping someone would come so he could be checked in.

Dr. Gerry Townsend was as 'Type A' as they came. He

adhered to a rigid schedule and despised any and all deviations from it.

"Townsend isn't even in his lab yet," a girl said.

Isaac glanced at her but didn't know who she was. "I know. I'm supposed to be setting it up before he gets there."

Curtis laughed. "You guys don't get it. I heard Townsend chewing out Diaz here last week. He's already on probation. Isn't that right?"

Isaac glared at the turnstile and longingly lifted his gaze to the elevators beyond. The others kept talking, but Isaac ignored them. If he waited there, Townsend would get him kicked out of his internship. He couldn't lose his position, even if he had to bend the rules.

Isaac inhaled deeply through his nose, ran toward the turnstile, and hopped across as Curtis's shouts echoed behind him. He raced toward the door to the stairway and slammed it open, then ran up the steps, taking them three at a time.

Winded and thighs burning with exertion, he yanked open the door to the ninth floor and peered down the corridor. Seeing no one, he ran. His shoes squeaked on the polished floor with the rapid, desperate cadence of someone running for their life. He barely slowed down to turn into the adjacent corridor. A door opened ahead and a long counter-grav cart entered the hallway. Lab equipment was precariously stacked atop it. Isaac jerked to the side, but his foot got snagged on the edge of the cart and he tumbled to the floor. He rolled a few times and stopped.

The cart wobbled, but then miraculously seemed to become still.

"Isaac! Oh my gosh, are you okay?"

He looked up and saw Julian's blond-haired, slender form hastening toward him. Julian reached out a hand to help Isaac to his feet, but the lab equipment teetered to the side and began spilling to the floor. Julian rushed back toward the cart. Isaac joined him and began picking up stacks of storage kits.

"Thanks," Julian said.

"The least I can do." Isaac helped him restack the cart.

Julian snickered. "Careful or you'll use your word allotment for the day."

Isaac frowned. "Huh?"

"You're normally pretty quiet. Go on, I got this. You look like you've got someplace you've gotta be."

Isaac gave him a quick nod but slowed his pace down the corridor. He didn't need to cause any more accidents.

He made it to the genetics lab and looked through the window at the dimly lit interior. Could Townsend be running late? Nope. He heard the geneticist's voice echoing from farther down the corridor. He was close. He must have gotten called into a colleague's office on his way to the lab.

Isaac entered his security access code and the door to the lab unlocked. The automatic lighting came on as he walked inside, and he quickly grabbed one of the lab coats from a peg and slipped on a pair of gloves. Heading straight for cold storage, he entered the retrieval code for Dr. Townsend's scheduled experiments for the day.

Hearing Townsend's voice from just beyond the door, Isaac hurriedly brought up the lab stations' computer systems, but he wouldn't have time to get the kits deployed to them.

The door opened and Dr. Townsend walked in.

"Come in, Ella. This is where you'll be working today," Townsend said.

He took a few steps into the room and stopped.

Isaac looked up. "Good morning, Dr. Townsend."

Townsend's critical gaze swept the area, and Isaac imagined

him running up a tally of everything that was wrong with the day to that point. Right at the top of the list was a lab that wasn't properly prepped for the day's work.

Someone walked in behind him. "This is quite the lab, Dr. Townsend," she said, and the geneticist looked at her and smiled pleasantly.

"Oh, I didn't know someone was already in here. Hello, I'm Mariella Kingston."

He nodded a little. "Isaac Diaz."

Townsend arched an eyebrow. "Looks like you're running a bit behind."

"Yes, sir. I'm sorry about that."

Townsend's eyes furrowed with consternation.

"I can help finish the prep here. Drs. Rostova and Solomon will be here shortly," Mariella said.

She looked a year or two older than he was, and her eyes gleamed with competency, but Isaac tried not to let his gaze linger for long. She had long, dark hair and her skin was a medium olive tone that drew his gaze to her high cheekbones. She was beautiful, and it was enough to send out all the trouble signals in his brain. He needed to focus and stay on task.

"I appreciate that, Ella. I'm afraid the interns rotate through here every so often, and it can disrupt the workflow from time to time," Dr. Townsend said.

A comlink chimed from the nearby wallscreen and Townsend walked over.

"Yes," Townsend said.

A face appeared on the wallscreen. Isaac's shoulders tightened as he recognized the security uniform of the man on the screen.

"Dr. Townsend, this is Marc from security. I believe one of your interns failed to follow the security check-in protocol for entering the research wing."

Townsend's eyes slid toward Isaac and narrowed.

Isaac's shoulders slumped a little and he set down the sample tray he'd been carrying. "I'm sorry, Dr. Townsend. I was running a little late this morning."

"Again?" Townsend said. "You were running late again?"

"I was, but there wasn't anyone at the security desk, and I had to get up here to prep the lab before you got here."

Townsend held up his hand and turned toward the wallscreen. "Marc, he's here. I'm sorry about this. It won't happen again."

"Thank you, Dr. Townsend. We had a short birthday celebration this morning, and that's why the desk was unattended for a few minutes. I'll go ahead and note this in the log," Marc replied.

"Perfectly understandable. I appreciate you bringing this to my attention. I'll take care of it from here," Townsend replied. The wallscreen went off and he turned his disapproving gaze toward Isaac. Biting his lower lip, he looked at Ella. "Ms. Kingston, would you excuse us for a few minutes? Perhaps you can check with Dr. Rostova."

Mariella set the sample tray down on the counter. "Of course."

Twin almond-colored eyes glanced toward Isaac, and she gave a sympathetic smile as she walked past him. He caught the sweet scent of honeysuckle with a little bit of jasmine. It was pleasant and reminded him of warm summer nights. Isaac resisted the urge to watch her leave, but he did inhale a little deeper.

The door hissed shut, and Dr. Townsend sighed heavily.

This is it. He's going to kick me out of the internship, ending the terms of my probation with Field Ops and Security.

"Isaac," Townsend began.

"Sir, I apologize for being late. It won't happen again. Please don't..."

Townsend pressed his lips together, forming a grim line. "This internship just isn't working out."

"Please don't kick me out. I need this," Isaac said.

Townsend regarded him for a few moments. "It's not the end of the world, Mr. Diaz. There will be other opportunities for you out there—opportunities that don't require adherence to a strict schedule and security protocols."

Isaac shook his head. "I need to finish this."

"I'm afraid it's quite impossible—" Townsend said and stopped as a chair squeaked from one of the offices across the lab.

Isaac looked over at the office and frowned. He hadn't known anyone was here.

A man walked out of the office, stretching his arms overhead and yawning. "Come on, Gerry. Give the kid a break. He was late. It's not like he set the lab on fire."

Townsend's lips curled as if he'd smelt something foul. "Mr. Franklin," he said in sharp, clipped tones.

The man had broad shoulders and dark, rumpled hair. His clothes looked as if he'd slept in them. "*Agent* Franklin."

"Agent Franklin," Townsend replied dryly.

Agent Franklin strode over to them and extended his hand toward Isaac. "Hunter Franklin."

Isaac shook his hand. "Isaac Diaz."

"Nice to meet you, Isaac," he said and looked at Townsend. "Good, strong handshake. He's a good kid. I hate that limp handshake crap some people use. Don't you?" Hunter said and looked at Isaac.

Isaac nodded once.

Townsend set his tablet computer down on the counter and crossed his arms. "Why are you sleeping in my office?"

Hunter shrugged. "I got here a few hours early and thought I'd take a nap."

"Don't you have anywhere else to stay? I'm sure Katarina would welcome the company. Her office even has a couch."

Hunter snorted. "Normally I would, but... I heard this was where all the action was." He glanced at Isaac. "You know what I'm talking about. This is the genetics lab with the power of creation right at your fingertips. Am I right, kid?"

Isaac didn't know what to say. He was about to get fired from the internship.

Hunter looked at Townsend accusingly. "Look what you did."

Townsend's gaze slid toward Isaac as if he'd just remembered he was still there.

Isaac backed toward the door. "I'll just go. It's fine."

Hunter shook his head. "No, it's not. Gerry, you don't have to be so hard on the interns who work here. You're developing a bad reputation because you go through so many."

"Indeed," Townsend replied. "But the ones that make it through are known for their excellence. I've given Mr. Diaz the same opportunities as everyone else who's walked through those doors. The same number of chances. Just like when you came through here."

"Rigid to a fault."

The two men regarded each other, and Isaac felt as if he could crawl under a rock or slink away.

"It's fine," Isaac said, retreating toward the door.

Hunter frowned. "Do you always give up so easily, kid? Didn't sound like you were giving up before."

"Perhaps it's a sense of decorum," Townsend said. "Mr. Diaz is taking responsibility for his actions. Not everyone gets what they want."

"Give me a break," Hunter replied. "Sometimes, being fair is more important than being right."

"Do you have any more pearls of wisdom from the CIB?" Townsend asked.

Isaac's gaze darted toward Hunter Franklin. When Townsend had referred to him as Agent Franklin, Isaac assumed he'd meant an agent with Field Ops and Security. He'd heard of the Colonial Intelligence Bureau before, but this was the first time he'd ever seen one of their agents.

The door chimed softly before hissing open and Isaac turned to see Mariella looking at him, her dark eyebrows raised in surprise. A group of people trailed behind her, and Isaac quickly stepped out of the way.

"Katarina! Maxwell! So glad you could join us," Agent Franklin said.

Dr. Katarina Rostova had sky-blue eyes and long blonde hair that was tied back. Isaac had seen her before but had never heard anyone refer to her by her first name. The other doctor, Maxwell Solomon, was a biomedical engineer. Isaac had only seen him a handful of times before. The four professionals began to greet each other, and Isaac was happy to have the attention off him.

Smiling at him, Mariella gestured for him to join her. "Why don't you help me finish setting up?"

"I don't know if I should. He was about to kick me out of the program."

She nodded. "I know, but did he actually do it yet?"

Isaac thought about it for a moment and shook his head. It had certainly been implied, but he hadn't actually said the words.

"Well then, it's a good time to make yourself useful," she said. "I prefer Ella, by the way."

They quickly set about preparing the lab workstations. Isaac avoided eye contact with Townsend, figuring that perhaps he could slip under the radar and continue with his internship. The three professors and CIB agent ignored them for the most part.

The door chimed again and Julian pushed a grav cart into the lab. Isaac helped him guide it to the storage area in the back of the lab where they transferred the biological samples into cold storage. Isaac began categorizing the samples into alphabetical order. The cold didn't bother him much and he liked the quiet. It took him about twenty minutes to check the new samples into the laboratory inventory system.

When he walked out of the storage area, he saw that the others had all sat down and Agent Franklin was speaking to them. More people had joined them while Isaac was away. Curtis glanced at him and smirked.

Agent Franklin noticed and looked over at Isaac. "Good, you're back. Why don't you join us, Isaac?"

Isaac walked over, not making eye contact with anyone. It felt as if everyone were staring at him, and he didn't need the attention. He headed for the rear of the group but didn't sit, preferring to stand.

"All right," Agent Franklin continued. "It's important to remember that the proposal is just for a few months and on a voluntary basis only."

"But it could be extended," Dr. Rostova said.

"The project could ask it of you, or you could elect to stay," Agent Franklin said.

Dr. Solomon leaned forward. "Why all the secrecy?"

"It's likely something the Mekaal Council hasn't approved for public knowledge yet," Townsend replied.

Dr. Solomon glanced at the others in alarm.

"It's not classified here," Agent Franklin said and looked at the other interns and students, "but I expect a little discretion from everyone."

"What they're asking for is almost unethical," Dr. Rostova said.

"Why, Kat? Infertility is an ongoing problem with the Ovarrow," Agent Franklin replied.

"What Deasira is proposing doesn't just affect infertility in females. They want us to help them alter their physiology, which would not only increase their fertility rates but the number of pregnancies they can have. This can lead to changes in their hormonal balance, which will affect their behavior," Dr. Rostova said.

Townsend nodded. "I agree. I don't know if they realize the implications of what they're asking us to help them with."

"It's really simple. They want to have more babies. The Ovarrow population suffered catastrophic losses in their war with the Krake, and two hundred years of faulty stasis technology has led to further decline. We helped them with the rapid aging issue they had when they came out of stasis. Why not help them with this?" Agent Franklin said.

"What's the CIB's role here?" Townsend asked.

"Officially, none. We need to keep this between the scientists, but we have a presence at the embassy in Shetrian. The Mekaal host a number of cross-cultural studies through our embassy in their city. However, unofficially, we observe key projects that may affect wide-sweeping change to the Mekaal."

Dr. Rostova tilted her head to the side and regarded Agent Franklin. "Are you assigned to the project?"

Agent Franklin smiled. "I am."

"That might be a problem," she said frostily.

"Not for me, it's not," Agent Franklin said. "Look, we're all professionals here. This is important work."

"Agent Franklin is right," Townsend said. "They're asking us for advice and perhaps some guidance. It's important to note that they're not asking us for our permission."

Dr. Rostova stood up and took a few steps, her hands resting on her slender waistline. After a minute, she turned toward the others. "There are moral implications they need to consider. This will affect them more than they think it will."

Agent Franklin nodded. "That's why I requested that you be on the team, Kat."

"Is that the only reason, Hunter?"

Isaac watched the two look at each other for a few moments.

"It's the only reason I'll discuss here, but if you'd like to talk about it over dinner tonight, I can see if my schedule is clear."

Dr. Rostova rolled her eyes. "My nights with you are over. As long as you can accept that, we'll be fine."

Agent Franklin chuckled. "Ouch. Loud and clear. But I just want to confirm your participation."

Dr. Rostova thought about it for a few moments and glanced at the others. "I will go and try to talk them out of this. There has to be a better way to achieve what they want."

"No one is going to script what you're allowed to say. Make your objections if you have them, but be respectful."

Dr. Solomon nodded. "He's right. We should have seen this coming."

"Why?" Townsend asked.

"The Mekaal are well aware of how our population has grown since the *Ark* arrived on New Earth," Dr. Solomon replied.

"What about the Konus? Will they be part of this?" Dr. Rostova asked.

"To the best of my knowledge, the Konus have no knowledge of Deasira's proposal," Agent Franklin said. He pursed his lips for a few moments. "It's not surprising, really. However, it's a safe assumption that the Konus struggle with the same issues regarding infertility."

The others remained quiet, and Isaac wondered why the students and interns were still in the lab. This meeting didn't involve them.

"Which brings me to the other half of this project," Agent Franklin said. "It comes with a valuable learning opportunity for the students and interns here. Just to reiterate what we're asking —it's a six-month work-study at the colonial embassy in Shetrian, home of the Mekaal. Upon successful completion of the project, you'll have recommendations that will help you pursue any academic program you might wish."

Ella raised her hand and Agent Franklin inclined his chin once. "I'm interested in the medical program at Sierra."

"I hear it's competitive," Agent Franklin replied.

"It is, but will it be dangerous for us to live in the Mekaal city?" Ella asked.

"Not really. The Mekaal are civilized for the most part. We have CDF soldiers assigned to the embassy, and most fieldwork in the area will come with a protective detail. They're our allies, and one day they might even become colonial citizens."

Townsend cleared his throat. "I doubt the Mekaal appreciate armed soldiers roaming around their city."

"That's not how it is. It's small arms, and as I said before, the CIB maintains a presence there. More than likely, it'll be someone like me there who's observing."

"How many assistants can we bring?" Dr. Solomon asked.

"Laboratory space is limited, but I'd say one or two per professor wouldn't be unreasonable."

Isaac glanced at Townsend. The geneticist regarded him for a few moments but didn't give any indication whether he'd allow Isaac to participate.

Agent Franklin went around the room, speaking to the various interns in attendance. About half of them declined. Agent Franklin seemed unperturbed by this.

"Mr. Diaz, we have yet to hear from you," Agent Franklin said.

"We've already settled this issue," Townsend said.

Isaac's shoulders tightened. That was it. His internship was over.

Agent Franklin's gaze narrowed toward the professor in annoyance. Then he looked at Isaac and rapped his knuckles on the tabletop. "Opportunity has knocked, Mr. Diaz."

Isaac glanced at the others. His gaze lingered on Ella, who smiled and nodded. Curtis Palmer shook his head. The other two simply waited for his answer. Palmer looked as if he were about to say something.

"I'd like to go," Isaac finally said.

"Just to be clear," Townsend said, "you're no longer my intern here."

"Yes. Yes, Gerry, we get it. You're a major hard-ass. What about you, Maxwell? Could you use another assistant?" Agent Franklin asked.

Dr. Solomon frowned and looked at Isaac for a second.

"What about you, Kat? I know you've commented on being shorthanded in the past," Agent Franklin said.

Dr. Rostova pressed her lips together, and Agent Franklin arched an eyebrow. "Come on."

Dr. Rostova nodded. "Yes, I think I can make use of Mr…" she looked at Isaac.

"Diaz, ma'am, Isaac Diaz."

Agent Franklin smiled. "Excellent. It's settled then. We'll be leaving in just a few days. There will be clearance checks, as well as some other things. Please inform your families …"

The rest of whatever Agent Franklin was saying seemed to slip away from Isaac with the startling realization that he'd just volunteered for something he wasn't sure he was qualified to do. But even more daunting was that he'd have to tell his parents. He tried to imagine what their reactions would be and didn't like it. He glanced at Ella, who was speaking with Dr. Rostova.

Curtis walked over to Isaac and put his hand on Isaac's shoulder. "Not a smart move there, buddy."

Isaac glared at him, and Curtis grinned as he left the lab. Isaac glanced at Agent Franklin, who smiled and jutted his chin toward the door. Isaac took the hint and left the lab.

4

ISAAC'S HEAD WAS SPINNING, and his eyebrows pushed forward as he tried to piece together what had happened. He'd been fired from his internship for Dr. Townsend, but Dr. Rostova had taken pity on him. He stopped walking and inhaled deeply. After a moment, he moved toward a large window where he leaned on the sill and peered outside. People were walking the paved paths across campus, weaving among the several decorative fountains placed along the way. The day was clear and bright, and he raised his eyes to look across the campus and the city beyond. Sanctuary was all he'd ever known. He'd visited the other colonial cities, of course, but not for very long.

He heard someone walking toward him and saw Dr. Rostova looking pointedly at him. She gestured for him to come to her. Had she already changed her mind?

"Mr. Diaz, do you have a few minutes to talk?"

Isaac nodded. "Yes, of course. Please call me Isaac."

Dr. Rostova led him toward her office where she gestured

with one slender arm toward a chair near her desk. "Please sit, Isaac."

After circling around her desk to sit on the other side, she activated her holoscreen and then looked at him. Pale blue eyes stood out from her tanned skin. Isaac had no idea what her age was, but she must be an authority in her academic field to hold a posting here.

"Do you know Agent Franklin?" she asked.

Isaac shook his head. "I just met him this morning. He was napping in Dr. Townsend's office."

The edges of her lips lifted, and her eyes gleamed in amusement. "I see."

"He put you on the spot, and I'll understand if you've changed your mind," Isaac said. "It's not a problem, is what I'm trying to say," he added hastily.

Dr. Rostova's eyebrows raised. "He put us both on the spot, but he was also right in so far as I'm concerned. I do have an open slot to fill, but first, I'd like to know what happened with you and Dr. Townsend."

Isaac told her. He recognized that the job wasn't his yet, and she was giving him an opportunity to claim the opening. His recounting didn't take long as he edited the facts to include only what had happened on that day.

"I see," she said. "I'm not able to see the details for your internship, so I have no idea what your qualifications are."

"Dr. Townsend had me doing mostly lab prep work, cataloging new samples, and cleanup. General admin-type duties."

Dr. Rostova leaned forward, rested her elbows on the desk, and steepled her fingers. Isaac shifted in his seat a little. The fact that she was a beautiful woman wasn't lost on him. "Isaac," she said, "if this arrangement is going to work between us, then you need to be completely honest with me."

"Understood, ma'am."

She tapped the holo-interface and a duplicate screen appeared in front of him. Isaac peered at his own record in the Colonial Research Institute's computer systems. There was an orange button highlighted to indicate there were special notes regarding his current status.

Isaac sagged a little. "Okay," he said. "My internship status is tied to an incident with Field Ops and Security. If I lose my current status, I'll have to report this back to the city and it will affect the terms of my probation."

Dr. Rostova leaned back in her chair with a thoughtful frown. He knew she wanted to know what trouble he'd gotten into that landed him in this situation. He didn't want to talk about it but couldn't see a way to avoid it.

"I had an aircar accident and there were some injuries. Some of them were pretty bad," Isaac said softly.

Painful, intense memories spasmed to the forefront of his mind—images he wished he could forget, along with all the pain he'd caused.

"I appreciate you telling me. I can see that it's not easy for you to talk about," Dr. Rostova said.

Isaac lifted his gaze to meet hers. She wasn't looking at him with the prejudice he'd come to expect once people learned of his past.

"What are you hoping to get out of this?" she asked.

Isaac gave her a long look. "I don't want to be held in a colonial detention center. The accident occurred before my eighteenth birthday. This internship was supposed to help me choose a career path."

"And you chose genetics?"

"It was the only one available in the life sciences department."

Dr. Rostova grinned. "Okay, so at least we're not completely off the mark here."

"I don't know what I want to do. I only know what I need to do right now, and I don't know if that's good enough for you to bring me along on this project. I promise that if you do, I'll work hard every day to be an asset and not a hindrance to you. I might not have the same qualifications as the other candidates that you're probably used to working with, but please give me a chance. I'm a quick learner and I won't let you down."

When Dr. Rostova smiled, she almost looked like a different person. One moment she could appear cold and reserved, but the next, she appeared genuinely friendly. "I believe you, Isaac. That's the only reason I'm willing to give you a chance. Welcome to the team."

Isaac smiled. "Thank you. Thank you so much. Is there anything you need me to do now? Is there some way I can help you with anything?"

"No, thank you, but that's very kind. We're already into the afternoon. Tomorrow morning, you and Curtis will get the field lab equipment together and ready for shipment," she said.

Isaac nodded and then frowned. "I'm sorry, did you say Curtis?"

Dr. Rostova nodded. "That's correct, Curtis Palmer. You'll be working together. I thought I saw you two speaking and assumed you knew each other."

Isaac felt a scowl start to form but smiled instead. "Yes, we know each other."

"Good, I'll send updates to your e-mailbox here. It'll have a packing list and other information. I expect we'll be leaving the day after tomorrow."

That was sooner than he expected, but it would have to be fine. He tried not to think about working with Curtis for the next six months.

"Do you mind if I ask you another question before I leave?" he asked.

Dr. Rostova glanced at her holoscreen, and Isaac heard several audible chimes. "Sure, but you'll need to be quick. These are only the calm before the storm of messages I'm about to receive."

"Oh, there's a privacy setting that'll disable the notifications for a while."

Dr. Rostova blinked several times, and he felt like he'd said the wrong thing. She didn't avoid work, and he was trying to convince her that he would work hard for her. "Never mind. I don't know why I said that. What I wanted to ask you was why you had such strong objections to what the Mekaal are proposing?"

Several more notifications chimed, and she pursed her lips. "Not exactly a small question," she said, regarding him. "We can talk about it while we're traveling. It's a bit of a hot topic right now, and I just don't have the time to discuss it."

Isaac nodded quickly. "I understand. I'll get out of your hair. If you need me for anything, just let me know. Even if it's later today or this evening. Middle of the night. Sunrise. Anything."

She smiled. "I like the enthusiasm, Isaac. If you don't hear from me later today, I'll see you here bright and early tomorrow morning," Dr. Rostova said.

She turned her attention to her holoscreen.

Isaac walked out of the office. Taking a deep breath and blowing it out with a smile, he pumped his fist into the air. He heard people talking from farther down the corridor and glanced to see if anyone was watching him. Agent Franklin stood outside

Townsend's lab with a couple of people. He raised his chin and touched two fingers to the side of his head in acknowledgment.

Isaac waved and then headed toward the elevators. As he entered and selected the ground floor, his thoughts turned toward informing his family. He could almost imagine their reactions. He was a middle child, with two older brothers and three younger sisters. Would they even notice that he was gone? His father had tried to recruit him to work in the family restaurant, but that wasn't what Isaac wanted. He'd spent plenty of time working there while growing up, but the Salty Soldier wasn't for him. Endless cleanup, meal prep, or cleaning the coffee makers came with the added bonus of watching his father swap stories with the CDF soldiers who frequented the place. He wanted something different. The question of what he wanted had come up often, especially as he'd gotten older, and Isaac didn't know the answer. He only knew that there were things he *wasn't* interested in, and that included the family business.

ISAAC USED the public tram system to travel back home and spent the time preparing what he was going to say to his parents. He was under no illusions that they'd like what he was going to do, but they were his parents and they deserved to hear it from him in person. They were probably at the Salty Soldier, but he didn't want to show up if they weren't there. It was Tuesday. His mother would be home in the afternoon. He could tell her first before approaching his father.

Sanctuary had an elevated train that made it easy to travel the entire city. There were offshoots for tram systems that had expanded the city's interior. Sanctuary was always expanding, and

Isaac had become quite familiar with public transit since he was no longer allowed to operate an aircar.

The tram reached his stop and he got out. The walk home passed by in a blur of half-formed thoughts. His neighborhood was still mostly forested, but there were other houses that had been built in the area. He'd seen pictures of the basic HAB units the early colonists had used and was glad he'd never had to live in one of those.

As he approached the property, he saw several aircars taking up all the designated landing pads, along with one N-class rover that he recognized immediately. Connor must be visiting. It looked like he'd have an audience when he told his parents that he was going to live in Shetrian for the next six months.

Gritting his teeth, he walked determinedly toward the front door and entered his home. He walked through the entranceway into a grand, open kitchen. Beyond was a wall of windows to the outside courtyard. There were a dozen people outside, lounging and looking to be having a good time.

His mother spotted him through the window and waved. She wore a concerned frown.

Isaac walked to the nearly transparent door that slid to the side, allowing him to pass.

"Is something wrong? You're home so early," his mother said.

"We finished up sooner than I thought. What's all this?" he asked, inclining his chin.

"This is just an after-war-game get-together that I convinced your father to have here instead of at the restaurant. You know how he gets. If he's there, he'll start working instead of relaxing," she replied.

Isaac scanned the crowd but didn't see his father anywhere.

"Are you sure there's nothing wrong? Is there something on your mind?" she asked.

"I need to talk to you and Dad about my internship."

His mother frowned and was about to say something when his father entered the room.

"Isaac, give me a hand with this, will ya?" his father said.

He was carrying a cooler of beer, and Isaac grabbed the handle on one side.

"We'll set it over here."

They walked through the throng of people, carrying the cooler off to the side and out of the way.

Connor joined them, helping them lower the cooler to the ground. "How much of this stuff do you keep here?"

His father grinned. "I have a small brewery in one of the sheds out back. I've been practicing with a couple of recipes. Going to add a few of them to the menu."

Connor smiled at Isaac. "Hey, Isaac, how you doing?"

"I'm fine. How were the games?"

"They were fun. Next time you should join the civilians. Might be fun."

His father grinned and took a swallow of his beer. "You've got the wrong one for that. Isaac hates that stuff. You should get Tomasz next time. He should be finished with SAR training by then."

Isaac looked away, clenching his teeth a little. Slighted already. That hadn't taken long.

"I'm sure he'd do just fine," Connor said.

Isaac smiled a little in response.

His father looked at him and frowned. "You're home early today. What happened?"

Simple enough question, but it sent spikes of irritation along his scalp. His mother joined them, grabbing a beer from the cooler and opening it.

"I need to tell you both something. It's about my internship," Isaac said.

His father's gaze hardened. "You didn't get kicked out, did you?"

Isaac shook his head. They always seemed to expect him to fail. "No, I didn't get kicked out. There's a big project that became available at the Research Institute and I volunteered to participate. I'm going away for a while—six months. It's for a field assignment."

His mother's eyes widened. "Six months! Where is it?"

Isaac licked his lips and swallowed. "It's in Shetrian. At our embassy there."

Both his parents frowned at him, and his father's mouth hung open a little. "What? Say that again?"

"The field assignment is in Shetrian. There's a group of scientists going to our embassy there and I was one of the interns selected to go."

A blast of breath came from the back of his father's throat that sounded like a berwolf about to howl. His father glanced at Connor for a moment. "Uh, no you're not. Are you crazy? You can't go live with the Ovarrow. Six months! No."

Isaac felt the heat rise to his face. "I said I'd be living at the embassy."

"Don't give me that. The embassy is right smack in the middle of their city. What are you thinking? It's crazy there. You don't know anything about the Ovarrow. What the—Never mind. Tell them you can't go."

"I can't."

His father seemed to puff up. "Yes, you can. You can finish out your internship here. They're not making you go. You said yourself that you volunteered. Well, un-volunteer yourself."

Isaac shook his head and his nostrils flared. "No."

His father's eyes flared in anger. "What!"

"Juan," his mother said.

Isaac locked stares with his father. His back was straight, and he tried to relax his hands to keep them from clutching into fists. "I said no. I'm going with the science team."

"The hell you are. You're not even qualified for this. Did you lie about your qualifications? That's it, isn't it?"

Isaac gritted his teeth. It felt like everyone was staring at them, and they all seemed to go quiet. He stepped back away from them. "This was a mistake. I just came to tell you I was going."

His father stepped closer to him. "And I said you weren't going. Listen to me. I just have to make one call and I can stop all this from happening."

Isaac's hands balled into fists as he glared at his father. A scream gathered in his chest, moments from erupting.

"Maybe we should take a minute here to calm down," Connor said.

"Yes. Juan, go cool off," his mother said, moving between them.

Isaac stared at his father. He wouldn't look away. "I'm going with them. I don't care if you try to stop me. I'm going."

"Isaac," his mother said, "this isn't helping. Go and wait for me in the kitchen. Go."

His father's face was purple with rage, and he didn't care who saw him. They'd been building to this for years. His father spoke to his mother in angry bursts that Isaac couldn't hear. He clenched his teeth, wanting to scream in defiance. Then he glanced at the onlookers. He felt like they were all judging him, and he hated it. This had been a mistake and he needed to get out of there. He turned around and stormed into the house, hearing his mother calling after him, telling him to wait in the kitchen.

He didn't.

He strode to the front door and walked out, getting nearly to the road before he heard his father shouting for him. He quickened his pace. He wouldn't go back. He'd rather camp out in the forest than go back home. He started to run, pumping his arms and sprinting away. His breath came in controlled bursts, some of which carried a slight growl. All the pent-up frustration scattered his thoughts until the only thing he could focus on was the path in front of him. In the early evening, with blood pounding in his ears, he felt as if he were running for his life. But a small, rational part of his mind knew the truth. He wasn't running toward something; he was running away from everything, and he didn't care. He couldn't afford to care about it anymore. If he stayed, he'd never be free, but if he left, he might not ever be able to come home. But he couldn't go back, so the only choice he had was to keep going forward. Each step took him farther from home, and an ache formed at the back of his throat. When the six months were over, he'd find a way to stay there or go somewhere else. No matter what happened in the next few months, he was certain that going back home would never happen.

5

"Do we get hazard pay for this?" Jackson asked.

Riley kept his gaze on the video feeds from the reconnaissance drones they had deployed. "Absolutely, plus bonus pay and an all-expenses-paid vacation to a destination of your choice."

Corporal Jackson looked at him. "Why do you have to ruin it for me, Sergeant? Bad enough we're deployed way out in the middle of nowhere."

Riley inhaled deeply and sighed with contentment. "The CDF provides travel to exotic places with sterling accommodations. Nothing like some fresh air in the morning. Could be worse. You could've drawn rabbit duty on this fine day, Corporal Jackson. Would you like to be one of the rabbits?"

"No, thank you, Sergeant Riley."

"You sure?"

"Yes, Sergeant!"

Riley wasn't surprised. It took a special kind of crazy to run with the ryklars, but he'd done more than enough of that over the last eighteen months. The best way to lead was by example.

"Those things scare the crap out of me."

"Well, gosh darn it all. We can't have that!"

Jackson grinned. "Why do they have four arms? It's the creepiest thing I've ever seen. And those damn nasty-looking claws... or are they talons? Whatever they are, they can tear through the battle steel of our combat suits, you know."

"That is true. It is a pickle. I'll give you that."

Jackson's helmet turned toward him. "I don't talk like that."

"Why Corporal Buck Jackson, you do too. I love it. It's one of the reasons they promoted you. You're a good old boy. You work hard, and you're trained in the use of deadly weapons. You just have some ryklar phobias to work out."

Jackson sighed. "Kristensen, Rockwood, Zerneck, and Green are moving into position. There has to be more than one pack of ryklars here."

"You're right about that. There are several in that cohort. It's mating season."

Jackson looked at the drone video feed that showed clusters of ryklars scattered throughout the hillside. Ryklars looked as if they wore the pelt of an old-Earth leopard, tannish and spotted, which allowed them to easily blend into the multiple New Earth landscapes. "So?"

Riley shrugged. "They can get it on all year long, but this is where they gather to see who gets lucky and who doesn't. Tensions are high. Those ryklars will be in a killing mood."

Jackson nodded. "I haven't seen so many before. The mission must be working because there are fewer ryklars around."

"That it is, in this region of the continent anyway."

"Should I send an update to Lieutenant Harlan?"

Riley glanced at the time. "Go ahead and give him a time estimate for when our squad will get into position."

Jackson recorded a quick update and sent it via comlink. "How many of these missions have you been on, sir?"

Riley had to think about it for a few seconds. "A lot. I've been doing it a while. Spent my fair share being the rabbit for those ryklars to chase."

"Have there ever been any casualties?"

Riley stared at him. "You kidding me?"

Jackson didn't respond right away. Then said, "Uh, no, sir."

"There's a reason we're doing this. Ryklars are dangerous to keep around. The control signals help, but they've been genetically modified for war. People have been killed by them. We can either keep culling their numbers or find them another planet to live on. Relocation is the best option."

"I know that. I meant on these missions, sir."

"Yes, Corporal Jackson, soldiers have died on these missions," Riley said.

Jackson checked his rifle. It was almost an unconscious, conditioned behavior.

Riley closed the video feeds and started creeping forward up the hill. The ryklars were extremely difficult to sneak up on. They could conceal their body heat from sensors and had a highly acute sense of smell.

Jackson followed him. He should probably say something to help calm him down. He wasn't the first soldier to get the jitters before an op like this. Riley had them himself sometimes, but he embraced them. Others called him a thrill-seeker, but he'd take this duty over a dull guard stint any day of the week.

They reached the top of the hill and stopped. There were several small hills for the next kilometer, forming a shallow valley. Ryklars were an apex predator. They were highly efficient killing machines that could be controlled by high-frequency sound waves that drove them into a frenzy. Ryklars in a frenzied state would attack anything that crossed their paths. Certain frequencies enticed the ryklars toward the source. Ovarrow had used these signals during their wars to force the ryklars to attack their enemies. But the Ovarrow also fought among themselves, as well as the Krake. Ryklars were set loose in their cities, and anyone who didn't get to shelter quickly enough became collateral damage. It was a brutal tactic, but Riley knew some of the Ovarrow's history. General Gates had made sure they knew the importance of their mission, along with guidance to refrain from judging the Ovarrow too harshly. The Ovarrow did what they had to do to survive. Riley wasn't going to judge them, but they'd created a problem that needed to be addressed. Ryklars roamed the continent, and sometimes the old automated ryklar-activation signals triggered the apex predators into a frenzy. The CDF had made a concerted effort to disable the signals, but Riley was under no delusion that they'd found them all.

He opened a comlink to Lieutenant Harlan.

"J squad is in position, Lieutenant. As soon as you give the word, we'll execute," Riley said.

"You're the one."

"Linson still not in ready position?"

"That would be affirmative."

"The longer my squad has to wait, the more of a chance our asses will get burned in the fire."

Harlan didn't respond right away, so Riley waited him out. "Give me options," Harlan finally said.

"Send the mobile gateway to our waypoint first and make Linson's team wait. They're already running late. Couldn't they just slow their approach and adjust accordingly?" Riley asked.

He didn't know Linson's precise location, but Lieutenant Harlan did.

"Approved, Sergeant. We'll do it your way. Good luck."

"Thank you, sir," Riley said and closed the comlink. He activated a comlink to his squad. "J Squad, thanks to my awesome powers of persuasion, I got us moved up to the front of the line. You can thank me later. Are you ready to kick a nest of ryklars?"

A chorus of "Hell yeahs" came over the comlink in response.

"I'll take on a whole cohort of them, sir," Emma Zerneck said.

Rockwood laughed. "See, I told you. Put a tiny woman in a Nexstar combat suit, she goes from unobtrusive to mighty and ready to kick ass."

"Who needs a combat suit?" Zerneck replied.

"Easy there, tiny," Rockwood said.

"We'll settle this in post-op, Rockwood," Zerneck said.

"Only if we're naked. I'd be down with that."

"Dream on, big guy."

"Sounds like we're all ready. I've pushed the location for the mobile gateway out to all of you," Riley said.

"Serious question, Sergeant," Rockwood said.

"Go ahead."

"Since there are more ryklars here than expected, why don't we use the control signal to send them through the gateway, sir?"

"Oh geez, why didn't I think of that? The key is to get them to go through the gateway in a somewhat controlled manner. Just tossing a gateway near them with a signal going creates a killing frenzy among them. We're not trying to hurt them. We just need them to go away," Riley said and paused for a moment. "Right then, Rockwood, you get to go first."

The others grinned.

"I look forward to serving my squad to the best of my abilities, Sergeant," Rockwood said in a well-rehearsed, even tone.

"I know you do. Now take point," Riley said.

Rockwood and Zerneck began running toward the ryklars. On the other side of the valley, Green and Kristensen waited a few minutes and then began their run. Ryklars would sometimes attack on sight, but not always. Larger cohorts like this needed some prodding before they'd give chase.

Riley had the recon drones deploy concussive charges and dozens of ryklars began moving. The senior alphas scanned the area, looking for threats. Seeing the CDF soldiers running on the outskirts of the valley, they began running toward them, screeching at the betas to get them to join the hunt.

Ryklars had two sets of arms. Their inner arms, which were smaller, were used for precision attacks, but the outer arms were much longer and more heavily muscled. When a ryklar charged, they used those powerful arms, along with their thick, burly legs, to propel their bodies into a high-speed gallop. Their top speeds on rough terrain could outperform any colonial rover, but they couldn't outrun Hellcats. Air superiority usually trumped ground forces. CDF soldiers in Nexstar combat suits could run nearly as fast, but the ryklars were more agile. They were relentless pack hunters that were capable of sprinting short distances at high speeds, but they could also run for longer periods of time to wear out their prey. Ryklars' bulky, bulbous heads had thick tentacles that covered powerful jaws with rows of sharp teeth, and their loud screeches pierced the valley.

Anticipating where the two groups of squad mates were heading, several groups of ryklars broke away from the main pack. Smaller packs joined the chase, clearing out the middle of the valley.

"Let's go," Riley said.

"I'm with you, Sergeant," Jackson said.

They ran down the hill through the middle of the valley at a dead run. The combat suits' AIs assisted the wearers' movements, enabling strength and agility that would otherwise be outside their capabilities.

They ran toward a hill and quickly headed up. Several stragglers noticed them and screeched a warning. Answering ryklar calls echoed through the valley.

Jackson was able to keep pace with Riley. He seemed to have gotten over the jitters now that they'd started their run. Soldiers had to learn to master their fear. If they didn't, accidents happened. He was glad Jackson hadn't tripped. Falling at these speeds tended to damage the combat suits, and there were ryklars that would be only too eager to shred the suits to get at the juicy middle.

Riley glanced to his right and saw a ryklar galloping nearby. A CDF Hellcat flew overhead. Hanging underneath it were several long metallic cables that were attached to a mobile arch gateway. The Hellcat flew toward the waypoint, and the squad followed. The airship set the gateway down about five hundred meters ahead of them, then flew away. Rockwood and Zerneck ran along the edge of the valley with a large group of ryklars chasing them. Riley looked at the other side of the valley and saw Green and Kristensen's locators appear on his internal heads-up display, showing him their positions.

They closed the distance to the gateway and Riley initiated a short-range ryklar activation signal. Two ryklars caught up to them and knocked into Jackson, lashing out with their claws. He stumbled into Riley, almost knocking him off-balance. Jackson fired a stunner round at the ryklars and they backed off a little. The ryklars' bearded tentacles went from a dull gray to blood red.

Both he and Jackson managed to get their feet under them, and Riley howled in excitement.

Jackson sped ahead of him and went through the inactive gateway.

"Come and get papa bear!" Riley bellowed.

Dozens of New Earth's most dangerous predators galloped behind, gaining on him. Riley saw a slight shimmer appear in the middle of the gateway and glimpsed a wide-open field of green beyond. He then activated a secondary comlink that amplified the high-frequency sound waves, drawing more of the ryklars toward him. Several meters before the gateway, he leaped high into the air. The combat suit's actuators enabled him to leapfrog over the gateway as he tossed the secondary comlink toward it. The comlink attached to the top of it and altered the signal to appear to be coming from just beyond the gateway. Riley landed on the other side and heard the ryklars running through. They were in such an agitated state that he doubted they noticed him. The only indication that the ryklars had breached the gateway was the abrupt cutoff of their screeches and growls.

Riley continued onward and caught up to Jackson, who waited for him over a hundred meters away.

"Green. Kristensen. You're up," Riley said over comms.

The CDF soldiers acknowledged and led their frenzied group of ryklars toward the gateway.

"We're coming in hot, sir. Another cohort has joined this one," Rockwood said.

Riley turned toward them. They were running at max speed and had several large groups of ryklars chasing them. He cursed.

"They're coming in too fast," Jackson said.

There was nothing Riley could do. The CDF teams were going to arrive at the same time as the ryklars, and the ryklars were as likely to combat each other as they were to go through the gateway.

Riley opened a comlink to Lieutenant Harlan. "We need an emergency extraction," he said and explained the situation.

Manipulating smaller groups of ryklars to go through mobile gateways was much easier than the larger groups. Dividing them up with multiple teams usually worked, but not this time.

"I'll alert the nearest Hellcat. Stand by," Harlan said.

The comlink session went on standby and Jackson gestured for his attention.

"Sergeant, I'm detecting a secondary ryklar signal," Jackson said.

Riley frowned and checked the recon drone feeds. Jackson was right. There was another signal being broadcast. The rogue signal was interfering with theirs at the mobile gateway.

He increased the intensity of the signal on the mobile gateway. He could still get the closest ryklars to go through. Green and Kristensen were first to arrive at the gateway and he watched as they circled around it. Rockwood and Zerneck were just a few moments behind. Riley seized a recon drone feed to get an aerial view. There looked to be a couple hundred ryklars closing in on the gateway. Bulbous heads with crimson-bearded tentacles raced forward without any cohesion.

Riley opened a comlink to his team. "Abort mission. Don't stop at the gateway. Change ammunition type to incendiary rounds."

CDF standard-issue rifle was the AR-74 that had a nanorobotic ammunition block capable of forming multiple types of munitions. Incendiary ammo could burn through armor, as well as the toughened hides of the ryklars, and increased the damage above what a standard round could do.

Riley aimed his weapon. "Covering fire. Let's try and give them some breathing room."

Jackson brought his weapon up and began firing in short, controlled bursts.

Riley aimed for the ground behind the fleeing soldiers. Large pockets of dirt burst into the air at the charging ryklars. The predators flinched away from the small explosions, causing several to stumble into each other.

He only wanted to slow them down, but if they kept pushing forward, he was going to have to shoot to kill. Jackson followed his lead.

Riley looked at the gateway. Several groups of ryklars clustered around it. They kept shaking their heads and pounding the ground with their outer fists. Fighting broke out among the groups. A few dozen had followed the CDF soldiers past the gateway.

An alert appeared on his internal heads-up display. The rogue signal had moved to a place behind Riley's location. It had increased intensity to a staggering degree, rendering the one at the gateway useless. The effect on the ryklars was immediate. A chorus of screeches and howls came from all the ryklars in the area.

"What the hell just happened?" Jackson asked.

Riley gritted his teeth and looked at the hordes of ryklars being driven into a frenzy. "Shoot to kill."

This operation had quickly gone from high-risk routine to a fight for their lives. Their weapons fire tore into the nearest ryklars, but they kept charging. Riley knew they wouldn't relent no matter how many he killed, but he kept firing until the rest of the squad reached him.

A comlink came to prominence and Riley acknowledged it.

"Sergeant, this is Lieutenant Peters on Hellcat E-74. We're fifteen minutes out from your location."

"You need to get here faster than that. This is an emergency evac, danger close," Riley replied as he fired his weapon.

"Understood. We'll get there as soon as we can," Peters said.

"When's the evac coming, sir?" Rockwood asked.

Riley told them.

The squad had been steadily retreating while firing their weapons at the ryklars. "We need to run for it. Hellcat is coming from that direction."

"That's the same direction as that rogue signal," Jackson said.

"Can't the Hellcat take it out? I mean, it's coming from that direction anyway," Rockwood said.

"Good thinking!" Zerneck groused. "Tell the Hellcat that's coming to pick us up to go take out the rogue signal instead."

A few moments passed and Rockwood replied. "All right, tiny, it was a bad idea."

They continued running over smalls hills in the valley, pausing to fire at the ryklars and then moving forward.

Riley knew they couldn't keep this up. "Listen up," he said. "We're going to make our stand at the edge of the valley. We'll have the high ground, and we'll hold them off until the evac gets there."

Riley checked that their locator beacon was activated, and the CDF squad headed for the waypoint. It was a solid plan—get to the high ground and then unleash their full armament on hordes of ryklars coming to kill them. But once they reached the edge of the valley and glimpsed the surrounding area, things really started to unravel.

"Holy hell, we're going to die out here!" Green shouted.

"Then we'll die fighting," Riley said.

Jackson locked gazes with him and nodded.

"Rockwood, Zerneck, and Jackson take east. The rest of you are with me, holding west," Riley said.

He glanced skyward, hoping to see a CDF Hellcat flying towards them, but the skies were clear.

Over the next few minutes, they fired their weapons at the ryklars, but they kept coming. They were circling around and pushing in on all sides.

"Conserve your ammo. Controlled bursts!" Riley shouted.

More and more ryklars darted toward them, avoiding being shot. One barreled its way past the front line. Riley heard Zerneck scream as she fired her AR-74 on full auto, chewing through the ryklar's massive chest. It sank to the ground and its innards slapped the dirt in a grisly mess.

They were moments from being overwhelmed when Riley heard the high-pitched whine of the Hellcat's engines, followed by the heavy gauss cannon as it unleashed an onslaught of 30mm projectiles. The ryklars closest to them were split in half. Blood splattered the piles of bodies littering the ground.

Other ryklars avoided fire from the heavy gauss cannon, and Riley growled as he continued to shoot his weapon.

Rescue lines dropped from the Hellcat. The CDF soldiers stepped into the boot and grabbed the line, then covered the others while they did the same.

"Time to go, sir!" Jackson shouted.

Riley spun and hastened toward the remaining rescue line while the others continued firing their weapons. He stepped into the boot and it attached to his armored foot, but before he could be lifted, something big slammed into him, pushing him toward the ground. Riley heard the others shouting as he tried to regain his feet. A ryklar howled as it tore at his armored back. Riley jerked his elbow back and twisted around. His elbow hit something solid, but he had no idea what. He tried to bring his weapon around but didn't squeeze the trigger. If he did, there was a good chance he'd hit the Hellcat or one of the others.

The ryklar let go of his combat suit and Zerneck screamed while she fired her weapon at it. Riley stood up and saw the ryklar tumble away. Two rescue lines dangled nearby. He grabbed one and shoved it toward Zerneck. She took it and started to rise into the air as the line was retracted. Riley took the other one, feeling the line become taut moments before he was whisked into the air. Several ryklars leaped up, attempting to get at him. He fired his weapon at them. Then he saw Zerneck fall past him. One of her legs was missing, and three ryklars clutched her as she hit the ground. Then more piled on top. Zerneck screamed in pain as the ryklars tore her to pieces. Riley kept shooting his weapon, trying to clear them off, but there were too many. His back hit the edge of the Hellcat and the others pulled him in.

Rockwood screamed. "We have to go get her."

He started toward the edge and Riley grabbed him. "She's gone. Look!" He gestured toward the rescue line and the remains of Zerneck's leg. The combat suit had been severely damaged.

"No! Dammit!"

More ryklars stormed the area as the Hellcat rose into the air. Riley looked at the others. They'd all made it except for Zerneck. Had she not helped save him, she might have survived.

Riley clenched his teeth and cursed.

KOUKAX WATCHED the CDF Hellcat fly away and looked back toward where the squad of soldiers had been. They'd lost one of them to the ryklars.

He glanced at his own soldiers. They were lying on the ground under the cover of the foliage around them. Their armor had helped them avoid detection from the CDF. He'd taken this scout group to investigate the rumors—rumors that had just been proven true. The colonists were attempting to rid Bhaneteran of the ryklars.

Koukax placed an armored hand on the soldier next to him. "Deactivate the signal."

"At once, Commander," Seomus said.

The ryklar signal went offline.

"We'll stay here until nightfall. Then we head back to Renoya to regroup."

His scout force gestured their acknowledgment.

"The Konus endure," Koukax said, invoking the motto that had sustained them since the great awakening.

6

Noah Barker stared at the data on the holoscreens as if they had just betrayed his best friend in the whole galaxy. It was as if the universe had some kind of vendetta against him for trying to succeed where so many engineers and scientists throughout history had failed. God really did have a sense of humor.

He inhaled deeply and pressed his lips together as he stood in his lab at the science research station Terra. He then looked out the window. From the station, he had a clear view of the moon and New Earth just beyond it. New Earth's rings shone even brighter from off-planet than the brilliant display from his home. He suddenly realized he'd lived longer here on New Earth than he had on Old Earth. His fortieth birthday was rapidly approaching, but he still looked as if he were in his mid-twenties.

He sighed.

Old Earth was a distant memory, and New Earth was more of a home to him than anywhere else. Kara had brought up his birthday the other day. She was likely planning some kind of party for him.

"We're part of a small minority of colonists who actually remember Earth," Kara had said to him.

His wife's words had stuck with him, and his brain wouldn't let them go. They persisted in his mind like an annoying song that he just couldn't get out of his head.

The door to his lab opened and Kara walked in. She stopped a short distance from him, hips cocked to one side. Her blonde hair skirted an inch below her jawline, and eyes the color of warm honey regarded him. The edges of her lips were the color of frozen strawberries and lifted into a flirty smile. Being married for as long as they had had given him more insights into another person than he'd ever thought was possible. Within the passing of a few seconds, they could gauge each other's temperaments and share a brief moment's respite in each other's company. He loved his wife more now than when they'd first met.

Noah tilted his head toward the phalanx of holoscreens. They were like a strike team that had just brought back bad news.

"Look, hon, I found another way how not to crack FTL."

Kara scanned the data on the screen. She could read faster than anyone he knew, and it was something to see. "Structural integrity is lost in transit," she said, coming to stand next to him. She rubbed the middle of his back in slow circular motions and the tension eased out of him a little.

"Just a little decomposition of mass, and the fact that it's way off course," Noah said and frowned. He looked at her. "I've never failed at something so consistently in my entire life."

Kara grinned. "Well, it's not just you. There's a team working to help you."

Noah nodded in mock severity. "It's a group effort," he said and shook his head. "I just don't get it. The only consistent result is that I manage to destroy anything we try to propel. The

Ovarrow somehow managed to link two gateways across vast distances of space."

"They weren't trying to use it for traveling. They were trying to bombard the planet."

"That's the big question. We're not exactly sure what they were trying to do. We've only observed the results," Noah said. He made a swiping motion and all the holoscreens disappeared. "At least we got subspace communications out of it."

"I know you thought it was going to be easier to figure out than this, but you have to realize that most major scientific breakthroughs happen on top of a mountain's worth of work. Sometimes it takes decades," Kara said.

Noah nodded. She wasn't saying anything new. "I know. It just feels like it's right there at the edge of our grasp. Or I can see the top of a mountain, but the higher I climb, the farther away it becomes."

Kara arched a blonde eyebrow. "Regretting not going on the *Ark II?*"

"No," Noah said with a laugh. "I meant the proverbial 'we' as in humanity. I don't want to leave New Earth."

"Then why have you put years into trying to solve this?"

Noah regarded his wife for a few moments. "I thought it was a team effort."

She chuckled, her eyes gleaming. "You know what I mean."

"I don't want to leave New Earth permanently, is what I guess I'm trying to say," he replied, feeling a thoughtful frown pulling his eyebrows together. "If we could make this work, we could support the second colony and travel back to Earth someday. Figure out if there are any survivors. Not to mention explore other worlds. I don't believe this is where we're meant to stay. We might have avoided a war with the Krake altogether if we could've simply left the planet."

The war with the Krake had been eight years ago, but it had been a close battle, and the colony was almost lost.

Kara nodded. "And the Ovarrow?"

"They could come with us."

"You're assuming they'd want to leave the only home they've ever known."

Noah shrugged. "Between that and annihilation, which would you choose?"

"That's a little too simplistic a choice."

"Sometimes simple is better."

"Or it's just convenient for the simple-minded."

Noah grinned. "You've got me there. I guess I walked right into that one. You really stuck the landing."

Kara threw her arms around his neck and kissed him. "You're just tired."

He'd married this woman fifteen years ago and he never tired of how her lips felt against his.

"I slept fine."

She shook her head. "Not that. Mentally. I think you need a break. I know I do."

Noah blinked a few times and considered it. "We could take a shuttle to Phoenix Station and visit Sean and Oriana."

"And get roped into one of their projects? No, thank you. I told you I want to unwind a little bit. We should go planetside for a while. Give the entire team some downtime. They could use a break too."

Noah glanced out the window toward New Earth and his eyes drank in the sight of a planet vibrant with life. Terra Research Station had gardens and a place to rest, but they weren't long-term substitutes for standing on solid ground.

"How long do you want to go away?" he asked.

Kara shrugged and pursed her lips. "A couple of months, maybe."

Noah's eyebrows shot up. "Months! Are you serious?"

"Yes, I'm serious. A couple of weeks isn't going to cut it. Everyone on the team is wound up tight, and sometimes taking a step back to get some perspective is what you need to take a giant leap forward."

Noah slowly shook his head and smiled a little. "Now you sound like Sean trying to talk me into doing something."

Kara kissed him again, then leaned toward his ear and whispered. "I'm pretty sure Sean doesn't do this." She nibbled on his earlobe and then kissed his neck.

Noah sighed with pleasure.

A notification chimed and came to prominence on one of the holoscreens.

"We need to meet with the rest of the team," he said.

Kara pulled away from his neck and smiled at him. "This way, we can balance the bad news with something good."

"It's almost like a compliment sandwich."

Kara frowned. "A what?"

"A compliment sandwich. You know, when you hide a bit of criticism between two compliments."

Kara regarded him for a moment. "Not the analogy I would have chosen."

"Close enough."

"If you say so."

7

CONNOR GLANCED at the clock for what seemed like the umpteenth time in the past hour. He rolled his eyes, thinking of his own lack of focus at the moment. He'd spent the last six hours reviewing proposed updates to the CDF charter that was going to be sent for colonial approval in the coming weeks. The Colonial Defense Force was a military that had similarities to the NA Alliance military of Old Earth, but there were also significant differences. The NA Alliance military had been born of multiple nation-state militaries that had joined together to become the NA Alliance. It'd taken decades for it to mature into the military that he remembered being part of. The CDF was maturing as well, and this was an important step in its life cycle. He'd been a key contributor in creating the CDF during a time when it hadn't been clear that the colony required an active military to defend it.

Connor recalled his earlier days as part of Field Ops with bemusement. The colonists had come from all walks of life. There were scientists, engineers, builders, doctors, and all kinds of people with various skills. There were even people from former militaries but not that many. And then there was him and the Ghosts. They were the ones who weren't supposed to be part of the colony. Every member of the Ghost Platoon would have faced a significant amount of time in a military prison until such time as their innocence could be proven, but there were no guarantees.

Admiral Mitch Wilkinson, an old family friend of Connor's, had taken action on his behalf. Wilkinson must've anticipated how events would unfold for Connor and the rest of the Ghosts, which was why he smuggled them aboard the *Ark*. They'd all had their lives altered because of it, and not everyone had adjusted to colonial living.

Connor hadn't thought of the admiral in such a long time. He'd long since put his past behind him, and he wasn't quite sure why reviewing the updated CDF charter reminded him of Mitch Wilkinson. Maybe it was because they shouldered similar burdens of leadership—the burdens of generals and admirals. These were burdens Connor took extremely seriously. In the short time that the colony had been established, it had faced two significant extinction-level events—existential level events. On Old Earth, the enduring conflict had always involved people fighting among themselves. It had been the same for thousands of years, but the Vemus had changed things. They were some kind of bacterial viral pathogen that modified human DNA. And not just human DNA, but mammalian DNA. Colonial scientists theorized that the Vemus pathogen was of alien origin. The records indicated that it had come from deep within Old Earth's oceans, but how it got there was anyone's guess. The Vemus proved to be one of the strangest and most terrifying enemies Connor had ever faced. Then there was the Krake, an entirely different alien species, who'd been in another class of enemy altogether.

Connor shook his head. His job was to anticipate what third type of enemy they might face in the future. The fact that he couldn't have imagined the first two enemies didn't even matter. He'd already faced the unimaginable, so what else was left? It was those kinds of questions that occupied his thoughts, and probably the reason he kept checking the clock.

Nathan wanted them to focus on more domestic-type threats —the kind of threats that could exist among themselves and their neighbors. Having a common enemy did unite people, and species for that matter. It was easy for them to put their differences aside, even if they didn't agree on how best to deal with the threat. He supposed he should feel relieved that he could look over solutions as to how best to defend the colony under relatively peaceful circumstances. And he was thankful, but it was also a little bit boring for him. But he couldn't pass it off to someone else. He had to review what was being proposed. This was his chance to influence the direction of the CDF charter. It would be easier to make changes now than after it was ratified.

Connor glanced at the clock again and initiated a shutdown of the holoscreens in front of him. He'd had enough for today.

He left his office and walked to the corridors that led toward the airfield nearby. The soldiers saluted him, and he nodded a greeting toward the people he passed. They were all familiar faces and were used to seeing Connor. This wasn't always the same when he traveled to other CDF bases throughout the colony, especially among the younger recruits. They typically looked at him with a sense of awe, as if he weren't a soldier like them. It was helpful when they needed to listen, but it quickly became tiresome.

He exited the building and walked toward a row of aircars. His vehicle powered up as he approached and began to hover above the ground. The sleek craft was black with crimson lines that went from the nose to the back. Technically, his aircar was a civilian model, but it had quite a few upgrades that'd he'd either modified himself or had a few CDF engineers install while off duty. Most aircars didn't have weapon systems, countermeasures, or increased armor, nor could they go at speeds that would challenge a Talon-V fighter.

He transmitted his authorization and the side door opened, closing itself after he climbed inside. He brought up the flight control systems, which went through a quick check, and all systems were ready to go. Some of New Earth's engineers were trying to figure out a way to make the aircars capable of space travel, and they might figure out a way to do that eventually, but he wasn't going to hold his breath. Most colonists didn't need to travel into space with a frequency that would demand they be able to do it with their day-to-day mode of transportation.

He entered the coordinates for his home and the aircar ascended. The flight home was uneventful, and the sun would dip below the edge of the world soon. He'd expanded his home to include several buildings beyond the main house after the Krake war ended. They'd had to expand their home after Ethan had been born, too.

Connor noticed another aircar that was occupying the visitor landing pad, but he didn't recognize it. Someone was probably visiting Lenora. He initiated the landing sequence and the aircar's automated driving system brought him in for a smooth landing.

He climbed out and heard his wife calling to him from their courtyard behind the main house. Connor walked along the path and saw Lenora speaking with Noah and Kara.

Connor smiled and then eyed Noah for a moment. "Don't tell me you broke Terra Station."

Noah grinned and shook his head. "No, but not for lack of trying."

Connor gave Kara a quick hug and then kissed his wife. He glanced toward the house.

"Lauren and Ethan are sleeping over at a friend's house tonight and then they'll be going to the lake with their class tomorrow."

Connor whistled in appreciation. "We've got a rare night off. I guess we're going to get crazy tonight."

The others laughed.

Connor looked at Noah. "I thought you weren't returning for another three months."

Noah glanced at Kara for a moment and then looked back at Connor. "We needed a break from the station."

Connor nodded. "How long are you in town?"

"We've been back on New Earth for two weeks. We were in Sierra for a bit and now we're here. And we're hungry, so will you feed us?"

"You show up unannounced and now you want to be fed?" Connor said and grinned.

"Yes, because that's the kind of guy I am."

A short time later they had finished eating and evening had settled on them. New Earth's rings lit up the night sky toward the south, but farther north they could see the stars. It was a warm summer night, but the humidity wasn't as bad as it was going to be in a few weeks.

Lenora and Kara had finished off a bottle of wine while Connor and Noah were working on their third glass of bourbon.

Noah looked at his wife. "You were right. I needed this. I just had to say it out loud and give you the credit you deserve."

Kara lifted her chin in acknowledgment. "You could never go wrong by telling a woman that she was right."

Lenora made an *ahem* sound and Connor pretended not to understand. He looked at Kara. "The same applies for men, too."

"Oh, we know that already," she replied and grinned wickedly.

Lenora joined in.

Connor polished off his bourbon and set the glass down on the table. "So, did you figure out FTL yet, or are you still destroying things?"

"Connor!" Lenora admonished. "These things take time, and I know it's not from lack of effort," she said, nodding toward Noah and Kara.

Noah bobbed his head to the side with a guilty smile. "No, I can still destroy things with the best of them. There are thousands of ways *not* to achieve FTL."

Connor nodded and looked at his friend for a few moments. "So, you're taking a break for a few months and then you're going back at it?"

"That's the long and short of it," Noah replied.

Lenora and Kara stood up and walked toward the house.

"Have you thought that maybe it's just not possible?" Connor asked.

"Only a few hundred times a day, especially…" Noah let the thought go unfinished. Then he said, "There are plenty of theories asserting that it should be possible, but we lacked the capability of producing the energy required. The best I can come up with is that the Ovarrow stumbled upon something. I feel like we're close. And I know I've said that before, maybe once or twice anyway."

"I think I've heard that a couple times from you before."

"Fine," Noah said and smiled. "I don't think it's impossible; I just think we're doing it wrong."

"Well, the Ovarrow here didn't stumble onto it."

Noah's eyebrows raised questioningly.

"Do you remember the underwater city where we found the arch? Before the city became submerged there were Ovarrow there, but we think there was a group of Ovarrow from another universe that were more advanced. They were trying to find the Krake homeworld and recruit other Ovarrow to defeat them."

Noah frowned. "I've heard this before, but I can't remember what they were called."

"That's just it. We don't know exactly what they were called. The only name we can go by was given to us by the Gesora. Remember them?" Connor asked.

Noah nodded. "I read the mission reports. They were our allies from one of the alternate universes."

"Leading up to the Krake attack, there was a group of Ovarrow that had reached out to the Gesora. They called themselves the Bhatdin. Intelligence analysts couldn't determine whether this was a Krake ploy or if there was an actual group out there—a group of Ovarrow capable of more advanced technology than we thought possible."

Noah drained his bourbon and set the cup down. "It's interesting. I'll give you that. But I don't see how it helps."

Connor stood up. "Let me show you something. Side project of mine."

"Of yours?" Noah asked. Then said, "As if running the CDF wasn't enough to do, not to mention being a father."

Connor shrugged. "It's just something I've been working on since the end of the Krake war. It's something both Lenora and I have put some time into."

Connor led him toward a large outer building away

from the main house. He palmed the identification plate and the doors opened. There were several work benches inside, along with a rover that was partially covered for storage. Beside the rover were several racks of field equipment.

"Are those weapons containers?" Noah asked.

Connor nodded. "I also have a bunker below with a tunnel that connects to the main house. There are a couple of outside entrances to tunnels that connect to the bunker as well."

Noah nodded. "You can't be too careful. The bunker, weapons, a highly modified rover. I'm surprised you don't have a fully armed Hellcat tucked away somewhere."

Connor grinned. "You never created a version of the MPS with flight capabilities."

Noah chuckled and then looked around the workshop. He noticed an AR-74 that was disassembled on a workbench, and next to it was an Ovarrow plasma rifle. "You certainly like to tinker."

Connor shrugged. "It's not on the scale of making FTL work, but it's interesting. Lauren even has her own rifle, scaled down to something she can handle. She shoots pretty well with it, too. Among the top in her field class."

"Not surprising. She's your daughter. Do you bring her in here?"

Connor shook his head. "Not here. We built a smaller workshop for the family."

Noah smiled. "You've really embraced being a father."

"Well, yeah. It's fun. You should try it some time."

Noah chuckled and rubbed the back of his neck. "Someday for sure. The colony has grown quite a bit without our contribution."

"You guys all right?"

"Oh yeah, we're fine. To be honest, taking time off was Kara's idea."

Connor regarded his friend for a few moments. Noah had turned his attention toward another part of the workshop. "Why are you pushing so hard for this? FTL, I mean."

Noah turned around and leaned against the workbench. He crossed his arms. "I really believe I can make it work. The whole team does."

"I understand that, but what happens if you *do* make it work? What then?"

"It opens so many opportunities. We can support the second colony. Explore other star systems. Maybe even send a survey team back to Old Earth. The probes we sent still have another eighty years left on their journey. We sent them an update so their fabricators could build a subspace transceiver, but I can't remember when we'll receive a check-in from them."

Connor had heard Noah give these reasons before, but there was something more he wasn't saying. Connor simply stared at him, deciding it was better to wait him out.

Noah sat quietly for a few seconds and then seemed to arrive at a decision of his own. "I know there hasn't been any evidence of the Krake being active in the alternate universes, but what if they were? Or maybe there's something else out there that wants to wipe us all out."

Connor inhaled deeply and sighed. "Hopefully not."

"That's just it. Hope isn't a strategy. I must have heard you say that a thousand times over the years. I want to make FTL work so we'll have some options other than surviving at all costs. The more the population of the colony grows, the more our previous solutions won't work. Could you imagine building stasis pods for 1.2 million colonists? Not to mention the Ovarrow.

And that's just now. What about fifty years from now, or a hundred?"

"I didn't know you felt so strongly about it."

Noah rolled his eyes a little and shook his head. "I know how it sounds. I don't think about it all the time."

Connor smiled in understanding. "Just when you need motivation to keep pushing forward. To go that extra step. I understand what you're saying, Noah. I really do."

Noah sighed. "I know *you* do."

Connor scratched the stubble of his beard. "All right, come on over here. I've got something else to show you."

He led Noah over to the far side of the workshop where he opened an access panel and inputted a security code. Then, an opening appeared in the floor nearby and interior lighting came on. There was a set of stairs leading down.

"Of course you have a second level. Do these lead to the bunker?" Noah asked.

"No, this is just a sub level," he replied, and Noah arched an eyebrow toward him. "Hey, this was years in the making."

He walked down the stairs and into another work area. There were storage containers neatly stacked over on one side of the large room. Connor led him toward a mini command center.

"You call this a side project," Noah said while looking around the workshop.

Connor brought up a couple of holoscreens and opened the folders that had his data on the Bhatdin.

"These are some of the things we've pieced together about the Bhatdin over the years. The data came from a variety of sources. Lenora found some of the information during her research and the Mekaal have added to it, but what you're seeing here are some of the things we can't explain that have to do with the Ovarrow. The Ovarrow had their own nation-states, which had various factions that had dealings with a group that introduced multiple types of tech to them. Many of the records were lost, but there is definitely a pattern here. There was a faction of Ovarrow that seem to have introduced advanced technology."

Noah frowned in thought. "Well, it's not just the Ovarrow. The Konus had some Krake tech that they were using as well. You think there were competing factions that were trying to manipulate the general population?"

"That's right, and the Konus having access to Krake tech just makes it more complicated."

Noah peered at the data on the holoscreens. "I wonder if there are any records of the work done with the arch gateway that was found under that lake."

Connor smiled. "There are some records, and we've been back-tracing them to see what we can learn about them."

"Like what?"

"Ideally, if they're not from New Earth, then where did they come from? More importantly, where did they *first* come to New Earth from? Maybe they had a base of operations. There might be data in there that could be useful. Something to maybe help you with what you're doing."

Noah arched an eyebrow. "You think they knew how to achieve FTL?"

Connor shook his head. "No, but they were definitely involved with those gateways. It's crazy to think about how close they were to figuring out where the Krake homeworld was. Maybe they actually knew where it was and were working on a way to bombard them from this universe. I don't believe it was chance that the space gate was near Sagan."

"But the Ovarrow didn't have the technological capability to go into space."

"You're right, they didn't, but they could manipulate Krake

technology, and the Krake could've had a space gate in our universe. In fact, the one that Sean found could have been theirs and that's what the Bhatdin used. I'm sure we don't have it all worked out nice and neat, but it's interesting."

Noah nodded slowly. "It is."

"I'm glad you agree. Are you up for some fieldwork?"

"Fieldwork?"

"Yes, Lenora and I are taking a little trip, looking for more evidence about the Bhatdin. You and Kara could join us if you wanted."

Noah considered it for a few moments and pursed his lips.

"You don't have to decide right now. We can go talk to them about it, but I thought you might be interested."

"Oh, I know *I'm* interested, but I'm not sure about Kara. She was keen on some downtime."

"Think of it as a camping trip," Connor said and smiled.

"It couldn't hurt to work on something else for a change, even if it's indirectly related to what I'm trying to do," Noah replied.

8

THE NEXT DAY Connor was alone in the sub-level of his workshop. Several amber-colored holoscreens were active with regional maps, each displaying a highlighted waypoint. These were the areas they were going to search for evidence of the Bhatdin. This sort of exercise was right up Connor's alley. He enjoyed the hunt for information, as long as it also included work in the field. And learning about the Ovarrow had been critical for their own survival on New Earth.

Noah and Kara had left that morning to put their own travel kits together. It wouldn't take them long, and Connor had more than enough stuff to make up for what they lacked. The resources for this trip were coming from their own personal items, as well as support from the Colonial Research Institute and the CDF.

Lenora walked down the steps to the sub-level wearing a thoughtful frown.

"What's going on?" Connor asked.

She walked over to him and glanced at the holoscreens for a

second. "Victoria reached out to me. She wants you to persuade Diaz to come with us."

Connor's eyebrows raised. "Come with us? Why?"

"She said she needs him to get away for a while."

Connor considered it for a few moments. "I don't know if this is such a good idea."

Lenora held up one of her hands. "I know. I told her, but she's really worried about him."

"And Isaac."

Lenora nodded. "It's been months since they've spoken. She sounded really upset. She said the men in her life are tearing her family apart. We need to help them."

Connor inhaled deeply and sighed. "I can try to get him to come."

Lenora smiled. "You'll do more than try, love."

"I can't force him to come."

"I know. No one expects you to do that." She shook her head. "It's not black and white. Diaz hasn't been the same since Isaac left. It's hit him really hard."

Lenora was right about that. They'd been there when Isaac told his parents what he was going to do. Diaz hadn't reacted to it well, and Connor couldn't blame him. He might not wholly agree with him, but as a father, he understood wanting to keep a child out of danger.

"She wants us to take him to the Embassy in Shetrian and get them to talk to each other."

Lenora nodded. "Ideally, yes."

Connor shook his head. "He's as stubborn as they come."

She laughed. "Look who's talking."

Connor grinned and rubbed his chin. "Point taken. I'll talk to him, but what about the other preparations?"

"I'll take care of it. The rest of the expedition is meeting at the Colonial Research Institute. Is the CDF side taken care of?"

"Yes, there's a squad that'll be joining us."

"Just one?"

Connor shrugged one shoulder. "Well, there's me."

Lenora smiled and slipped her arms around his waist. "You're all I need."

"You're a smooth talker," he said and kissed her.

"I learned from the best."

Connor closed the holoscreens and followed Lenora out of the workshop, thinking about how he was going to coax Diaz into their little excursion. Diaz had taken up permanent residence in Sanctuary, with the occasional CDF reserve duties that sometimes called for travel. His life was comprised of his family, running the Salty Soldier, and being active within the CDF veteran community. He'd had enough of exploring, but Connor thought he knew a few ways he could get Diaz to at least consider joining them. If all else failed, he could tie him up and make him come.

CONNOR WALKED toward the Salty Soldier. Voted the most popular restaurant in Sanctuary by visitors and soldiers alike, what had started out as a singular place to eat had expanded into multiple themed buildings, giving the place an experience to be had, as well as delicious food. He headed toward the center building, catching a healthy whiff of cooking that made his mouth water. Patrons gathered at outside tables, eating and drinking. All the buildings had been constructed with rich hardwoods, stained a rustic brown, and copper furnishings. He walked on a pathway of wide, darkened-hardwood planks that smelled of longevity and good times, as if the restaurant had always been there.

Diaz spotted him as he walked in the front doors.

"Connor! What are you doing here in the middle of the day? Did Lenora kick you out already?"

Connor grinned and crossed the entranceway heading toward the bar where Diaz was standing. "What? I need an excuse to come in here?"

"Never. What's up? Want a beer?"

Connor had thought of a couple of different ways he could broach the subject but dismissed all of them.

"Sure."

Diaz retrieved and opened two dark bottles, then passed one over to him.

Connor took a healthy swallow. It was deliciously smooth with a slightly bitter flavor that sported notes of coffee and chocolate. He swallowed the brew and lifted the bottle up appreciatively. "That's good."

Diaz nodded. "It's one of the better batches we've made."

"Micro-brewery is working out well, I see."

"So far. We've had a couple of duds but nothing too drastic. I got the idea from Nathan and his bourbon."

Connor took another swig from the bottle. "Are you going to start making bourbon? Give Nathan some competition?"

Diaz shook his head. "Nah. I like what he's done and I'm happy to serve it here."

His friend regarded him for a few moments, and Connor knew he suspected something. Middle-of-the-day chats at the bar weren't something Connor normally initiated. Time to get this over with.

"I stopped by to see if you were up for a little camping trip."

Diaz narrowed his gaze suspiciously. "Camping?"

Connor nodded. "Yes, camping."

"This weekend?"

"A little longer than a weekend. A couple of weeks."

Diaz's eyes widened. "Weeks! I can't leave for that long. We're updating our menus again, and I have some new chefs coming in from Sierra. There's even some talk about opening more restaurants in other cities."

"Really? I hadn't heard that. Where?"

"Sierra and New Haven for sure."

"That's amazing. Congratulations," he said and raised his bottle.

Diaz smiled, looking pleased, but Connor could see the strain around his eyes. This was a front.

"I'm afraid I can't take no for an answer."

Diaz lowered his bottle. His mouth opened as if he were going to speak, but he just blinked a few times instead.

Connor raised his hand in front of his chest. "Just hear me out. Victoria's worried about you. She thinks you need to get away for a while."

Diaz rolled his eyes and looked away. "We just had the war games a few months ago. Doesn't that count for something?"

"It does," Connor agreed. "But not to our wives."

Diaz shook his head. "Lenora is in on this too?"

"She's not in on anything, Juan. You haven't been the same since Isaac left."

Diaz shut his mouth and his expression became guarded.

"Has it really been months since you spoke to your son?" Connor asked.

Diaz set his bottle down on the bar. "Are you going to give me parenting advice now?"

"Do you want me to?"

Diaz sighed explosively. "The kid doesn't know what he's getting himself into."

"We can't control them."

"Like hell we can't." Diaz banged a fist on the bar and shook his head a little. "You're right, we can't, but it doesn't mean I won't say my piece. I never trusted the Ovarrow, and now he's there in that damn city. It's not what he thinks it's going to be. They're not who he thinks they are."

Connor was quiet for a few moments. "He's there, and there isn't anything either of us can do about it."

Diaz rested his hands on his hips and looked at Connor. "You're lucky your kids are small. When they grow up, they become a real pain in the ass with their think-they-know-better-than-us garbage." He grabbed his beer and began walking away. "Thanks, but no thanks, Connor."

Diaz walked into the kitchen. Connor drained his beer and followed his friend.

Diaz whirled around and glared. "What are you gonna do?"

The kitchen staff nearby stopped what they were doing. Diaz was the boss here, and his staff was sensitive to his moods.

Great, now they had an audience.

"We're not done."

"I said we are," Diaz said and looked around at the kitchen staff. "Get back to work."

The staff hastily returned to their duties, but you could tell they were still listening to them.

"Juan, come on. It's me. Would you just talk to me?"

Diaz bit his lower lip and shook his head. "I told you already. I don't have the time for it right now."

"Just hear me out. Somewhere else, maybe?"

"Fine," Diaz said and strode past him back out to the bar area.

Connor had seen Diaz angry plenty of times. He needed to be careful or Diaz would dig in his heels even more.

"You can't do this. Not here."

"Do what?" Connor asked.

"Try and bully me into getting your way."

"Is that what I'm doing?"

"Isn't it?"

Connor shook his head. "It's not. I'm here as a friend."

"I appreciate it, but the answer is no."

"Give me a break. Push back whatever you've got planned for the next few weeks and get out of town. Maybe it'll give you some perspective."

"I have plenty of perspective. You could say I have a plethora of perspective."

Connor arched an eyebrow. "A plethora? Seriously?" Diaz didn't answer him. "Ten years ago."

"Connor! Don't you dare bring that up!"

"Ten years ago," Connor began again. "You remember? Me trying to do everything I could to get us ready to fight the Krake. I almost let it consume me. What did you do?"

Diaz rolled his eyes. "It's not the same."

"Yes, it is. You're putting up barriers rather than trying to fix things with your son."

"I didn't tell him to leave! He did that on his own."

"He was angry. I know Isaac's been in trouble a few times, but like it or not, this is important to him."

Diaz blew out a breath. "The damn Ovarrow."

"No, it's not just about them. Don't you get it? He's trying to figure out what he wants."

"That's just it. He doesn't know what he wants, and now he's around *them*. It's not safe there. He's not prepared for this."

"Have you tried to talk to him since he left?"

Diaz looked away for a few moments and shook his head.

"You can do it in person if you come with me. See what Isaac is doing. Maybe you'll even start to mend this rift between the two of you. Isaac isn't a kid anymore," Connor said and paused for a few moments. "We're going to investigate a couple of old Ovarrow sites, and we'll be near Shetrian. We can visit the embassy if you want."

Diaz swallowed hard and then lifted his gaze to his friend.

The door to the restaurant opened and Victoria walked out. "Pack your bags, Juan. You're going with Connor."

She strode toward him, and Connor gave them some room to speak. Mostly, it was Victoria speaking and Diaz nodding a few times.

"I'm asking you to do this for me," she said to Diaz. "I know you don't like it and you don't approve, but I also know you love all your children. Isaac needs you. You're two sides of the same coin, and I'm not going to lose him because you're stubborn."

Diaz pressed his lips together a little and took a deep breath. "He's not going to want to talk to me."

Victoria tilted her head to the side, her expression softening. "Then *make* him talk to you. I know if you show up and apologize—"

"I've got nothing be sorry for."

"Yes, you do. Isaac doesn't need our approval anymore."

Diaz was quiet for a few seconds. "All right. I'll go with Connor. I'll go to the embassy in Shetrian and check in on Isaac, but I'm not apologizing."

Victoria hugged him fiercely. She let him go and smiled a little at Connor, then hastened back into the restaurant.

Diaz just looked at Connor.

"Had to bring out the big guns," Connor said.

Diaz snorted. "I should've known. When do we leave?"

9

Civilian aerial transport vehicles—C-cats—had changed over the years as the colony evolved. They were no longer the de facto transportation option. The use of C-cats had given way to aircars, which required fewer resources to produce, but they wouldn't fade from use entirely because of their storage capacity. The base design for a CDF troop carrier had a foundation in the C-cat specifications. They could be modulated to perform any number of duties, and they were easy to maintain. As such, many C-cats stayed in service for a long time. They were mainly used in shipping equipment and supplies among the colonial cities, but various groups that worked in the field utilized their services as well.

Connor stood in front of hangar twenty-one at Quick's Airfield just outside the city of Sanctuary. The airfield provided services to just about anyone who required the use of shipping large equipment fast. The hangar doors were fully retracted, and a Hercules class C-cat fit snuggly inside, if only just barely. Connor watched as the ground crew guided the behemoth out of the hangar and then proceeded to load their equipment. Four N-Class rovers were driven up the loading ramp.

"Maybe he changed his mind," Lenora said.

"He'll be here," Connor replied.

An aircar flew overhead and landed nearby. Noah and Kara climbed out.

"I thought you said this was a small camping trip."

Connor smiled. "It's all relative."

"Are you kidding me?" Lenora said. "Do you know how many times I've gone into the field with hardly any equipment at all? No more."

Noah glanced up the loading ramp and whistled appreciatively. "If you have a few HAB unit kits in there, I'd think you were establishing another FORB."

Forward Operating Research Bases—FORB—were used for long-term expeditions.

"We've packed everything but the HABs," Connor replied.

Noah nodded. "I feel like I could've brought a few more toys of my own for this. Where are we going again?"

Connor chuckled. "Just twenty or thirty kilometers east of here."

Noah blinked several times and then shook his head. "You almost had me there."

Connor smiled. An audible chime came from his wrist computer. He opened his personal holoscreen and read the notification, then looked at Noah. "We're heading pretty far afield. We'll be thousands of kilometers away from here, or any other inhabitants for that matter. Hence the larger-than-average team for this."

"I saw a CDF squad inside. Who else is coming?"

"A couple of Lenora's students, a team of Mekaal, and a salty guest of honor."

"You're bringing Ovarrow on this trip?"

Connor nodded. "Sepal. He's a historian. Lenora has consulted with him before. It helps to have Ovarrow with us, and he's got a protective detail with him."

"All right. I guess you've been putting this expedition together for a while then."

"About once a year, if we can. It used to be just me, Lenora, and a handful of other people, but we've expanded."

"I'm surprised Dash isn't here. This would be right in his wheelhouse."

"He couldn't get away this year," Connor said with a shrug.

"I haven't heard from him in a while. Where's he been hiding lately?"

"Hiding?"

"You know what I mean."

Connor glanced around for a moment. "He still consults with the CDF."

"He's off-world?"

Connor nodded. "He's on a scouting mission."

"Scouting mission. Where?" Noah asked and then shook his head. "Never mind, I'm sure it's not something you can disclose."

The CDF still fielded scouting missions to alternate universes, searching for signs of a Krake resurgence.

"Dash teaches scout forces about both Ovarrow and Krake technology. He's actually got a team of trainers that help him. They're pretty good."

"Have they ever found anything?" Noah asked.

Connor shook his head.

Noah sighed. "That's good."

"Agreed."

"Dash is one of the good ones. I'm glad he's doing all right,"

Noah said. "So, who's the guest of honor?" he asked and frowned. "Wait. Did you say 'salty'?"

Another aircar flew overhead. It was black and tan with the Field Services logo on the side. Connor looked at Lenora. She stood a short distance away, conferring with the ground crew. She looked at him and he inclined his chin once with a smile. She touched two fingers to the side of her head in a salute.

"What's that about?" Noah asked.

"Just husband-and-wife stuff. She didn't think he was coming," Connor replied.

The aircar landed nearby and Diaz climbed out. He looked at the fully loaded Hercules class C-cat and rubbed the top of his head.

The aircar's side storage compartment opened, and Diaz reached inside for his travel kit. His lips thinned as he walked over to Connor.

"God, what's got him all stirred up?" Noah asked.

"Just you wait," Connor replied quietly and looked at Diaz. "Cutting it kinda close."

Diaz snorted. "I'm right on time," he said and looked at Noah. "Hey, kid, how you doing?"

"Kid?" Noah said with a grin. "It's good to see you too, old man."

Noah's good nature was infectious, and Diaz's stony facade softened. "You, too. I see Connor roped you into coming along."

Noah smiled. "I volunteered."

"There's a surprise."

"What?"

Diaz shook his head. "Nothing. I didn't get much sleep last night."

"That excited, are you?" Connor asked. Diaz simply stared at him. "Would it help if I told you that I have a present for you on board?"

Diaz chuckled. "Oh boy, a present just for me."

"You're gonna love it."

"I'm sure I will," Diaz replied and gestured at the nearest ground crew. "Can you load that crate over there?" he said, gesturing toward a storage container that had been deposited near the aircar.

"Yes, sir."

The ground crewman trotted over to the container and carried it up the loading ramp.

"What's in the container?" Noah asked.

"This is a camping trip, right?"

Noah glanced at Connor and they both nodded.

"I brought beer."

Connor grinned. "Now we're fully packed."

Lenora called out to him and gestured toward the C-cat.

Connor looked at Noah and Diaz. "Time to leave."

"Saved the best for last," Diaz said.

They started walking up the loading ramp.

"I'm trying to remember the last time we did something like this," Noah said.

They'd just cleared the ramp when Diaz suddenly stopped walking. The loading ramp began to retract into the C-cat.

"What's wrong?" Noah asked, peering ahead of them.

Diaz whirled around. "There are fucking Mekaal here!"

Noah went silent and glanced at Connor.

"Yes," Connor replied.

Diaz glared at the seating area.

"You want out?" Connor asked.

He considered it for a few moments and then shook his head. "No."

"Good, now stop acting crazy or you'll scare them. You know how you get sometimes."

Diaz sighed and began to walk. "Don't think I've forgotten about that present."

Connor smiled. "You're gonna love it."

Noah waited for Diaz to get farther ahead of them and leaned toward Connor. "Is he all right?"

Connor inhaled deeply and shook his head. "No."

Noah bobbed his head once.

They walked past the rovers and other storage containers and then through the doorway to the passenger area. There was plenty of seating available, and Diaz headed straight toward the CDF squad on the right.

Connor opened a data comlink to the pilot and gave him the all-clear to depart.

"I'll leave you to it," Noah said and went to sit with his wife.

Lenora stood in front of everyone, and Connor joined her. He looked at the group of Mekaal soldiers.

They stood up and saluted Connor in the Mekaal tradition.

"First Fist Urret, thank you for joining us," Connor said. "Did you have a chance to speak with Sergeant Tui?"

"I have not," Urret replied.

"There'll be plenty of time for that during the flight," Connor said.

The engines of the Hercules spun up, and soon after, the massive C-cat rose into the air.

"Can I have everyone's attention, please?" Lenora said.

Silence descended on the group almost immediately and Lenora smiled. "Thank you. Just a few words to kick off this expedition. Many of you have probably already reviewed the briefing of our expedition goals, but we have some late additions who haven't had a chance," she said and paused for a moment.

"We're searching for evidence of the Bhatdin. We believe they are a race of Ovarrow that came here from another universe hundreds of years ago and may have influenced events that led to the latest ice age. Intelligence gathered by the CDF from Ovarrow civilizations in other universes indicates that the Bhatdin were waging war with the Krake by helping others fight them. Their true origins are unknown, but it's believed that their homeworld was lost during their war with the Krake."

Noah raised his hand and Lenora inclined her chin once. "How many other places do you think the Bhatdin were in?"

"We're not sure exactly. Some of the leads are flimsy at best, but a few dozen civilizations had rumors of outside help. It's not a lot to go on. The Bhatdin operated in secret as much as they could," Lenora said and turned toward the others. "One of the questions we get is why bother looking for the Bhatdin at all? The Krake were defeated, so why do this?" She paused for a moment before continuing. "The pursuit of knowledge is one of the foundational cores not only of the colony but of humankind. The Mekaal are equally interested in learning more about the Bhatdin. As we search these sites, keep in mind the amazing history we've already uncovered. Perhaps we'll make a few more discoveries while we're here."

Lenora looked at Connor, handing the introductions over to him. "I couldn't have said it better myself. I just want to remind everyone that the places we'll be visiting have been undisturbed for a long time. Security details will go with all the teams. Both the CDF and Mekaal soldiers are here to help keep us all safe. Sergeant Dave Tui and First Fist Urret will organize the security details that go with the away teams. However, everyone is expected to do their part to keep us all safe both at camp and while we're away."

Lenora went to sit with her students and Connor walked to where Diaz sat. "Come take a walk with me."

Diaz stood up. "Lead the way."

Connor walked back toward the storage area and opened the door. There was a platform of field equipment and he read the tags on the outside. After he found the one he wanted, he opened it and pulled out a smaller container that was a little over a meter in length, handing it to Diaz.

"I had this made for you," Connor said.

Diaz opened the container. He grinned. "Would you look at that," he said, reaching inside to pull out a tri-barreled shotgun. The polished chrome gleamed in the light, and the handle was made of a pearl-colored composite. The stock had an etching of the Salty Soldier on the side.

Diaz glided his fingers over the stock appreciatively. Then, he narrowed his gaze toward Connor for a moment. The edges of his lips lifted, and he grinned. "Damn it, Connor, I love it. But you didn't have this made in the last few days."

Connor shook his head. "No, it was going to be a birthday present, but I figured you'd like it sooner rather than later."

Diaz nodded. His gaze continued to slide up and down the shotgun appreciatively.

"Friends?" Connor asked.

Diaz set the shotgun back into the case and closed it, looking at Connor with a somber expression. "Always."

10

THE N-CLASS ROVER was parked a short distance away. Connor gave the cable attached to the winch a firm tug and then connected it to the mid-section of the harness before using his foot to flick a rock over the rim of a collapsed rooftop. It ricocheted a few times as it fell over forty meters to the dimly lit ground below. The recon drone scouting the area had dropped several amber glow sticks that marked the bottom.

Connor looked at Lenora.

"Ready," she said.

Diaz adjusted his harness so it would fit over his thick chest. Then he attached the tether cable and gave it several jerks before he was satisfied it was going to hold him.

Noah muttered something while he fumbled with his harness. "Sorry, I'm trying to remember how to do this. It's been a while."

"Anytime now," Diaz replied.

Connor sighed in mock irritation. "Seriously, Noah, we could have been back by now."

Noah chuckled while he checked the harness. "If I don't do it right, I could fall and hurt myself. You guys wouldn't want that to happen to me, right?"

Connor glanced at Noah's setup and frowned.

Noah's eyebrows raised. "What? Is something wrong? Did I miss a step? I thought I did it right. It looks fine, I think. What?"

Connor leaned over and peered at Noah's harness. Then he grabbed the straps and leaped over the rim, pulling his friend with him. Noah screamed, and Connor laughed as they shot through the air in free fall for a couple of seconds before the winching mechanism applied tension to their cables, slowing their descent.

Noah reached the ground first and hunched over, grabbing his knees and gasping. "You bastard. You nearly gave me a heart attack. I can't believe you did that."

When Connor's feet touched the ground, he detached the cable and watched it retract up to the Rover. A grin bubbled up from this chest. "You were taking too long."

"Taking too long!" Noah shook his head. His facial expression danced between a grin and slight irritation, as if he couldn't decide whether he was mad at Connor. But after the confusion of falling so far, so fast, he realized that he was fine. He shook his head. "I see how it is now. You better watch your back."

Connor smiled. "That's the spirit."

Noah grinned.

"You've got to admit it was funny, right?"

"You know what they say about payback."

Connor chuckled.

The others soon joined them, albeit in a much slower descent.

Lenora looked at Connor with a hint of exasperation. "You just can't help yourself."

"Sometimes I can't. I really can't."

Her blue eyes flicked upward, and she smiled.

They had spent the better part of the morning scouting the outskirts of an Ovarrow city. The Mekaal couldn't agree on its name, and Urret and the other Mekaal soldiers deferred to Sepal, who had narrowed it down to a couple of possibilities. Lenora had wisely suggested that he should bring back whatever data they found, along with general observations, to be reviewed by the historians at Shetrian.

The Mekaal had always respected Connor because of his military prowess and the fact that he'd been instrumental in preparing them for the Krake. When the Mekaal learned of the colonial war against the Vemus, it had solidified Connor's reputation to the human equivalent of legendary status.

As the Mekaal interacted with the colonists, they'd begun to embrace some of the colonial practices, particularly among scientists. Scientific peer review was an essential ingredient of significant progress. It took time, and on occasion, appeared to be stagnant, but it was necessary. Even though the Ovarrow practiced a rudimentary form of peer review, the process was often fraught by misinformation and suppression of opposing viewpoints. Connor thought that as the Mekaal learned more of humanity's history, they'd realize that they'd had similar struggles to those that had plagued the Ovarrow civilization, and not only had humanity overcome these challenges but had become better for it. This had forged the foundations of a bond between the Mekaal and the colonists, though there would always be challenges on both sides.

Connor glanced at Diaz for a second. What the Mekaal and

the colonists needed was time—time to live and grow in such a way that allowed for the newness to become ordinary. But Diaz wasn't the only colonist who had strong opinions where the Ovarrow were concerned.

"We should clear the way so the others can come down," Lenora said.

The rest of them detached their cables and moved off to the side.

Diaz looked at Noah. "If there were any ryklars in the area, they sure as hell know we're here."

"There haven't been that many around lately. Haven't you noticed? Maybe they've migrated somewhere else," Noah replied.

Diaz looked at Connor for a few moments, considering. Connor knew why there were fewer ryklars—not just here but throughout the region. The CDF had been relocating them to another planet, and the operation was being carried out without the knowledge of the general population. A few Mekaal leaders knew of the undertaking, but that was about it.

Noah looked around, taking stock of their surroundings, including remnants of ancient machines that had propelled multiple assembly lines. Exposure to the elements had left them covered with dirt and moss in some areas. Moisture glistened in the vicinity, but beyond the gaping hole above them, things looked better preserved.

Noah inhaled and sighed. "This wasn't at all what I was expecting."

"What *did* you expect?" Connor asked.

"Not tracking logistical supply lines used between cities or exploring old factories."

Connor shrugged. "You can learn a lot by tracking supply chains."

"You think the Bhatdin used supply chains to help the Ovarrow fight the Krake?"

"Not exactly," Lenora said. "They'd introduce new manufacturing methods, and then those improvements would make their way into a supply chain. Like improvements for composites used in construction, for example. We trace these improvements, looking for a pattern that will lead us to the source."

Noah considered this for a few moments. "I guess it beats randomly searching one abandoned city after another."

"It helps narrow the search grid," Connor said.

Diaz snorted. "Your grid is still the size of the entire continent."

"Yeah, it is," Connor agreed. "That's why we have Sepal and Urret's team with us."

Diaz's eyes went skyward for a second. "Oh joy. We're saved."

Noah looked at Diaz with a thoughtful frown. "You can't possibly hate them all."

Diaz regarded Noah for a few moments, then rolled his eyes and blew out a breath.

"Come on, really?"

"Fine, they're not all bad, but they could be better," Diaz said.

"The same could be said about us."

Diaz replied with a grunt of acknowledgment.

They were soon joined by Urret, two other Mekaal soldiers, and Sepal. Six cables hung in the air, and Connor shared the waypoint with the others.

Diaz looked at him questioningly.

"Just in case we get separated," Connor answered.

Noah walked next to Sepal. "You're a historian?"

The Ovarrow's head bobbed as he walked. "I have multiple

skills, but to answer your question directly, yes, a part of my duties is keeping and sharing knowledge of historical events and practices."

Noah frowned and the edges of his lips quirked a little. "That's a lot for anyone to take on."

The Ovarrow shared a common ancestry that included reptiles, which gave them the vertical pupils that most colonists found unsettling until they got used to them. Sepal looked at Noah and his gaze grew in intensity. "Execution of my duties has always been to the level of my peers as required. My proclivity for processing information is beyond the normalcy for my kind."

Noah looked at Connor. "I think something is getting lost in translation here."

"Yeah, you're almost insulting him."

Noah's mouth hung open a little and he glanced at Sepal. "I didn't mean to. If I've offended you, please accept my sincerest apologies."

"Give me a break," Diaz scoffed.

Sepal looked at Diaz.

"He was just asking you a couple of questions. No need to be so uptight about it."

Sepal cocked his head to the side.

"Wait a second," Connor said. "The Mekaal take their assigned roles seriously."

Diaz shrugged, unconvinced. "Well, so do we. What's your point?"

"The point is that the Mekaal make their decisions based on the capabilities of the individual. There is no room for bruised egos when it comes to assigned tasks. Everyone's place must be in service of all. They earn their places among their peers."

"Well, what's his problem then?" Diaz asked and looked at Sepal.

Sepal seemed to relax. "There is no problem here, but there seems to be an increase in an emotional response from you. Yes, there is a marked increase in temperature that suggests a hastiness for anger."

Diaz blinked several times and Noah laughed.

"What are you laughing at?"

"I just think it's funny that he called you emotional."

"That's a new one," Connor agreed.

Diaz looked as if he was deciding whether to be offended by the Mekaal historian. Instead, he smiled wolfishly. "I'm one big bundle of joy. Now, let's take a look around."

They began to explore the factory. Connor thought they might have found a warehouse, but he'd been wrong.

"Emotional," Diaz grumbled to himself. He looked at Connor. "Watch out! I'm thinking of expressing my emotions vehemently."

Connor snorted and kept walking. Lenora came over to him. Her personal holoscreen was running an analysis program that attempted to recreate the area they were in.

"See the walls over there? Same artwork."

"Company logo, maybe," Connor said.

"Could be. At least we're seeing a pattern."

"I don't get it. What's so important about the logo?" Diaz asked.

"We've seen it at other locations. They all seem to have something to do with industrial sites," Lenora replied.

Diaz shrugged. "It could just be a regional thing."

"True," Connor agreed. "We need to find their control systems."

Noah looked around. "They were using a fair amount of automation, but I doubt anything here would work again, even if we ran power to it."

They continued walking between long industrial lines that looked to have fallen into disrepair, and it was impossible to determine whether the factory had been in use before the ice age. It could have been shuttered before the ice age was triggered.

Lenora and the others put on smart-glasses that would allow them to see better in the dim light and also helped them identify known systems the Ovarrow used. The data was stored in their wrist computers. The Mekaal soldiers wore night-vision goggles because the glasses the colonists used wouldn't sit right on their almost non-existent noses. Connor, Diaz, and Noah didn't need the smart-glasses because they had higher functioning implants —built-in artificial lenses that could do much more than enable them to see in the dark. The CDF had standardized the use of basic implants for all soldiers. The wetware was proven tech that humanity had been using for a long time. Connor had tried to convince Lenora to upgrade her implants, but she'd refused, preferring to use wearable tech.

They continued to explore the factory ruins, eventually splitting up to cover more ground quicker. Sepal and the Mekaal had gone off exploring on their own, while Connor and the others went in a different direction.

They found a series of ramps that led down to the lower levels. Age had left gaping holes in some areas, exposing the substructure that held everything together. Connor went first, moving along the support walls and pausing to attach a rope for the others to hold onto. He made it past the patchwork section and gestured for the others to follow.

"It's hard to believe there's this much structure down here," Diaz said.

"Technically, when we made that initial drop from the rooftop, we landed on the ground floor," Connor said.

"The landscape has changed that much around here?" Diaz asked.

"In some places," Lenora replied. "There's an ongoing effort to study how the ice age changed the topography."

Diaz frowned. "Where?"

"At the research institute."

"No, I meant what areas are they studying?"

"Oh, everywhere. We've been mapping the planet's surface since before we arrived here," Lenora replied. Diaz pinched his lips together. "They use the data we've already gathered to pick sites for field research and then try to establish a baseline by region."

"Scouting for bunkers really advanced those efforts quite a bit," Connor said.

Noah sneezed and then coughed. "Are they still finding bunkers?"

"Not in our region, but there's still much of the planet left to explore. The problem is that there isn't a record of the bunker sites or where they're located," Connor said.

"The Mekaal have good ground transportation available, so they can extend their search area," Noah said.

Diaz sneered. "Not if the Konus have anything to say about it. They've been around a lot longer." He paused and looked at Connor.

"Forty years before we found them. Getting closer to fifty years now."

Diaz nodded.

Lenora called out for Connor. She'd gone ahead and was peering at a closed door.

Connor caught up to her. "Did you find the control panel?" he asked.

Lenora frowned and shook her head. "It's not where I

expected it to be." She ran her fingers along the wall left of the door.

Connor looked around the door, searching for a control panel, but the walls were smooth and featureless. He frowned and glanced at the floor. There were several floor panels that he could just about make out. He put down his tool kit and rummaged through the contents, pulling out a pry bar and a small plasma torch.

"Did you find something?" Lenora asked.

"Maybe," he replied and gestured toward the floor panels.

Lenora backed away from the door and peered at the ground.

He knelt down and pushed the edge of the pry bar into the edge of the panel, working the hardened edge in under the lip by moving it side to side.

"Come on, put your back into it," Diaz said and grinned.

Connor pulled the pry bar up and then pushed the end farther inside. As he worked it in, the floor panel began to come apart. Hundreds of years had fused the tightly fitting panels.

Diaz came to his side and shoved his own pry bar into the opening. Together, they forced the opening wider and then heaved. The floor panel popped up with a metallic groan and a clang. Underneath was more subflooring, but those came out with minimal effort.

"Noah, pass me the portable power generator," Connor said.

Noah handed Connor a small rectangular box with a few power cables wrapped around it and then knelt down, looking at the cables in the floor. "That one right there?" he asked, pointing to an old power line.

"Go for it," Connor said.

Noah connected the generator and turned it on. Then, Connor raised his wrist computer and scanned for the door control interface. He quickly found it, and multiple sections of the door pulled away in swirling pieces faster than he could count.

"Keep it connected," Connor said. He'd prefer to avoid being trapped on the other side once they went through.

Connor peered inside the control center, and the light from his wrist computer reflected off multiple computer stations. Ovarrow consoles had a circular base that came up from the floor and widened at the top. Typically, the computer interface was projected onto a mesh screen, but as expected, the mesh display screen had long since deteriorated.

Lenora walked to the nearest console and connected a portable holographic interface. A few moments later, an amber holoscreen appeared, and an Ovarrow translator outputted the data in a format the colonists could read.

They went to the other consoles and connected a data exfiltration device. They'd found that it was easier to extract all the data they could from local storage and do their own analysis with the vastly superior computers they'd brought with them.

"This one only has local storage," Noah said.

"I've got one that connects to a backup system. Shouldn't take long to retrieve what's there," Connor said.

A comlink notification appeared on his HUD.

"General Gates, do you copy?" Sergeant Tui asked.

"I read you."

"We're not alone at this site, General. There is a Konus scout force making its way into the city southwest of our camp. They've got at least forty soldiers with them."

The others looked at Connor. "Understood, Sergeant. Task a recon drone to keep an eye on them."

"Yes, General," Sergeant Tui replied, and the comlink disconnected.

"Son of a... Konus?" Diaz groused.

"How far are we from their city?" Noah asked.

"About seven hundred kilometers," Connor replied.

"Do they normally venture out this far?"

"They can, but none of our reports have shown them in any of the areas we're planning to visit," Connor said.

Lenora stowed their data storage devices in her pack.

"Should we contact them?" Noah asked.

"Are you kidding me?" Diaz said.

"No, I'm not kidding. We're here and so are they."

They both looked at Connor.

He'd rather avoid contact with them if he could. Communication with the Konus wasn't cordial in any sense of the word. The CDF had fought the Konus when they'd tried to invade Shetrian and absorb the Mekaal into their numbers. The conflict had cost a lot of lives, and in the years since, there had been few efforts at establishing diplomatic relations with the Konus. Connor wasn't involved in any of that.

The Konus were rigid in their approach to survival. Their methods were based on practices that had existed before the ice age. The differences between the Konus and Mekaal had become more prevalent over the years. The Mekaal had chosen to ally with the colony and adapt their civilization to embrace human values. According to their histories, there'd been a time before the Krake when the Ovarrow civilization had embraced many similarities to the nations of Old Earth. The Mekaal were more militaristic than the colony, but the Konus were quick to go to extremes. They viewed 'survival at all costs' as a societal norm. And now they were here.

"We'll talk about what to do about the Konus back at camp," Connor said.

"I'm finished here. I need some time to review the data we've gathered," Lenora said.

"I'd like to take a look at it, too," Noah said.

Lenora smiled. "Of course you will."

"Don't you want to keep searching here?" Diaz asked.

"There are a few more places to check, but I think this room had the real payload we were searching for," Connor replied.

11

THEY RETURNED to camp and began reviewing the data they'd been able to retrieve. Connor left Lenora, Noah, and Kara to work on it.

He accessed the recon drone video feeds. They'd been monitoring the Konus as they began to explore the city, likely searching for a place to camp. There were only a few more hours of daylight left, and Connor had to decide what to do about the situation. Betting on avoiding them wasn't a reliable option. All the Konus had to do was explore the city and do a proper survey to detect that they weren't alone there either. The Konus always traveled armed with weapons, and the colonists did the same. Most of the continent would be considered wild frontier except for established population centers. Traveling without some kind of protection was a quick way to an early grave.

Connor closed the video feed and walked to the rover. He opened the storage compartment in the back and transmitted his credentials to the weapons locker, which chimed an acknowledgement and opened. He'd only been carrying a CDF predator pistol, but with the Konus so close by, he needed something with more stopping power. He reached into the locker and pulled out one of the AR-74 assault rifles, standard issue for CDF soldiers because of its versatility and toughness. Loaded with nanorobotic ammunition, the AR-74 could fire different types of projectiles with both explosive and nonexplosive rounds. The default was set for controlled bursts firing three rounds each but could easily fire at full auto. It was just a good all-around weapon that was easy to train with and yet flexible enough to adapt to the capabilities of a real marksman. Connor was an excellent shot, among the best in the colony. There were a few soldiers who could compete with him, but none were with him here.

He heard someone walking toward him and looked up to see Diaz coming around the corner of the rover. His gaze flicked toward the assault rifle, and he smiled and nodded his approval.

Connor gestured toward the weapons locker. "Want one?"

"I've already got mine, thanks to you," Diaz said, gesturing with his thumb toward the tri-barreled shotgun that was attached to his backpack.

"We can't afford to get caught off guard."

Diaz looked at the other assault rifles in the weapons locker. "You've brought enough, but how many people know how to use them?"

Connor scratched the skin above one of his eyebrows. "Lenora knows her way around one. I don't think Noah and Kara have practiced all that much recently, but if push came to shove, I believe they could step up if needed. The students definitely have never used one. They'll stick with the civilian rifles they're cleared to use. Urret and the rest of his squad are familiar with them, but I expect they'll prefer to use their own weapons. Are you sure you don't want one?"

Diaz shook his head. "I'm fine with this." He pulled out the shotgun. "This baby will get the job done if it comes down to it. What do you intend to do?"

Connor closed the locker and then the storage compartment. "Come on."

Connor walked to where the CDF squad was waiting for them. Urret and the other Mekaal soldiers were also there.

Sergeant Tui stood up and the other soldiers did the same.

"General Gates, the Konus scouting force is heading in our direction," Sergeant Tui said.

Diaz shook his head.

"That simplifies things," Connor said.

"So, we're going to pack up camp and head to the next waypoint?" Diaz asked.

"Negative," Connor said and looked at Sergeant Tui. "Who's your tech specialist?"

"Specialist Cora Weps, General," Tui replied and gestured toward a female soldier standing nearby.

When Connor looked at her, Specialist Weps stood up straight but not quite at attention.

"Do you have a comms drone in your kit, Specialist?"

"Negative, General. They're back aboard the ship. I can go retrieve one."

Connor shook his head. "Not necessary. We'll use the recon drone. I want you to fly it toward the Konus. Slow and steady. Let them see it coming."

"Yes, General," Specialist Weps replied.

Connor watched as she dropped the stealth protocol and engaged the indicator lights so the drone would be easy to spot.

"What are you going to do?" Diaz asked.

"I'm going to tell them we're here."

"What for?"

"They're heading in our direction. I'd much rather they know we're aware of them than give them the impression that they've snuck up on us. Specialist, I'll take it from here," Connor said.

"Passing control to you, General Gates," Weps said.

A data comlink came to prominence on Connor's wrist computer. The recon drone hovered nearly seven meters in the air. Twenty Konus soldiers were walking toward it. They must have sent a smaller group to scout in a different direction. They were searching the city on foot, but they must have reached the area somehow.

Connor engaged the drone's holo-projector and a holographic image of him appeared on the ground in front of the approaching Konus.

Ovarrow skin tones favored their reptilian ancestry in various tones of browns and tans, but there were also paler skin complexions, as if they'd covered themselves with gray-colored ash.

Several of the soldiers gestured toward Connor's holographic image. A few raised their weapons a little but didn't aim them at the drone.

"Hello," Connor said. "I'm part of a colonial survey team that's scouting the city. I just wanted to let you know we're here. Our camp is a few kilometers away."

One of the Konus stepped forward. "Have you been following us?"

"No, I assure you that we're just as surprised to find you here as you are, no doubt, that we're here."

The Konus's eyes flicked up and down. "I recognize you. You're the CDF General Connor Gates."

Connor heard Diaz mutter something, but he ignored him. "That's right. Who are you?"

"Shuno. I'm First Fist of this scout force."

"What brings you here?"

Shuno cocked his head to the side, which was the Ovarrow equivalent of keeping their guard up. "I could ask you the same thing."

Well, he'd asked the question, and he wasn't surprised to have it turned back around on him. "We're scouting the city here, looking for salvageable material."

Shuno regarded Connor for a few seconds. "We are doing the same."

"You're pretty far from home."

He knew this statement would irritate the Konus, but irritation went both ways sometimes. Throughout his interactions with Ovarrow on multiple worlds, he'd learned that there was a time and place for being polite. This wasn't one of those times.

"What are you doing here?" Connor asked.

One of the other Konus said something that the drone's microphone couldn't detect well enough for the translator to provide a translation. Shuno inclined his chin toward the other soldiers, and they began walking back the way they'd come. After a few moments, Shuno followed them.

Connor sighed and killed the comlink. He passed control of the drone back to Specialist Weps. "Keep an eye on them," he said.

"Yes, General," Weps replied.

Diaz grunted. "Such a warm reception. He didn't answer your question."

"Yeah, I know. But at least they know we're here."

"General, do you think the Konus will be a problem tonight?" Sergeant Tui asked.

Connor wished he knew. "We'll do a watch rotation."

"Understood, General."

Connor looked at Diaz. "Stop looking so smug. Let's go see if the others learned anything from the data we got."

As they were walking away, Urret quickly caught up with them. "General Gates, we'd like to help."

Connor looked at the Mekaal soldier. "All right, coordinate with Sergeant Tui."

"Thank you, General," Urret said.

The Mekaal soldier gestured toward his companion, and they hastened over to Sergeant Tui.

Urret followed Connor and Diaz.

Diaz looked back toward the soldier for a second and then at Connor. "Are you sure you don't want to leave? Maybe call in a few more squads at least?"

"If it comes to it, I will. I'm more interested in what they're doing here."

"You think he's lying to us?"

Connor shrugged. "I'm sure they're here to scout, but for what, I'm not sure."

Urret quickened his pace until he walked abreast of them. "They could be searching for more of my people in stasis. There could be bunkers hidden in the area."

Connor considered it for a moment. "It's possible."

"All we need is to get involved in a dispute between the Konus and Mekaal," Diaz said.

"Calm down. The likelihood of a bunker hidden inside the city is remote at best."

"How do you know?"

"I don't know. Maybe it's because I've spent a lot of time looking for them over the years. They didn't build bunkers in major metropolitan areas," Connor replied.

"He's right," Urret said. "Cities were being destroyed. Bunkers would have been built in remote locations."

Diaz blinked and looked at them. "What if this place is different? You can't even agree what the name of it is."

"All right, Juan, you're right. We can't rule it out. No one can, okay?"

Diaz inhaled and nodded.

Urret looked away from them in the direction the Konus were located. They couldn't see them, not with remnant buildings and overgrowth in the way. Even if they climbed one of the taller buildings, Connor doubted they could spot the Konus. That's what the recon drones were for.

They continued walking toward where Lenora had set up her equipment, and Connor caught snippets of conversation as they approached.

"There's no way Connor is going to go for that," Noah said.

"We'll see," Lenora replied. "Sepal, what do you think?"

Connor walked around a stack of equipment and saw his wife and the others speaking inside a tent. The walls had been rolled up, allowing the occasional breeze to come through.

Sepal looked as if he'd been scowling.

"Go for what?" Connor asked. "Did you find something?"

Lenora smiled and nodded enthusiastically. "We did. The same company logo that we've documented from the other sites. However, this time it was written into the software they used on the manufacturing line."

"What's so special about the logo?" Diaz asked.

"I'll show you," Lenora replied.

She opened a holoscreen and displayed the spherical logo they'd seen before. "Looks simple enough, right? Just a group of spheres, but check this out." The grouping of spheres changed as if they'd been pulled apart, forming a model of the star system. "The analysis AI was able to determine the measurements of the spheres, and based on their locations, saw that they could be interpreted as distance measurements. They line up with each planet in this star system. Noah confirmed it for me."

Connor's eyebrows raised and he looked at Noah.

"It's true. I'm having trouble believing it, but it's true."

"Could it be a coincidence?" Connor asked.

"That's what I thought, too," Lenora replied. "I thought the AI was just pointing out something that didn't measure up."

Noah nodded. "So, I put the data into a navigation program and it's a match. Not just a match, but down to the actual distance from the star. There're even hidden computational inputs to account for their orbits."

Connor stared at the star map on the holoscreen. "Why put all that in a logo?"

"Wouldn't that alert the Krake?" Diaz asked.

"That's a valid point," Connor said.

Lenora shrugged. "I don't know. Maybe it's a calling card of some sort, which is why I want to speak to the Konus about it."

Connor blinked several times and frowned. "You want to talk to the Konus about this?" he asked, gesturing toward the holoscreen.

"I do."

Diaz grimaced. "Oh man that's…" he muttered.

Connor didn't know what to say. He wasn't sure it was a good idea, but it also wasn't something he could outright forbid. Lenora would just march right over and ask them herself.

"Help me understand why this is even a possibility," Connor said.

Noah's eyebrows raised and he glanced at Kara for a second.

Lenora shrugged. "They've been around a long time. They've explored more of the continent than we have. And there are more of them, which means there might be someone among them who knows more about who the Bhatdin were," she said, gesturing toward the holoscreen.

Connor thought about it. She made some good arguments. "What do you think, Sepal. Have you seen this before?"

"I can't recall it. I would need to craft a search of our archives," Sepal said.

"Fair enough," Connor replied. "We could go through diplomatic channels to see if the Konus are willing to cooperate."

The edges of Lenora's lips lifted and her eyes gleamed. Connor knew she wasn't willing to wait.

"Or we can ask the Konus who are already here. It might be worth finding out what they're doing here anyway," Lenora said.

Connor snorted. He should've known better. "Okay, but let's wait until morning," he said and told them about contacting them via the recon drone.

He also wanted to know why the Konus had ventured so far from their home. Lenora's query would give him an excuse to find out more.

Noah walked over and stood next to Connor. "So, Konus, huh?"

"Yeah."

Noah tilted his head to the side.

"It'll be fun. It's all part of the package."

Noah grinned. "I figured. Anyway, regarding the Bhatdin, I think you're really onto something with them."

Connor smiled. "It's interesting. I wonder what happened to them."

"Did they go into stasis? Did they go to another world? Did they all die? I wonder how many of them there were," Noah said.

"Exactly," Connor replied.

Diaz blew out a breath. "I'm glad you're having such a good time."

Connor glanced at Noah and they both shrugged. "I doubt the Konus came all the way out here to start a fight. Let's just keep a level head."

Diaz smiled with half his mouth. "I'm emotional, remember?"

Connor laughed, and Noah and Diaz joined in.

12

SHADOWS FELL in sharp slants from all the tall trees and buildings, turning the remnant streets and sidewalks into bands of light and darkness, but the night passed by uneventfully. The Konus had set up camp just a few kilometers away.

Connor decided to take the direct approach. After a quick breakfast, they climbed into the rovers and began heading toward their potential rivals.

"How long until we get to Camp Konus?" Diaz asked, his mouth twitching with amusement.

"Shouldn't take long," Connor said.

Camp Konus... Leave it to Diaz to assign labels that would instantly cement themselves in everyone's mind. Diaz had told Connor how he'd come up with the 'Salty Soldier' name for his restaurant on a whim and just went with it. Connor smiled a little at Diaz's nickname for the camp because it had already stuck in his head. Even the others in their group were now referring to it by that name.

Connor drove the rover. Gnarled tree roots invaded the old

city streets, which meant they had to take their time, but the terrain wasn't anything the rovers couldn't handle. Connor had firsthand experience at pushing the limits of the N-class rovers.

Diaz looked at Lenora. "I still can't believe you want to talk to them."

"Think of it like this," she began. "If all our interactions with the Konus are through ambassadors and the CDF, then that's the only basis they'll have to interact with us. We're more than that, and if we open communications to include efforts like this, maybe we can improve relations with them."

Diaz pursed his lips in thought. "I hope you're right. I really do."

Connor smiled to himself. Diaz had no issues expressing his opinions, but with Lenora he'd always been more respectful. He often said she was the sister he'd never had.

The Konus had taken up temporary residence in one of the taller buildings, and Connor spotted a couple of scouts on the roof. He kept the rover at a constant speed as they slowly approached the camp and stopped about thirty meters from the building.

Connor looked at Lenora. "I'll get out first, along with Tui and the others. Give us a few minutes and I'll signal for the rest of you to follow."

Lenora nodded. "We'll wait here."

Connor looked at Noah and Kara, and they each gave him a nod.

"Let's go, Juan."

Connor grabbed his rifle and stepped out of the vehicle while Diaz got out on the other side. Sergeant Tui and the rest of the CDF squad exited the second rover and spread out, staggering their formation. Then Urret and his squad of Mekaal soldiers did the same.

Connor looked up at the scouts and heard more Konus soldiers from inside the building.

"First Fist Shuno, I'd like to speak with you," Connor called loudly while walking ahead of the others. He was exposed and he knew it. It was a calculated risk.

Konus soldiers walked out of the building and took defensive positions. They wore a pale green metallic armor that protected their chests and arms, and even though they didn't aim their weapons at the colonists, they were ready for action should the need arise.

Shuno walked out of the building and regarded Connor. Irritation flickered over his face and was gone.

Connor walked toward him for a few paces and stopped. Diaz stood a short distance behind him to his right. Connor's rifle hung from the straps with the barrel toward the ground, freeing his hands.

"We just want to talk. Are you willing to do that?" Connor asked.

Shuno walked toward him, and one of the Konus soldiers followed him. The rest stayed behind. Their armor covered parts of their bodies, but it appeared to be lightweight and suitable to quick movements—standard for scouting missions. Traveling with thirty soldiers put them at a platoon-sized deployment, and Connor thought it was a safe bet that a few Konus soldiers carried heavier weapons than the long plasma rifles the others carried. Only fifteen Konus soldiers had exited the building, but the two scouts remained on the rooftop. Where were the rest of them?

"General Gates," Shuno said. The Ovarrow translator had given him a generic human accent that was easily understandable. "Are there more soldiers with you?"

Not the most tactful question, but Connor supposed the

question was fair enough. Shuno was trying to figure out how much of a threat they were.

"As I told you yesterday, we're here scouting the city. I only brought a small scout force with me, but as you are well aware, more can be here quickly if there is need," Connor said and gestured skyward.

Shuno raised his gaze and then looked behind Connor when Urret walked up to stand next to Connor.

"Mekaal," Shuno said.

The Ovarrow translator had been refined over the years to give an accurate conveyance of tone that implied the mood of a statement. However, Connor didn't need a translator to understand that Shuno had made it sound like both an accusation and disdain at the same time.

"Konus," Urret replied in what was more of an acknowledgement than any sort of terse statement.

"So, you're servants of the colonists?" Shuno asked.

"No, we're their companions."

"Are you in command?"

Urret hesitated for a moment then said, "No."

"They are here as my guests," Connor said.

Shuno regarded Connor for a few seconds. "Are they free to leave? Would you allow them to join us?"

"If that's what Urret and the others want."

Shuno's gaze flicked toward Urret. "You should join us. Only together can we be as we were."

"That's the problem. The Konus seek to rebuild a world that is gone. We seek to build a new world with new alliances," Urret said and looked at Connor.

"You betray the sacrifice of the Mekaal by being subservient to the invaders. The Mekaal used to be strong," Shuno said.

"Do you seek to test us?" Urret replied.

Shuno didn't blink. "I would like that very much."

The two Ovarrow glared at each other.

The exchange had been quick, and Connor needed to intercede before things got out of control.

"We're not invaders, Shuno."

Shuno turned toward him. "Not invaders? You come to Bhaneteran uninvited. You take what doesn't belong to you. You manipulate my people to join you. And there are things that you do in secret—things that you think no one knows about, but we do. You brought the Krake here and nearly killed us all."

Bhaneteran was what the Ovarrow called New Earth.

"We stopped the Krake and destroyed their homeworld. There was a cost that affected us all, but it's the cost soldiers pay —yours, mine, theirs," he said, tilting his head toward Urret. "We've bled for this world. Bhaneteran is as much our home as it is yours. We're not going anywhere, and it's time for the Konus to accept it."

"We accept nothing. We've endured war with the Krake, and we can endure an occupation by humans."

Diaz puffed out a breath and glowered at Shuno. "Was it war with the Krake that destroyed your cities? I thought you did that on your own."

Shuno glared at Diaz.

Connor also looked at Diaz, and his friend simply stared back at him. "Shuno," he said, turning back toward the Konus officer. "I don't want to get into any kind of debate with you. I only wanted to discuss what we found here."

"Never before have your kind wished to discuss anything with us."

"For good reason—" Diaz began and then clamped his mouth shut.

Connor was getting irritated with the whole situation. He

looked back at the rover where Lenora and the others watched them. They leaned forward and Lenora bobbed her head once. He sighed and turned back toward Shuno.

"We found something. We'd like you to take a look and see if you recognize it. That's it. If you don't want to do it, we'll be on our way."

Shuno looked at Urret and the other Mekaal, and then at the CDF soldiers before his gaze returned to Connor.

"Why would I help you?"

"Because you lost your world. You scout these old cities for resources, but I suspect you also search for answers."

Shuno frowned in thought.

"You're survivors of a holocaust. Don't you want to know more about your own history?"

"It's gone. It doesn't matter anymore," Shuno replied.

"How can you learn from it if you don't study it? Would you repeat the same mistakes? What if your historians are wrong about the past? What if there is more to it than the Krake invading your world and manipulating your entire civilization?"

Shuno looked at Urret. "This is what you're doing? You search for answers?"

Urret seemed to relax a little. "It's how we can improve and become stronger."

"Like them."

"There is much we can learn from them."

Shuno turned away. He stepped toward his companion and the two spoke softly.

Connor shared a look with Urret but didn't say anything. They had to wait. Normally, he got a sense of the direction a given situation would go in most negotiations, but he didn't have an inkling one way or the other in this one. He looked at Lenora and gestured for them to wait. He'd kept a comlink open so they could listen to what transpired.

Several more Konus soldiers joined Shuno and they spoke for a few minutes. Connor watched them, but he couldn't hear what they were saying. The other Konus soldiers deferred to Shuno, which confirmed to Connor that he was the highest-ranking officer here. Shuno was getting feedback from the others, which they seemed to give in quick, straight-to-the-point responses. He and Shuno might be on opposite sides of multiple issues, but he recognized an experienced leader when he saw one.

Shuno dismissed the others and watched them return to their original locations. He then walked back toward Connor.

"I will listen to what you've learned, and in return, you will answer my questions."

"I'll answer what I can," Connor replied. He turned toward the rover and gestured for the others to come out.

Lenora exited first, followed by Noah, Kara, and Sepal. The students remained inside the vehicle.

"This is Lenora. She's an archeologist who's been studying your civilization for over twenty years," Connor said. He wouldn't disclose that Lenora was his wife. They didn't need any more information than what was absolutely necessary. "This is Sepal, a Mekaal historian who is working with us to find answers."

Shuno's gaze lingered on Sepal for a few seconds in mild disapproval.

Lenora cleared her throat. "Thank you for agreeing to speak with us," she said and told him about the Bhatdin. "Their existence is suspected on multiple worlds accessed through the arch gateways."

Shuno listened intently. "We know of the gateways, but not

of any of the Ovarrow on other worlds. The gateways were of Krake design. We didn't use them."

"That isn't true," Connor said. "The first gateway we encountered was among the ruins of one of your cities. We've found others elsewhere. They couldn't all have been controlled by the Krake."

Shuno's face twisted between a sneer and a thoughtful frown. "Then whoever used them are unknown to me."

"Yes, but do you know anything about the Bhatdin?"

"That name is unknown to me."

"What about this logo?" Lenora asked and used her wrist computer's holoscreen to show them what they'd found.

Shuno peered at the logo, and Connor thought he recognized it. "Where did you find this?"

Lenora opened another holoscreen, which appeared beside the one with the logo. "It was in the ruins of a factory not far from here. I can share the location and you can go there if you want, but the consoles have deteriorated and they don't have any power."

Shuno considered this for a few moments. "How were you able to extract this information?"

"We brought portable power cores designed to be used with your systems and technology. We were then able to extract the data from those consoles."

"How much of the data was intact? Our experience is such that very little is accessible."

"We've observed the same, but we're able to put the pieces together and run our own analysis to rebuild what's missing. It's not perfect, but it helps. We've found intact data cores at other sites, which also helps fill in the gaps," Lenora replied.

"The data is reliable," Sepal said. "We've learned much from what they've discovered. We'd be willing to share what we've learned with you."

Shuno's gaze narrowed suspiciously. "To what end? Why would you do this?"

"Knowledge of our history is meant to be shared. With it, we can come to a common understanding of what transpired, but this idea of the Bhatdin might answer some of the discrepancies in our understanding of the wars before the great freeze. There are more answers to be found."

Shuno frowned in thought. The Konus had been the first to emerge from stasis over forty years ago, and they'd kept their presence a secret. They were focused on rebuilding their society, but no matter what Shuno claimed, Connor had witnessed a thirst for knowledge to help them make sense of what had happened to them. And it wasn't just the Konus and the Mekaal. He'd witnessed the same longing on other planets with other Ovarrow. The Krake had divided them and set factions of Ovarrow against each other through a brutal form of scientific study. It was highly manipulative and would have lasting consequences for generations to come.

"I don't know what that symbol means. It looks similar to others I've seen, but I've never seen this exact one," Shuno said.

Lenora nodded once. "Do you know of anyone who might recognize it? We're searching for it at other sites. We want to find out all we can about the Bhatdin."

"I must confer with my superiors. I can try to contact them via comms, but we might be too far away to get a reliable signal," Shuno said.

"We can help with that," Connor said. "There's a colonial comlink available at Chenesh. You could use that."

"That is unacceptable since the communications would be monitored by you," Shuno replied.

Lenora looked at Connor. She wanted him to think of a solution that would work.

"What if we amplified the signal from your own comms device and had it broadcasted from ours? That would simply make the signal more powerful so you could reach the people you need to," Connor offered.

Shuno thought about it for almost a minute. "I will contact Chenesh this way, but Warlord Tritix might command that the link be severed."

"I understand. We'll wait here for your reply. Give us a few minutes to set things up on our end and then you'll see a new communications node available to you. You can initiate contact then," Connor said.

"Understood," Shuno replied.

The Konus officer turned around and headed back to their camp.

Noah joined Connor and Lenora. "To be honest, I didn't think they'd help."

"They haven't yet," Connor replied. He looked at his wife. "But it's more than I thought they'd do."

"Don't do that," Lenora replied. "Don't minimize what you did. He wouldn't have even spoken to me if it weren't for you and Urret."

Shuno left a squad of soldiers outside their camp, presumably to keep an eye on them.

"They'll help if it's important to them," Connor said.

"Or they're trying to work some other kind of angle," Diaz added.

"He's right. There has to be something in it for them."

Lenora looked at the Konus camp for a few seconds. "I told them we'd share what we learned with them. What else do they want?"

Diaz grinned a little.

"What?" Lenora asked and looked at Connor.

"If they know about the Bhatdin or that logo, they'll seek to negotiate for more," Connor said.

"Always pressing for an advantage," she said and shrugged. "They can ask."

Connor smiled. "That's right; they can ask. The question becomes how much we're willing to give."

"Maybe they'll be more cooperative than that."

Connor wasn't convinced but said, "We'll find out."

Specialist Weps and Sergeant Tui walked over to them.

"General, they've initiated comms to Chenesh."

"Thank you, Specialist."

Diaz glanced toward Connor. "Can you monitor what they're saying?"

"Are you kidding? Decipher a signal within another signal? No way. No how," Connor replied and nodded his head.

Diaz frowned and then inclined his chin in understanding.

They could decipher Konus communications, but if they spoke in code, it would be more difficult to make sense of what they recorded. He'd ask Urret to review it later.

About an hour had passed before Shuno returned from camp.

"I've spoken with Warlord Tritix," Shuno said.

Connor was impressed. Warlord Tritix was the leader of the Konus military. The fact that Shuno's report had gone up the chain of command was a good sign that the Konus were taking this seriously. Connor also suspected that his presence helped Shuno's report get priority treatment.

"I transmitted the data you shared, and it was reviewed by a member of our archivist team," Shuno continued. "Preliminary searching revealed that the Bhatdin's symbol does exist, and we have a list of associated locations."

"That fast?" Diaz asked.

Lenora nodded. "Don't forget, the Ovarrow's written language is more symbolic than ours."

"That doesn't explain anything."

"Subtle variants in the Ovarrow language can change the entire meaning of their statements," Lenora said. "It would be easy for them to construct a query to search for the Bhatdin symbol because their language is based off imagery and symbols. They can pack more meaning into a single image."

"If you say so," Diaz replied.

Connor looked a Shuno. "Will you share those locations with us?"

"Only if certain concessions are granted."

Here it comes, Connor thought. "What are they?"

"Warlord Tritix wants you to allow us to investigate these locations with you."

Connor glanced at the Konus soldiers outside the camp.

"All of us," Shuno said.

Connor felt the others looking at him, but he focused on Shuno. Now the negotiations would begin.

13

ISAAC SPLASHED cold water on his face, using the shock of the cold to help him wake up. He put some soap on his hands and washed his face and neck. That helped him wake up a little, too, but what he really needed was more sleep. He'd burned the midnight oil last night... several nights... and it was starting to catch up with him.

Julian walked into the bathroom and eyed him for a moment before he grunted. "Rough night?"

Isaac puffed out a breath and glowered at him briefly. He rolled his shoulders and stretched his neck from side to side, feeling a few pops that drew forth a sigh.

"Just studying," he said and picked up his toothbrush to begin brushing his teeth.

Julian set his kit on the sink and pulled out his razor for shaving. He squirted some shaving cream into his hand and rubbed the lather onto his face. "You know what I heard about the other day? The CDF has implants available to reduce the number of hours we need to sleep."

Isaac spat into the sink and swished some water in his mouth. He yawned. "I could use those."

Julian made a few calculated swipes with his razor and paused to nod. "Right. That would be great. The only issue is that prolonged use can lead to anxiety."

Isaac grabbed a towel and dried his face. "Doesn't sound so bad."

Julian chuckled. "I was kidding. It's not worth it. Just get some more sleep instead of studying."

Isaac shook his head. "I can't. I have some catching up to do. I'll be taking the placement tests next week."

Curtis walked into the communal bathroom and glanced at Isaac, then rolled his eyes. "Give it up. You're never getting into Sierra's medical program."

After months of living together in a dormitory at the colonial embassy in Shetrian, he'd gotten used to Curtis's attitude. They'd never be friends, and a few scuffles had instilled a smidgeon of cooperation, at least in front of other people. Curtis loved to point out everything Isaac did wrong, but that didn't happen as much as when they'd first come here.

"Afraid I'll take your spot?" Isaac asked.

"You'd have to get in first, which you probably won't."

"Curtis," Julian said, annoyed, "it's too early in the morning for this crap. Give it a rest."

Curtis shrugged, but he still smirked with knowledge that only he was privy to.

"I'll get in," Isaac said and began packing up his toiletries.

"Sure, you will," Curtis replied.

Julian growled. He was a good deal shorter than the rest of them, but he more than made up for it with his attitude. "I'm serious. It's too damn early in the morning for the two of you to get into it. I don't want to have to do something we'll all regret."

Curtis's gaze slid toward Julian. "Don't hold back because of me."

Isaac stepped toward him. "What is it with you, Palmer? Can't go through the day without proving what an asshole you are?"

Curtis sniggered, looking pleased, and held up his hand in a placating gesture. He turned toward the mirror and began running his fingers through his hair. "Why'd you wait so long to take the placement tests anyway?"

Julian arched an eyebrow toward Isaac. "That's a good question."

Isaac shrugged. "I hadn't decided to take them until I was here."

Curtis grinned. "After you found out Ella was going, you mean."

"She might have talked me into it."

She hadn't, but there was no need for Curtis to know that.

"She's way out of your league," Curtis said, and Julian shot a glare in his direction. "Just stating the obvious. We've been here for months. If he hasn't made a move by now, it's not going to happen."

Isaac chuckled. "Struck out again, I see."

Julian grinned. "You're just mad because she sees right through you."

Curtis shrugged. "It's just a matter of time, boys," he said and looked at Isaac. "At least I'll get to keep trying."

"I don't know," Julian said and pressed his lips together, considering. "Isaac's been studying pretty hard. I think he's going to get in."

"And if he doesn't, he can always fall back on his family connections," Curtis replied.

Isaac frowned. "What family connections?"

A smirk touched his mouth, and he arched an eyebrow in amusement. "Seriously?"

Isaac knew he should walk away, but he wanted to knock that self-assured smirk right off Curtis's face. It would feel great for a second or two, maybe even a few minutes, but it would be a mistake—a mistake he couldn't afford to make.

Don't do it, Isaac, he thought to himself.

"What the hell are you talking about?" Julian asked. He was almost done shaving.

"His family is friends with quite a few influential people. I'm sure they could get Isaac into whatever program he wanted."

Isaac scowled and felt the heat rush to his face.

Julian shook his head. "So what?"

"So, it means he gets to play by different rules than the rest of us. It doesn't matter whether he's qualified or not."

"That's crap," Julian said, scowling. "It's not a popularity contest. You get the scores, make the grade, and they measure your performance against everyone else that applies for that cohort. It doesn't matter who anyone knows."

"Believe whatever you want," Curtis said and glared at Isaac before turning his attention back to his own morning routine.

Isaac shook his head and began packing his stuff. Curtis was still trying to get a rise out of him, but he wasn't going to let him. If he denied the accusation, he'd validate the argument. He glanced at Curtis while he primped in front of the mirror.

When Isaac started to walk out of the bathroom, Curtis snorted loudly. Isaac gritted his teeth, whirled around, and stormed up to him. Curtis reared back with a hungry gleam in his eyes.

Isaac snarled, getting right into Curtis's face. "Nothing has ever been handed to me."

Curtis shoved him back and his eyes went wide when Isaac

pulled him off-balance and used his own momentum, guiding him toward the wall. Isaac had the momentary satisfaction of seeing the complete shock on Curtis's face as it became red with anger.

"Go ahead," Isaac invited. "Put your hands on me again."

Julian stepped between them. "All right, that's enough!"

Isaac watched Curtis, hoping he'd come at him so he could deliver the beating he deserved. Curtis had been pushing Isaac's buttons since before they'd come to the embassy.

"Seriously," Julian said. "I'll report the both of you and you'll get tossed out of the program. I don't want to have to do it, but I will. Isaac, you're done in here, right? Go on, get out of here."

Isaac needed to be in Shetrian because of his probation as an extension of his internship. He was so close to finishing that for it to come apart now would be beyond foolhardy.

He stepped back toward the door, and Curtis smiled at him, delivering a promise. They weren't finished. Isaac returned the smile in kind and left the bathroom.

A short while later, Julian walked into the room they shared. He paused in the doorway and said, "Do you think Curtis spends all his time just thinking of the stupidest things to say?"

"He probably has a checklist of them to get through on any given day," Isaac replied.

Julian laughed. "You can't let him get to you."

"I know," Isaac replied and gave Julian a sidelong glance. "I know."

"I doubt he's gonna report what happened."

Isaac smiled with one side of his mouth. "He won't. It was self-defense."

He knew enough about the law to determine that he shouldn't get into any trouble, but with his record, it would be a very thin margin.

Julian pressed his lips together and nodded. Crossing the room, he opened the metallic storage container where his clothes were kept and proceeded doing the sniff test on several garments. He pulled on a shirt and then gave his underarms a sniff, shrugging. "Oh, I've been meaning to ask if you could put in a good word for my cousin. He's applying to the CDF corps of engineers. You do have family connections, right? Can you help me out here?"

A laugh bubbled from Isaac's mouth. "I'll get right on it."

The idea of using any family connections to get into the medical program in Sierra was absurd. He'd never even thought about it, but he did wonder if others thought that way. Just because Curtis didn't like him didn't mean he was wrong.

Isaac shook his head. He couldn't control what other people thought.

They left the dormitory and headed to the cafeteria. The colonial embassy housed everything the residents needed in one convenient location. They'd hardly left the embassy grounds for the first few weeks while they went through training that educated them on Mekaal customs to help them fit in better while they were living in Shetrian. Since those first few weeks, Isaac had gotten to explore the city many times.

Shetrian was the name the Mekaal had given the city. It used to be home to a couple of million Ovarrow, but the Mekaal population was just under fifty thousand, and there was plenty of room to expand.

Isaac and Julian scanned the room as they carried their trays of food, spotting Ella eating with Jordan. The interns stuck together as much as they could. Kanin grabbed a seat next to Jordan, leaving an open seat next to Ella. Julian inclined his chin in the direction of the open seat, and Isaac sat down next to Ella.

Jordan yawned, her mouth opening impressively wide. "Good morning," she said.

"Had the night shift again?" Julian asked.

Jordan nodded. "Last time."

"Townsend is such a hard ass. Why can't you work the day shift like everyone else?"

Jordan shrugged. "It's not as bad as all that. He didn't insist I do it. I volunteered to help keep us on schedule." She looked at Isaac. "Weren't you his intern for a while?"

Isaac shoveled a large helping of scrambled eggs with hot sauce into his mouth and nodded. He chewed and swallowed. "I survived for two months before getting the boot."

Kanin giggled. "Two months and then he got rid of you."

"I was late a few times, which he didn't appreciate."

Ella sipped her coffee and then gave him a sidelong look. "You've done much better with Dr. Rostova."

Isaac nodded.

Julian grinned. "Who wouldn't?"

Ella set her cup down and frowned, managing to make such a simple thing elegant and beautiful. "What's that supposed to mean?"

Julian rolled his eyes and took a large bite from a biscuit he'd stuffed a few pieces of bacon into. "Come on. We're just supposed to ignore the fact that she's a beautiful woman?"

Isaac tried to focus on the food on his plate while failing to ignore that the three girls were watching him with the intense scrutiny that could only be achieved by members of the opposite sex.

Julian smiled and nodded. "There, you see. Isaac agrees."

Isaac lifted his gaze. "No, I don't. She's a lot nicer than Townsend."

The girls looked unconvinced.

"Working in Townsend's lab, you felt like klaxon alarms were about to go off if you made the slightest misstep. We work just as hard for Dr. Rostova, but she's nowhere near as high strung as Townsend."

"And she's gorgeous," Julian added.

"Right," Isaac said and frowned. "No…" He shook his head. "I give up."

Julian tilted his head to the side. "All this could have been avoided if you'd just admitted that she's drop-dead gorgeous."

Ella stared at him for a moment and then her eyebrows lifted. "You're blushing," she said, her eyes gleaming. "He's blushing. You're attracted to her."

This was going to be one of those days where Isaac wondered how he'd gotten here. "I am not."

Ella's gaze narrowed and she giggled, then said in a small voice. "Isaac has a little, itty bitty crush."

Isaac laughed, finally giving in, and the others joined. "Now you know my secret. You've all figured me out."

Curtis walked over and sat down at the other end of the table near Kanin. "What secret?"

"Isaac's in love with Dr. Rostova," Kanin replied.

Curtis regarded them for a few moments and then took a bite of his sandwich. "She's easy on the eyes."

Julian slapped the table a few times and laughed.

"You guys are so lucky," Jordan said. "We're stuck with old Townsend and happily married Dr. Solomon."

"Weren't you leering at Agent Franklin the other day?" Isaac asked.

Jordan's eyes flicked toward Ella, and Isaac saw that her cheeks went slightly pink.

Ella looked as if she'd gotten caught with her hand in the cookie jar.

"Oh, I get it now," Isaac said with a grin and then added, mimicking Ella's tone, "Someone else had a little, itty bitty crush, too."

Ella laughed and gave him a playful slap on the arm, her eyes gleaming, and he felt his mood lift considerably.

They finished eating breakfast and headed over to the labs in the basement of the embassy. Curtis, having arrived later, stayed behind. Jordan kept him company, getting another cup of coffee.

Ella walked next to Isaac. "Something happen this morning?"

Isaac arched an eyebrow. "Could you be more specific?"

Ella's eyes went skyward for a second. "You and Curtis seemed to be ignoring each other more than usual at breakfast."

Isaac shrugged. "Oh, that. That's nothing."

Ella regarded him, looking unconvinced.

Julian and Kanin headed toward the labs at the far end of the corridor.

Sometimes when he was around Ella, he couldn't get comfortable in his own skin.

"Honestly, it's nothing. Just a little argument in the bathroom before breakfast."

"Oh," she said.

Isaac frowned. "What's that supposed to mean?"

Ella was about to respond when a nearby door opened and Dr. Townsend walked out. He propped the door, and his gaze flicked toward Isaac for half a second before settling on Ella.

"Good morning, Ms. Kingston. Mr. Diaz."

"We're right on time today. All is well with the world," Isaac said.

Ella's gaze darted toward him.

Townsend twitched his head to the side. "Thank God for small miracles."

Isaac gave a half-hearted laugh that died away as Townsend

walked past them. Once he was out of earshot, Ella said. "What are you doing?"

"I don't know why I said that. It just came out."

"You're in rare form today."

Isaac nodded. "I think I've been cooped up for too long."

They walked into the shared lab. The wide space had been divided up according to the visiting professor's specialty. They heard a few people speaking from inside one of the cubicles.

"Deasira, you have to be patient," Dr. Rostova said.

"I *have* been patient. We have irrefutable proof that this can work."

Isaac slowed down just outside the door, and Ella gestured for them to go inside. He walked in first and saw Dr. Rostova standing by a workstation with Deasira, whose jade-colored eyes looked more feline than reptilian.

The Mekaal population was only thirty-three percent female. Female Ovarrow had more delicate features than their male counterparts. They had pebbled skin similar to a reptile but were warm-blooded. Less pronounced pointy protrusions stemmed from their shoulders and elbows. Their brow lines were much less severe than their male counterparts, making their heads softer and less angular. They were lean and strong. Ovarrow weren't graceful by any stretch of the word, but the females of the species managed to display a little finesse in their movements. Like humans, Ovarrow were omnivorous, but they preferred to consume more animal-based proteins.

"Do you need to be alone?" Isaac asked.

"No," Deasira said. "You need not be shielded from our discussions."

"She's right. Come in and get started," Dr. Rostova said and then turned her attention back to Deasira. "We proved that it's possible, but the original plan was for the changes to be temporary until we could find a better solution. At this point, we can't reverse the changes."

Isaac went to a nearby workstation and Ella took the one next to him. He logged in and checked the list of tasks for him that morning.

"You think because I want to move forward that I don't understand the potential outcomes? I assure you that I do," Deasira said.

Dr. Rostova shook her head. "I know you do. I just want to do this right and minimize the risk to your people."

Deasira was silent for a few moments. "Our population is in decline. It's not going to get better. The data we received from the Konus prove that. They've been out of stasis for much longer than we have."

"Can you really rely on their data?"

"We have no choice."

"Yes, you do," Dr. Rostova said. "You do. There's always a choice."

Isaac shared a glance with Ella as they both tried to focus on their workstations. He felt like this was a conversation that should be had without them in the room, but the Ovarrow were different in that they didn't hide uncomfortable conversations. They treated anyone who reached the age of maturity as an adult. And with so few Ovarrow children being born, most of his interactions with them had been among adults.

"We lose ground to the Konus with each passing cycle."

"I know that, but the effects on you—"

"Are worth the risk for our survival. Animals across Bhaneteran use a heat cycle to procreate. I know you think it's primitive. We'd be introducing a primal base that could have enduring consequences for future generations. You might be right about it, but at least there would *be* future generations of Ovarrow. We'd get the one thing we need."

Isaac had heard similar discussions about their work. They were trying to increase fertility rates among the Mekaal. The most promising method included increased hormones, which would affect their behavior. The Ovarrow had used a primitive method for stasis that had had severe side effects, one of which was rapid aging. Colonial scientists had solved that one, but infertility was something that had taken years for them to recognize as an issue. Infertility had only affected the females of the species, who had trouble becoming pregnant, and an even smaller percentage of them carried to term.

"We'll need to collect more blood samples," Dr. Rostova said.

Isaac recalled when she'd been against the project and tried to convince Ovarrow scientists to be more cautious, but they hadn't agreed. Dr. Rostova was now trying to help them as much as she could while minimizing the risks.

"Agreed. We need a baseline to establish how much genetic diversity there is among my people," Deasira said.

"It'll take time. We'll need to visit the clinics to collect the samples."

Deasira didn't reply right away, and Isaac could feel the Mekaal's gaze on his back. "They can help us. We can leave this morning and meet back here by the end of the day."

Isaac looked away from his workstation and Ella did the same. Dr. Rostova regarded them.

"Dr. Rostova," Ella said, "I've been trained to collect blood samples. Deasira's right. If we split up, we could reach all the clinics today."

Dr. Rostova pressed her full lips together in thought. "You can't go out alone."

"I can help her," Isaac offered.

Dr. Rostova's lips twitched. "So helpful, Isaac. Thank you. Ella will need assistance with carrying all those samples."

"He's good at lugging stuff for me," Ella agreed.

Isaac looked at Ella and saw that one corner of her mouth quivered. He turned back toward the others. "I've been reviewing the training for collecting samples. I could do it, too."

Ella's eyebrows raised as she looked at him.

"Good," Dr. Rostova said. "You can both go, but you'll need a protective detail to go with you. Get your kits ready and meet us at the entrance."

They closed down their workstations and set about gathering the equipment they'd need. Deasira and Dr. Rostova left them.

Ella laid the stuff she was bringing on the table and then looked at Isaac. "I didn't know you were doing that kind of training."

Isaac shrugged. "I've been studying."

"For what?"

He hadn't told her about the placement tests. Julian and Curtis were the only ones who knew.

"The placement test for the medical program in Sierra," he said.

Ella's eyebrows pulled together in a thoughtful frown, and then she smiled. "Really? That's wonderful. So that's what you've been doing," she said and then added, "I was wondering what you've been up to. You must have been working on this since we got here. Why didn't you tell me?"

"We were all busy and… I didn't want anyone to know."

"Why not?"

Isaac sighed. "Because if I don't do well enough, they'll reject me."

"Then you just take the test again and apply again. I think you'll do well, though," Ella replied.

Isaac felt the urge to smile, and he stood straighter.

"I wished you'd told me sooner. I could have helped you study."

"It's fine. I didn't want anyone's help."

Ella arched a dark eyebrow and tilted her head to the side, exposing the lovely lines of her jaw. "Because you'd have to thank them?"

Isaac frowned. "What? No!"

"Yes, it is."

"You're crazy."

"Nope, I know how you think," she said, and then she made her voice low. "I'll do it on my own or not at all!"

Isaac's jaw slacked a little, and then he grinned. "My voice is lower than that."

Ella laughed. "I can still help you."

"Maybe I don't need your help."

"Yes, you do. I'll quiz you. When are you taking the test?"

Isaac had never thought she'd be so insistent on helping him. "What's that look for?"

Isaac shrugged. "I just didn't expect … this."

Ella's gaze slipped into some sort of calculation. "Oh, I see. That's what you and Curtis were fighting about."

How had she guessed that?

"No need to confirm. It's not that important. So, when is the test?"

"It's after we get back to Sanctuary."

Ella nodded. "Not much time, but we'll have to make do."

"Ella, why are you helping me?"

"Not the best way to show your appreciation."

"No, I appreciate the offer, but you don't have to do this." He was used to doing things on his own.

Ella sighed and just looked at him for a moment. "I know

you were having a hard time when we left Sanctuary. Now, don't go thinking I'm taking pity on you. I'm not. But I had a study partner when I prepared for my placement test, and it really helped."

Isaac considered it for a few seconds and then nodded. "Thanks," he said.

The bonus part of this whole thing was that he got to spend more time with her. That had to be worth something.

They finished assembling their field kits and packed up two duffle bags with a cooling core that would preserve the samples they were going to collect. Isaac swung on his backpack and then picked up the heavier duffle bag. He shifted his shoulders a few times, moving the padded section so it was comfortable. Ella did the same and grabbed the smaller duffle.

Isaac eyed her for a moment. "Want to switch?" he asked, lifting his bag toward her.

Ella's dark eyes flicked down to his arms. "You could use the workout."

Isaac glanced at his arms. They were lean, but he didn't have an overabundance of muscle. "In that case, I'll take yours," he said and made as if to grab her bag.

Ella grinned and moved out of the way.

They met Dr. Rostova and Deasira near the entrance to the colonial embassy. Two embassy rovers waited for them.

Dr. Rostova walked toward them. "Do you have everything you need?"

"I think we've got it covered," Isaac replied.

Dr. Rostova glanced down at their field kits and then accessed her wrist computer. She gestured toward the duffle bag that Isaac carried, and a packing list appeared on her holoscreen. She repeated the gesture toward Ella's bag.

"Looks like you've got everything you need. Some of the

clinics have already collected the blood samples we need, but you'll need to collect some. You'll be meeting with a healer named Jori. I think you might have met him before. He's worked with colonists a lot over the years," Dr. Rostova said.

"I know him," Isaac said and raised his hands above his hips, shaking them.

"What are you doing?" Ella asked.

Isaac smiled. "Jazz hands. Jori learned it from someone. I saw him do it before as a greeting."

Dr. Rostova smiled. "You're just full of surprises. Look, I know you've explored the city many times, but please be careful. Pay attention. Situational awareness—"

"Constant vigilance," Isaac and Ella said at the same time.

Dr. Rostova regarded both of them like a proud parent. "Good luck, and remember, this jaunt into the city wasn't planned. Keep that in mind."

Dr. Rostova walked to one of the rovers and looked at the driver but shook her head and hastened toward the second rover with a determined stride that made her ponytail bounce. "Switching rovers. You guys take that one."

Isaac walked toward the first rover and opened the storage compartment in the back. He unslung his duffle bag and loaded it in the back of the rover, helping Ella place hers next to his.

The driver's side door opened and someone stepped out.

"Come on, Kat, don't be like that," Agent Hunter Franklin said.

Dr. Rostova ignored him and climbed into the second rover.

Agent Franklin rolled his eyes and shook his head. Then he shrugged and smiled a greeting at Isaac. "Hey, kid. Looks like you guys drew the short straw. I'm your protective detail today. Climb aboard," he said and got back into the rover.

Isaac grabbed the handle, opened the rear door, and gestured to Ella. "Got your chariot right here."

Ella smiled and shook her head as she climbed inside, scooting across the back seat to make room for him. Isaac climbed inside and closed the door. A Mekaal soldier sat in the front passenger seat.

Agent Franklin gestured toward his companion. "This is Cohsora. He'll be with us today."

Cohsora didn't turn around. Instead, he kept watching the area just outside the embassy gates.

"That's very good, Cohsora. Constant vigilance even though we're in this peaceful city," Agent Franklin said.

"Luck favors the prepared," Cohsora replied.

Agent Franklin grinned. "You've been reading that book I gave you." He looked back at Isaac and Ella. "Famous quotes. A little bit of human philosophy."

"When did you get back?" Isaac asked.

"Some time in the night... or is it the morning? I can't remember. Doesn't matter, I'm here now. I've had a few cups of coffee; hence, all the talking."

"You were hoping Dr. Rostova would ride with you," Ella said.

Agent Franklin's shoulders sagged a little. "Yeah, I was. Kat is sometimes rigid... that's not the right word."

"Difficult?" Isaac asked.

Agent Franklin puffed out a breath. "Wiseass."

"What happened between you two?" Ella asked.

"Why, Mariella Kingston, are you prying into my personal affairs?"

"No," Ella said with a grin.

"Good, no time to discuss it now. Buckle up. We're heading

to our first stop. The schedule has very little in the way of wiggle room."

Agent Franklin had visited the embassy a number of times since they'd been there, but Isaac couldn't begin to predict when he would come through. He'd just show up. He'd tried to get them to call him by his first name, but Isaac wouldn't do it. It just felt wrong. Maybe one day.

There'd been a handful of other times that Agent Franklin was assigned to their protective details, but most of the time they were escorted by CDF soldiers. Sometimes agents of the CIB went with them, and Isaac wondered if they were on some kind of CIB covert operation, but as far as he could tell they weren't. He'd asked Agent Franklin about it once and he'd told Isaac that they were just there to observe, although he never elaborated on what they were observing.

Agent Franklin drove the rover through the embassy gates, and Isaac noticed him glance over at the second rover driving in the opposite direction.

Ella cleared her throat. She had her personal holoscreen active, and they began reviewing what they were going to do at each of the clinics.

Collecting blood samples from the clinics sounded simple enough, but as the hours went by, Isaac began to think he'd never know what to expect. Some of the clinics were only open part of the time, so if they missed them, they'd have to come back out the next day. They hadn't missed any yet, but it had been close a few times. And their reception was a little different at each clinic they visited. Some of the Mekaal wanted nothing to do with them, which included the healers. Others feigned ignorance, but a short conversation with Cohsora seemed to jog their memories. Maybe the Mekaal in general felt as if they'd been poked and prodded enough.

Isaac was becoming more comfortable with using a needle to draw blood from the Mekaal. No one liked to be pricked by a needle, but those first few times, he thought the Mekaal was going to lash out at him. Ella, on the other hand, was quite comfortable with it. She called it her bedside manner, which she assured him he'd get better at. Isaac wasn't convinced. He worked hard at everything he did, but making other people feel comfortable wasn't part of his skillset. It seemed that Ella could just set people at ease, whether they were human or Ovarrow. It also appeared to him that the Mekaal were more accommodating of Ella in general, and Isaac believed it was because she was a woman. There weren't many female Ovarrow among the Mekaal, which meant the males of the species were more accommodating.

"I wish we could tell them what we're really doing here," Isaac said.

Ella nodded. "I know, but we're not allowed."

They'd just gotten back into the rover and Agent Franklin was driving them to their next stop.

"Some of them know what we're doing, but they won't talk about it either," Isaac said.

"Just focus on the job we have to do."

Isaac leaned back and closed his eyes for a long moment. It would be nice to sleep for a little while. "They know we're keeping something from them, and it feels a little dishonest."

"It *is* a little dishonest. Do you think honesty is always the best medicine?"

Isaac sighed and shook his head. "Not all the time."

He closed his eyes and leaned back against the padded headrest. He was falling asleep and didn't know whether she'd replied or not.

All too soon, Ella shook him, and he had no idea how much time had passed. He opened his eyes and looked her, taking in her long dark hair that was tied off to the side and hanging in front of her shoulder, thick and lustrous. He blinked several times, looking at how her full lips fit together. The edges lifted as if a smile were moments from appearing.

"So beautiful," he said quietly.

Ella's eyes widened and her mouth opened a little.

His pulse raced as he suddenly became completely awake. "I'm up. I'm up," he said and glanced out the rover's window. "We're here. Time to go."

Ella opened her door and got out. Isaac did the same, rubbing his eyes and stretching. Agent Franklin was looking at him, so Isaac nodded in his direction. The agent walked over to him, leaned in, and said quietly, "At least one of us isn't striking out." He gave Isaac's shoulder a firm pat.

Isaac snorted and looked at the entrance to the clinic. It was a restored building. The bronze-colored alloy looked almost polished amid the dark walls. They were on one of the main streets that went through the heart of the city. The main administration building that was the seat of the Mekaal government was about a kilometer away. A few tall spires rose above the nearby buildings.

Isaac retrieved his field kit from the back of the rover and walked inside the clinic. A Mekaal walked toward them. He was older and more weather-worn, but he moved as if he were much younger than he appeared.

Isaac recognized him. "Hi Jori."

Jori paused in the middle of the room and raised his hands. Four long fingers shook as he performed jazz hands, and Isaac returned the gesture. "It's so nice to see you, Isaac."

Isaac smiled and saw Ella looking at him. He inclined his chin and did jazz hands toward her. After a moment's hesitation she returned the gesture.

A chuffing sound came from Jori, which was the sound of an Ovarrow grinning. "One of the best cures I've ever come across."

Jori was one of the most lighthearted Ovarrow Isaac had ever met.

"Come in. Come in. I have a lot of samples for you to take back with you," Jori said.

They followed Jori across the clinic. There were only a couple of Ovarrow here. The Mekaal healer guided them toward his cold storage unit and opened it. Isaac's eyebrows raised when he saw the rows of samples Jori had collected. They amounted to more than half of what they'd already gathered.

"How did you get so many?" Ella asked.

Jori looked around before he answered. "Very important work you're doing. Deasira is my colleague."

Isaac nodded. Jori knew of the project then. They began transferring the samples to their own portable cold-storage containers. Both he and Ella carried them out to the rover together. It took several trips, and he noticed that more Mekaal were gathering on the streets. They seemed to be waiting for something.

Isaac looked in the direction everyone else was watching and saw a procession of Mekaal vehicles driving toward them.

Agent Franklin walked over and peered in the same direction.

Ella joined them. "What's going on?"

Isaac shook his head. "I don't know."

Cohsora stood across the street and gestured for their attention. Agent Franklin looked at him.

"Konus envoy," Cohsora said, his mouth forming a grim line.

Agent Franklin was normally an easy-going person, but that was gone in an instant. Isaac could scarcely believe it. The CIB agent's gaze hardened, and he looked around as if surveying the area for potential threats.

He turned toward Isaac and Ella. "I need both of you to get back to the clinic and stay out of sight."

Agent Franklin hastened across the street to speak with Cohsora.

Isaac backed up and Ella leaned toward him.

"What did he say?" she asked.

The Mekaal lining the streets were speaking so fast that it was difficult for their translators to keep up, and it was getting difficult to hear.

"He wants us to go back into the clinic. Come on," he said.

They hurried back to the clinic and stood off to the side of the open doorway.

Jori walked over to them. "What's happening?"

"I'm not sure. There's a Konus envoy coming through here," Isaac said.

Jori looked out to the street in alarm. "Stay there," he said and moved toward the entrance.

"What are the Konus doing here?" Ella asked.

"I don't know."

Isaac knew that the Konus had once tried to invade Shetrian but had failed. The CDF and Mekaal soldiers had fought to protect the city. He'd never seen a Konus before.

Isaac moved to the other side of the doorway and peered down the street.

"What are you doing?" Ella asked.

"I just want to get a better look at them," he replied.

The commotion outside became louder. He peeked around the corner and couldn't find Agent Franklin, but he knew the CIB agent hadn't abandoned them. He glanced at the rovers, but they were empty.

The Mekaal vehicles came closer, sporting large, knobby tires suitable for rough terrain. The small convoy began to drive past the clinic and Isaac tried to see inside. Some of the vehicles looked more like military ground transports, open to the elements so it was easy for soldiers to get in and out of them. Ovarrow soldiers sat in the back. They wore green metallic armor and watched the Mekaal that had gathered along the street, their feline gazes surveying the area as they passed.

One of the vehicles stopped and a Konus stood up. He wore green metallic armor like the others, but his had a strip of gold that went down his arm, so Isaac assumed he was some sort of commander. The Konus turned toward the clinic. Jori stood in the doorway and stared back at the commander, who had a long scar that went from one of his cranial ridges down past his neck. He had the look of a veteran soldier that had fought many battles. The Konus peered into the clinic and Isaac thought he could see them. He backed farther into the shadows and gestured for Ella to do the same. He wasn't sure why they had to hide, but Agent Franklin wouldn't have told them to if it wasn't important.

The convoy began moving again, and the Konus commander stared at the clinic until they drove away. Mekaal lined the streets. Some of them shouted at the Konus, while others watched them with an odd sort of fascination.

Agent Franklin walked into view and gestured toward the rover. "Time to leave."

Jori wished them well. Isaac and Ella hastened to the rover and climbed inside. Cohsora joined them.

"What are the Konus doing here?" Isaac asked.

Agent Franklin shook his head. "I have no idea. I didn't know they were coming. Did you know?" he asked Cohsora.

"I didn't know either," Cohsora replied.

Agent Franklin swore. He put the rover into gear and drove

them away. "No more clinics today. We're heading back to the embassy."

Isaac listened as Agent Franklin opened a comlink to the other team. "Team two, head back to the nest. A general recall is going out," he said. He paused, listening. "Tell her I don't care. This is a security issue and they're to return to the embassy immediately. The same for all other away teams."

Isaac buckled himself into the seat and Ella did the same.

The rover increased speed as Agent Franklin drove them back to the embassy. Both he and Ella stayed quiet while the CIB agent spoke to the head of security at the embassy.

14

THE HERCULES CLASS C-cat began its descent, and Connor watched the squad of Konus soldiers that had come with them. Eight additional bodies were making even the inside of the Hercules start to feel a little crowded. It hadn't taken much in the way of negotiations to learn that Shuno hadn't really expected all forty members of his scout force to come with them in search of the Bhatdin. They kept mostly to themselves, but they did trade appraising looks with the Mekaal. Urret had positioned his team where he could keep an eye on the Konus. Sergeant Tui had the CDF soldiers located in two areas so that one was always covering the Konus. Connor didn't think Shuno had agreed to come with them only to try to do something like try to take them hostage or engage in some other kind of conflict. However, he didn't mind showing Shuno and the other Konus scouts that they were being watched.

Lenora sat down in the seat next to his. "What do you think?"

"I didn't expect the additional company."

"Neither did I, but I've been reviewing the locations Shuno shared with us. They're interesting."

Connor nodded. "They're nowhere near the Konus territory, so it's unlikely they're setting up an ambush for us, but as to whether those sites have anything to do with the Bhatdin, I'll need to reserve judgment on that."

"You think they're just using us to scout locations for them?"

"It's the perfect excuse. We're able to travel anywhere on this massive continent and they can't."

"I see your point."

"But if so, we'll quickly see through that kind of ruse after visiting a couple of locations."

Lenora inhaled deeply while she thought about it. "What will you do if that happens?"

"We'll go back to our original plan and continue investigating the locations we've mapped out. I'll arrange for transport to bring Shuno and the rest of his scout force back to their home as agreed." Connor looked at his wife and shrugged. "I wouldn't leave them stranded thousands of kilometers from home."

Lenora smiled a little. "I can think of someone who might."

Connor looked over to where Diaz was sitting. He had his personal holoscreen active with a video comlink to Sanctuary.

"I wouldn't rule it out either," Connor admitted. "Regardless, this is an opportunity for us to learn from each other. Better this than on a battlefield."

"I'm on board with that, but it's not quite the relaxing expedition I was hoping for. I'm not disappointed. It's just not what I was expecting."

"I agree, but sometimes it's the unexpected things that can make all the difference."

Lenora glanced at the Mekaal for a few moments. "Do you think they'll ever work out their differences?"

"Maybe when Lauren and Ethan are our age," Connor replied.

Lenora rolled her eyes and smiled as Connor continued speaking.

"They're not so different from us. Some of them want to rebuild the world they lost, make things as they were before the Krake invaded. How much of what we've built here is because it reminds us of Old Earth?"

"Maybe in the beginning, but what Lauren and Ethan build," she said and inclined her chin toward Diaz, "or any of the younger generations, will be based on what we've built here. This is their home, and I expect the inclination to hold on to designs and methods unique to Old Earth will eventually fade away. Not altogether, and not for everything. What I'm trying to say is that the longer we're here, we'll influence the world we build and who we build it with," she said and tilted her head toward the Mekaal, but Connor supposed she included the Konus as well.

They traveled in a northeast direction, flying over the bones of cities that had been destroyed. There were several holoscreens active throughout the seating area that allowed all of them to watch their progress. The Mekaal were familiar with colonial technology. The Konus had seen it before but weren't as familiar with it, and they watched the live video feed from the C-cat's sensors with keen interest. The Konus mostly used ground transportation, but they were beginning to resurrect their flying machines. The Mekaal were re-examining the engineering used for their own flyers, but they hadn't made as much progress. Between their scouting missions and their partnership with the colony, they hadn't created as much of a need to rebuild flyers with outdated designs. There was interest in adapting certain colonial designs for the Mekaal, but it would be years before anything was actually built and tested, let alone actually used in a widespread capacity.

The Hercules flew over their destination, making several passes as they did some aerial reconnaissance before selecting a place to camp and explore the area. The Konus had provided a city location that, according to their archives, had an association with the Bhatdin. Connor and Lenora reviewed the data and would focus their search in the industrial parts of the city.

They'd gathered around a large holoscreen inside the Hercules. Connor had ordered the pilot to hold this position until they picked a destination.

"This city looks older than most, but I didn't think we were far enough east for that," Noah said and looked at Lenora. "The architecture is different."

Lenora nodded. "Prewar and ice age. They used more elaborate designs because it was built for aesthetics."

Connor looked at Sepal and then at Shuno, wondering what they thought. Most of his experience with any Ovarrow was that they'd become a society with strict rules, all tailored toward survival and war. He thought it was important for all the Ovarrow to visit these old cities in order to imagine a life before the Krake. How would they ever move forward if they didn't take the time to learn about their past?

Connor looked at Sepal. "Do you know anything about them?"

Sepal stared at the video feed for a moment. "Dr. Bishop is correct. These ruins predate the ice age, but they didn't escape the war with the Krake."

"Not just the Krake," Shuno said.

Both the Mekaal and the Konus looked at him.

"Agreed, we fought these wars. We destroyed these cities and are as much to blame as the Krake are," Sepal replied.

"They failed to unite against the Krake. They were too concerned with establishing dominance," Shuno said.

"Sounds familiar," Diaz said.

The Konus soldier looked at him and then at Connor. "You refer to Warlord Kasmon's efforts to absorb the Mekaal into the Konus."

"I do."

Shuno considered this for a few moments. "The reasoning for that campaign was to help us survive. And to determine whether the CDF could successfully defeat the Krake."

Diaz looked at Connor. "Do you hear this?"

Connor nodded. "I don't approve of what Kasmon did, but that's not why we're here."

"Connor," Diaz said.

"Juan."

Diaz stared at him for a few moments and then looked away.

"I'd like to make a suggestion," Sepal said and waited for them to listen. "We've had success with tracking the Bhatdin at industrial centers, but the government buildings will have more information. I think we should conduct our search in those places."

The Mekaal historian gestured toward a grouping of buildings near the center of the city.

"Do you think the Bhatdin's address is just waiting for us?" Diaz asked.

"Yes," Connor said. "It's a good suggestion. The Bhatdin were hiding their presence in plain sight so that only someone with knowledge of the star system would be able to extrapolate that data. What if there's more data related to finding them?"

Lenora smiled. "A beacon."

"I'll tell the pilot where to take us," Connor said.

The Ovarrow city had once had parks throughout, but they were overgrown. At this point, only analysis by colonial computer systems could make a high-probability guess where those parks had been located. Connor wanted to avoid landing the Hercules on the outskirts of the city and having to drive the rovers in. They could do that if they had to, but clearing a landing field while minimizing the risk to the remaining structures was preferable. It would save them time.

They found a relatively open area where they only needed to clear a few trees to land the Hercules. The trees weren't far beyond saplings, and much of the shrubbery looked less than a year old.

"They must have had a dry season here," Lenora said. "It wouldn't take much for a fire to start. We can confirm this with soil analysis."

"Sounds like a job for a couple of students we brought with us," Connor said.

"It does, doesn't it? I'll go tell them," Lenora said.

The pilot landed the Hercules and they started gathering their field kits. They wouldn't need to take the rovers for this since they were close to the area Sepal had pointed out to them.

Diaz sighed and looked at Connor.

Connor checked his backpack and then put it on. "This is the fun part."

"I can't wait. I wonder if there will be a few ryklar packs waiting for us."

Sergeant Tui waved to them from the loading ramp. "Recon drones deployed. Ryklar deterrent signal activated. We'll know soon enough whether there are any in the area."

Diaz nodded and looked at Shuno and the other Konus. "Another parting gift that we appreciate."

"The ryklar populations have been in decline," Shuno said.

Connor kept his face impassive. The ryklar relocation program had been carefully guarded to avoid notice, but perhaps the Konus had learned of it somehow.

"Yeah," Diaz said. "That's a good thing."

"Only to some," Shuno replied and didn't comment further.

They left the ship and headed toward a complex of Ovarrow buildings that Sepal believed contained data repositories. Paved ramps connected the buildings in an elaborate network of walkways. There were remnants of columns, and Lenora told them that the walkways had once been covered so the Ovarrow who had frequented this area would be protected from the elements.

Connor watched Urret and his squad of Mekaal soldiers, as well as the Konus soldiers, survey the area. They kept careful watch on each other but were also in awe of their surroundings. Connor could appreciate it. He'd traveled to other Ovarrow worlds and had seen cities this size teeming with life. The Mekaal had come out of stasis from a world ravaged by war. Perhaps they could remember a city like this before it had been destroyed, but not the Konus. Shuno and the rest of his squad were young enough to have been born after. Their parents were the ones who had survived stasis. They'd been raised with an extremely disciplined mentality to put the highest importance of the Konus as a group above the individual.

Connor had witnessed various attitudes toward the Ovarrow's past. His own opinion of them had changed over time, but the divisiveness even occurred among the Ovarrow. Some resented the world that was, while others were envious of the life that came before. Then there were Ovarrow who chose to focus their efforts on building the future. They were survivors, much like the colonists, and they all had their differences.

They were walking next to a stone wall that was mostly covered with thick vines, the ends of which stretched out into the street. They made their way toward the Capitol complex, occasionally pausing to secure the area. Each group took turns exploring buildings along the street they walked down. Eventually, there was a break in the wall that was wide enough for them to walk through, and they made it onto the grounds.

With such a large group, Connor would have preferred that they split into smaller units to quickly explore the area, but he didn't think that was a good idea. With so much mistrust among the groups, it made the most sense for them to stick together.

"Where do we search first?" Noah asked.

"We're looking for data storage, which is likely located underground," Connor replied. He looked at Lenora. "What do you think?"

"We just need a control room. Something that would be connected to their computer systems," Lenora said.

Noah looked at the buildings. The domed-shaped rooftops had collapsed. "If we go crawling around in the wrong area, we could trigger further collapse. What about looking for power sources?"

"Let's hold up a second," Connor said.

The group came to a halt and the leaders came to them.

"A place as old as this isn't going to have any power," Connor said.

"Sepal," Lenora said, "what do you think our best chance is for finding what we need?"

"It's dangerous to go below. I would recommend trying to find the interior offices and see if we can use one of the consoles there," Sepal said.

Connor looked around. There were more buildings farther away from them. He frowned and then climbed to the top of the wall. "What about the guard towers? Secure check-in locations. They'd have consoles with direct access. Maybe we don't have to go inside any of these buildings at all."

"Do you see one?" Lenora asked.

"Yup, that way. Not far," Connor said and climbed down.

There were several guardhouses at the old entrances to the government complex, all in a state of severe disrepair.

"A place this big has to have a security operations center," Diaz said. He looked at Sepal. "Where would it be? Part of the main building?"

"I'm not sure," Sepal replied.

Connor engaged his personal holoscreen and brought up one of the drone video feeds. The drone flew over the complex and showed more areas where the rooftops had collapsed, along with several floors underneath. "Even if it was there, we can't get to it. This might be a bust. We don't have the equipment with us to start tearing things apart." He frowned and looked at Shuno, but The Konus just looked back at him. "What about a secondary security center off the main building? Ever come across one of those?"

Shuno looked at Connor's holoscreen. "Can your machine fly here?" he asked, gesturing toward an area.

"Yes," Connor replied.

Specialist Weps had the drone fly to where Shuno indicated. There was a smaller guardhouse between buildings that looked to be more intact than the surrounding area. The way the other buildings had collapsed around it had given it shelter.

"Let's go see what we can find there," Connor said.

They made their way through the campus by sticking to the walkways while the recon drone hovered outside the building they were searching for. Connor looked inside and the entrance was blocked. He stepped through the threshold and tried to peer through the wreckage.

"We can't get through that," Noah said.

Connor shook his head. "Specialist Weps, think you can get the drone through? I saw some open pockets in there."

"I'll try, sir," Weps replied.

She brought up the drone control interface, and the recon drone flew inside. She used its small cutting laser to slice through some of the debris blocking the path. It took her about twenty minutes, but the drone made it into the interior. The wreckage served as a barrier, but they saw a few consoles inside. Weps guided the drone toward the one that looked mostly intact. She opened the access panel and connected a power tap to the console. Then, using a power regulator program, she began to siphon some of the drone's energy into the console. Standard protocols called for them to use the least amount of power first and then gradually increase it until they could begin retrieving data.

"Clever," Noah said. "Good job, Weps."

"Thank you, sir," she replied.

Noah looked at Connor. "I like the new power regulator program."

"It beats burning out consoles. It's Lenora's design," Connor replied.

Noah looked at Lenora and gave her an approving nod. "Very impressive."

Lenora smiled and shook her head. "It's almost like I know what I'm doing."

"I didn't mean to say—"

Lenora grinned. "Gotcha. Some things don't change."

Noah gave her a slight bow.

"I'm getting a data connection. Beginning the extraction protocol," Specialist Weps said.

Lenora brought up her personal holoscreen and opened a data comlink to the drone. "Loading the search parameters we came up with," she said.

On their way here, Lenora had worked with Sepal and Noah to develop several search protocols designed for Ovarrow computer systems. The result didn't rely on the translator, and they were able to conduct searches much quicker. Search results began to populate a data window. Lenora made the holoscreen bigger so everyone could see.

"How does the search work?" Diaz asked.

"It looks for references to things we associate with the Bhatdin, like the planetary logo and a few other things. It then looks for other references associated with those things," Lenora said.

Shuno peered at the data. "Those are location references."

After a few moments, another entry appeared next to the list of location references. "And these are coordinates," Lenora said.

"Put them on a map," Connor said.

Lenora opened another holoscreen, and a map of the continent appeared. Bhatdin locations began to populate, and Connor watched as more locations appeared. They were all associated with the planetary logo. Most were from large Ovarrow cities, but then a waypoint appeared far to the north.

"I think we've found them," Connor said.

Lenora zoomed in on the northern waypoint. "There aren't any cities there as far as I know," she said and looked at Sepal.

"That is accurate," Sepal said.

"Why would they build something so far away?" Diaz asked.

"Because they didn't want it found," Connor replied.

"That's it? We just head up north? It's thousands of

kilometers away. Do you even have cold-weather equipment?" Diaz asked.

"We come prepared. All these other locations are Ovarrow population centers. We could travel to one of those locations to correlate the results, but that location right there just became ground zero for finding out more about the Bhatdin," Connor said.

"He's right," Lenora said and smiled.

"I'm glad you're excited, but how can you be so sure?" Diaz asked.

Connor snorted. "Because, like you, the Ovarrow don't like the cold."

Diaz glanced at Sepal and the other Mekaal. Several of them nodded—a human gesture they'd adopted. The Konus exchanged glances but didn't offer any comments.

"Sir," Specialist Weps said, "data extraction complete."

"Excellent, thank you," Connor replied.

They made their way back to camp. Now that they had a location for the Bhatdin, they had some planning to do. There were different kinds of dangers to be faced in the extreme north, and they needed to pull the most recent satellite imagery for the area. They'd camp here for the night and then head out first thing in the morning.

15

PEOPLE LOVED THEIR SLEEP. Connor looked over at Diaz's sleeping form and sighed. Connor had always been a creature of habit. He could easily adapt to snatching a few winks when required and push himself to his utter limits when he had to. He even had implants to assist with negating the requirement for sleeping for hours at a time, but those days were gone. Connor required a normal sleep cycle like most other colonists. A good day meant getting six hours' sleep. He just couldn't stay in bed for eight, so four to six hours were normal for him. CDF medical doctors believed he'd used his specialized military grade implants for so long that they had changed his circadian rhythms and his body had adapted to require less sleep.

The sun had not yet risen. They'd camped just outside the Hercules.

He made himself some coffee. Noah walked over to him and yawned, so Connor gestured toward the pot of coffee he'd brewed.

Noah nodded slowly and sighed. "We've been traveling so

much my body doesn't know which time zone it's in. Part of me was thinking we were back on Terra Research Station."

Connor sipped his coffee. "Could be all the fresh air."

Noah added cream and sugar to the coffee and stirred. He sat down next to Connor. "Maybe," he said and sipped. "Being up this early makes me think you're going to take me on one of those morning runs." He grinned a little. "Remember those?"

Connor chuckled. "You loved SAR training."

"It was more about the company. Me, you, Sean, Diaz. We had no idea what this planet had in store for us."

"Is that why you keep working on solving FTL?"

"What do you mean?"

"You know what I mean. This short history we've had here." New Earth had held no shortage of surprises for the colonists. The planet was as dangerous as it was beautiful, but the colonists had been up to the challenge.

Noah shrugged. "I'd just like to have the option. We were always meant to leave Earth. That was one of the primary drivers for the Ark Program. Colonize the stars, which didn't mean we stopped at the first habitable star system and never left."

"I understand that, but we haven't been here that long in the grand scheme of things."

"Kara worries I'm obsessed with it, but I'm not."

"Would you admit it if you were?"

Noah grunted and gave him a sidelong glance. "It takes one to know one."

"Ouch. Touché."

"We've learned so much since leaving Earth. We're able to generate power at levels above and beyond what they could. Traveling between universes is no mean feat either."

Connor refilled his cup. "We know how to use some Krake technology, but it doesn't mean we understand all of it."

"You're right. It'll take time. This is what I want to focus on for now."

"I'm sure you'll figure it out eventually." He sipped his coffee. "Seriously, if I had to bet on anyone figuring it out, it would be you by a long shot."

"Thanks for the vote of confidence. A lot of scientists and engineers have worked on this—theories that require us to generate the power of the main-sequence star—and there are even some that say we need to generate the power of a whole galaxy. There's no shortage of theories out there, even for the multiverse, which the Krake didn't even understand completely. So, yeah, I've got my work cut out for me. But what if I figure it out? Would you go back to Earth? See if anyone survived?"

"That's easy. No," Connor replied. "Even if you figure it out, taking a journey like that requires a lot of planning and preparation. But, no, I'm not returning to Earth. My life is here, Noah."

"What if Lenora wanted to go?"

Connor chuckled. "She doesn't."

"How do you know? Have you ever talked to her about it?"

"Yes, we've talked about it. This is our home. Lauren and Ethan are here," Connor replied and regarded his friend for a moment. "Would you go?"

"Yeah, maybe... I don't know. I think visiting the second colony is more within our reach before we go back to Earth."

They finished the rest of their coffee in silence. That was something he'd always liked about Noah. Sometimes they'd talk and other times they could both just sit there quietly. It made some people uncomfortable to do that.

Eventually, there was stirring among the Mekaal and Konus. Then the rest of the camp began to wake up. They spent part of the morning unpacking their cold-weather gear.

Diaz looked at Connor. He'd crossed his arms over his chest. "Minus thirty degrees is the average for that area."

Connor nodded. "I bet you wish you'd kept that beard you had."

Diaz grinned. "It might have helped."

Connor walked over to Shuno and the other Konus. "We only have enough cold-weather gear to accommodate four of you. The other four will need to stay aboard the ship until we can set up camp, but even then, they won't be able to go far."

"I understand, General Gates."

"Do you know anything about the region we're traveling to?"

"No, most Ovarrow stay in more temperate climates."

"Not even to explore?"

"I don't claim to know all our history, but if these Bhatdin have been difficult to find, then perhaps our destination makes the most sense."

Connor left them to finish packing up their equipment and load it back onto the Hercules.

Lenora walked over to him. "What was that about?"

"I was just asking if he knew anything about the northern regions."

"Did he?"

Connor shook his head. "No, but he made it sound like the Ovarrow didn't explore the colder regions."

"He might be right, or he's just speaking for the Konus. I bet there were Ovarrow who lived that far away. Even Earth had indigenous people who lived in the colder climates."

Connor glanced at Sepal and then looked at Lenora. "They seem to make a lot of assumptions. Or at least Shuno does."

"The Mekaal are more open-minded, but I've seen similar attitudes among them as well. And there's plenty of that in our own history."

"Let's hope they continue to learn," Connor said.

They packed up their camp and were soon on their way to the northern waypoint. Connor walked over to the CDF squad traveling with them.

"Do you have everything you need?" Connor asked.

Sergeant Tui gave him a firm nod. "We're well equipped, General. It's been a quiet trip so far."

"Hopefully, it'll stay that way."

It would take them over five hours to reach their destination. Meanwhile, Connor downloaded the survey data that colonial satellites had gathered over the years. Most of the topographical mapping occurred on the main continent. The northern regions were broken up by massive lakes, some of which were frozen over, making them indistinguishable from the snow-covered land. There were also glaciers, but they were farther north than the area they were traveling to.

Noah looked at the satellite image with a thoughtful frown. "Not as mountainous as I would have thought."

"That's a good thing," Diaz said.

"Agreed. It'll make finding a place to land easier," Connor said.

"I wonder how thick the ice is there," Noah said.

"I'm sure it's thick enough for most of us, but we'll do a quick survey. We have a few targets in the area already," Connor said.

Diaz arched an eyebrow toward him. "What do you mean 'most of us'?"

"Did I say that?"

Diaz nodded. "You did. Is this another comment about my weight?"

A grin bubbled up from Connor's chest, and he shook his head. "No, come on. That's not what I meant."

Noah's eyes widened. "That's not what you told me earlier."

Connor blinked and frowned. Then he smiled. "Having fun now?"

Diaz glanced at both of them, not sure who to believe.

"If you're that sensitive about your weight, maybe it's time to do something about it," Connor said.

"My weight doesn't bother me. I'm well fed, and I love it."

"Really," Noah said. "Because it sounded like—"

"Listen here," Diaz said. "You raise five kids and run an enterprise like mine. You wouldn't be scrawny anymore either."

"I'm not scrawny," Noah replied.

Connor rubbed his forehead and shook his head. "I think we can move on. Juan, I'm sorry if I hurt your feelings."

"Thank you, Connor. I appreciate it. I knew you cared."

Connor nodded gravely. "More than words, my friend."

Lenora laughed. "You guys are so cute," she said and looked at Kara. "I love you, bro."

Kara giggled. "I love you too, bro."

Connor's eyebrows raised. "If you're feeling left out, you could join us over here. We could have a group hug."

"And come between the adorable little bromance you guys have going on? No, thank you. We're just fine over here," Lenora said.

Diaz gave both Connor and Noah an appraising look. "Victoria would have enjoyed that."

"Maybe next time we'll bring her along instead of you," Connor said, and then quickly held up his hands. "I'm kidding."

Diaz smiled, but then his expression became somber. "I wonder how he's doing."

Noah frowned. "How who's doing?"

"Isaac. He's been doing a work-study program at the colonial embassy in Shetrian," Diaz replied.

"We'll be going there soon, but you could send him a comlink if you want," Connor said.

Diaz shook his head. "No. Comlink isn't good enough. I need to see him," he said and then looked at Noah. "You think figuring out FTL is hard? Wait until you raise a couple of kids. Each one of them is different, and it's your job to figure out what makes them tick."

Noah shrugged. "Doesn't sound so bad," he said, but when Diaz's gaze hardened, he quickly added, "I'm kidding."

Diaz's lips lifted a little, and he sighed. "I remember when he wasn't so sarcastic."

"They all have to grow up sooner or later," Connor replied.

"Give me a break," Noah said.

Diaz shrugged and gave Connor a knowing look. "Lauren is eleven so she's almost at that age, but just you wait until Ethan gets there."

"I'll enjoy them at any age," Connor replied.

Noah frowned and asked, "Why is it different if it's a boy or a girl?"

"Because we treat them differently, and because they are different."

"That doesn't tell me anything," Noah replied.

"Boys follow the father. Girls follow the mother. Cecilia and Tanya will always be my little girls. They're my daughters. Victoria has more of a firm hand when it comes to raising them. But Dominick, Isaac, and Sal are my sons. They're Victoria's little boys, but for me, I'm raising sons to be men. The relationship is different and sometimes it's a real challenge. They deserve the best from us."

Noah considered this for a few moments and said, "I understand what you're saying. You're probably right that I won't really know until we start our own family."

"You'll be a good father, Noah," Diaz said.

Noah smiled a little. "Thanks."

"Maybe you guys can explain something to me," Diaz said.

"Just one thing?" Connor asked.

"For starters. The search parameters and analysis of the data. How did it find this waypoint? It's not like the Bhatdin would forget about it once they left their base."

"Oh, we think they sent out multiple teams over the years," Connor said. "They could have had families of their own and wanted to point them to their home base. We knew what we were looking for, so it was easier for us to find it, but it could be different for someone coming after."

"Do you think the Ovarrow couldn't find it?"

"Only if they knew what they were looking for. They would need to understand the hidden details in the logo."

"Makes sense," Diaz said.

"At least we can be sure there aren't any ryklars there," Noah said.

Several of the Konus looked in their direction. Connor had supplied them with personal translators so they could understand what was being said.

"They're not cold-weather creatures. At least not this far north," Connor said.

Diaz nodded. "I'm sure there'll be something scarier waiting for us."

"Why do you think I gave you your birthday present early?"

"Because you felt guilty for bringing me on this expedition with not only the Mekaal but also the Konus," Diaz replied.

Connor smiled. "You know me well enough to know that I don't feel guilty about that kind of stuff. I just didn't want you moping around for the entire trip, so I gave you a new toy."

Diaz chuckled. "I do like it. Maybe I'll bring it to the next war games. There are a few officers I'd like to try it out on. Just practice rounds. I wouldn't want anyone to get seriously hurt."

Connor grinned. "You're on."

Connor sent an update to Field Ops and the CDF. They were deviating from their original set of destinations, and per the protocol, they had to file updates in the event that they became overdue. He received the system's acknowledgment and closed the comlink.

None of the topographical data indicated that there was any kind of structure in that region, but they would be able to scan much more closely than the satellites overhead.

"Nothing but a whole lot of white and some foothills," Diaz said.

They flew over the region of the waypoint, using specialized scanning equipment to map the area. The onboard computer would analyze the data and highlight any anomalies it found, which included structures not found in nature.

"These are the coordinates," Lenora said.

Connor peered at the holoscreen. "What about those foothills?"

Lenora just looked at him.

"What if they're not foothills? I'm going to have the pilot take us there for a closer look," Connor said.

The Hercules flew toward the foothills, and they began getting scan results that indicated a structure was covered with ice and snow. The parts that they could see had resembled foothills from a distance.

"Why is it located so far off course?" Diaz asked.

"It has to be the ice age. It could've moved the entire structure," Connor replied.

"It would have to predate the ice age. We'll be able to date it once we get inside," Lenora said.

The pilot made one more pass and their scan data updated. The AI provided a high-level view of the buried structure. These were just the parts that were exposed and looked to be more than a few simple HAB units. There were several corridors that extended away from the main rectangular structure, making it appear more like a bunker than anything else.

They landed a few hundred meters away from the structure where the scan results indicated the area was more stable. They could only see the top of the building, and they didn't want the weight of the Hercules to damage what could be a three-hundred-year-old bunker. They then sectioned off the interior of the Hercules so that the four Konus and flight crew remaining behind wouldn't freeze.

After donning their cold-weather equipment and climbing into the rovers, they crossed the distance to the structure at a steady pace in six-wheel-drive mode. On-board scanners helped them avoid fissures and gaps. They had plenty of daylight to work with because it was the time of year where it wouldn't be nighttime for a few more months. But that also meant it was the warmest time of year, which would impact the stability of the area. There was land somewhere beneath the snow and ice, but they weren't able to tell how much or whether they were driving over a lake.

"The temperature shouldn't vary at all, really," Noah said.

"Negative thirty degrees is cold, but it could be a lot worse," Connor replied.

Diaz looked at him and rolled his eyes. At these temperatures, every inch of their skin had to be covered. Their cold-weather gear included parkas that could handle the weather and could also fit the Ovarrow. Even though they had different proportions than the colonists, they were within the capabilities of the clothing because the smart fabric adjusted to the size of the wearer.

The closer they got to the bunker, the more it looked like an actual arctic base that had been there so long that it resembled a part of the landscape. They circled around the area using ground-penetrating radar and were able to find an entrance buried under the icy snow. They had equipment that would make short work of melting the snow enough for them to reach the doors.

Urret and the other Mekaal soldiers who had worked with the CDF for years were more comfortable with lending a hand. Shuno and the other Konus soldiers watched for a few moments, shifting their feet. Ovarrow in general weren't a people who'd stand idly by while there was work to be done, so Connor invited them to pitch in and help with the snow removal.

With everyone pitching in, they soon cleared a path to a door. The bunker entrance was attached to a small tunnel that led to the main structure, which Connor found similar to some of the bunkers he'd explored on the main continent. Perhaps the Bhatdin had shared the design with the Ovarrow. The main doors had been reinforced, undoubtedly for the purpose of not only withstanding the extreme temperatures but also an attack from outside. He doubted the complex could withstand an attack from Krake attack drones, but the material looked as if it had been built to last. And the Krake would have been hard-pressed to find this place if they were relying wholly on orbital surveys.

Specialist Weps checked the door. "I'm detecting a power source here. There should be a panel nearby."

After a few moments of searching, they found a circular panel to the left of the door, but it was frozen shut. A CDF soldier used a handheld plasma torch to warm the area and the panel opened. The interface reminded Connor of a Krake door-control system, but the language looked different.

Connor tilted his head to the side and pressed his lips together.

"Are you going to be able to translate that?" Diaz asked.

"Let's find out."

He enabled his Krake translator that had been given to him by a rebellious faction of the Krake. The program had stored multiple versions of the Ovarrow languages from hundreds of universes. Colonial scientists had studied it and had even been able to augment its capabilities. The translator included a security access module that went through an analysis of the screen prompts.

"Careful," Noah said. "There could be security protocols if we get it wrong."

Connor gestured for Sepal to join him at the door.

Sepal came over and looked at the interface. "I don't know the required sequence that will gain us entry."

"That's fine. I think I can get it," Connor said and ran a decryption protocol that would bypass the security.

The door unlocked and opened with a puff of air. Connor walked inside and interior lighting began to come on.

"I'm amazed the power is still working," Diaz said.

"We'll need to move quickly. There's no telling how long it will last," Noah said.

Amber-colored lighting illuminated the corridor that led to the bunker's main entrance.

"Looks familiar," Connor said.

Lenora nodded. "Standard Ovarrow bunker design we've seen, but we still don't know who built it."

Connor could always appreciate how Lenora refused to jump to conclusions. She often took an evidence-based approach to her research, which was one of the main reasons she was a leading authority in her academic field of study.

The floor tilted a little to the side, but the walls were still in good shape with no sign of structural failure. They walked to the main door and used the door control systems, hearing several clangs as the locking mechanism retracted. Connor pushed the door, which squeaked as it opened, and Diaz helped him open it the rest of the way. More lighting came on. They were in a reception area that was able to fit all of them.

Lenora checked her wrist computer. "Interior temperatures are rising, and it doesn't appear as if there's been freezing in here."

The interior walls were made from a dark metallic alloy. Located away from the main entrance was a console atop a pedestal that rose from the ground.

Connor approached and saw that there was no fabric screen like the Ovarrow consoles, but the design was similar. He waved his hand over the console and a green holoscreen flickered to life, but the screen was slightly out of focus and they were only able to see hazy images.

"That looks more like a Krake console interface," Lenora said.

"Yeah, but I don't think it is," Connor replied.

Noah walked around to the other side of the console. "Could be just an earlier version of it."

Lenora leaned toward the holoscreen and cleaned the projector leads. The holoscreen became clearer and they could see the symbols. "Not Krake. Definitely Ovarrow."

Sepal came closer and peered at the screen, and Lenora gestured for him to use the console. The Mekaal historian selected a few of the symbols and a map of the bunker appeared.

"There must have been hundreds of them living here," Noah said.

"Yes, but why here?" Connor asked.

Sepal selected a few other options, but the console appeared to have a limited interface. He looked at Lenora.

"It's fine. I think it must be just an information console and the interface is limited," she said.

Connor nodded. "We'll need to explore inside. Let's get a couple of recon drones ready and split up into teams."

Urret glanced at Shuno and then at Connor. "How many teams?"

"Three teams," Connor replied. He'd been expecting the question. "Sergeant Tui, pick three people to go with Shuno and his team to explore the dormitories and the other living spaces here," he said, gesturing toward part of the map. "Urret, your team can explore this region over here. Looks like it's some kind of maintenance area that also holds some other kind of equipment. The rest will come with me. There appears to be an engineering and control center. Here."

"General Gates," Shuno said, and Connor looked at him. "We don't need escorts for a simple scouting mission."

Connor regarded the Konus scout for a few seconds. "But you do need experts in using computing systems like this one."

Shuno looked at the CDF soldiers.

"I'll assign Specialist Weps with Schmiddy and Cooper as her backup," Sergeant Tui said.

Shuno was aware of Specialist Weps's technical capabilities. He looked at Connor. "Very well, I understand."

Connor wasn't about to let the Konus explore anything without someone there to prevent them from taking advantage of the situation. "We all have comlinks. Report in if you find anything interesting. We'll meet back here later on. When in doubt, don't touch anything. We're not under any time constraints."

They split up and each team took a different corridor to the areas they were going to explore.

"I thought Shuno was going to give you trouble about having escorts assigned to his group," Noah said.

"He's not really in a position to refuse. Plus, this place isn't like the other places they've scouted," Connor replied.

The interior of the bunker was in excellent condition considering its age and the harsh climate. As in the previous areas, there was about a seven-degree decline and the floor sloped downward, but the walls remained intact. The facility had shifted over the years.

Before they reached their destination, they walked past a number of empty rooms that held a few storage containers but little else. However, when they walked through the doors of the control center, they found several consoles stationed throughout the room.

"Each of these consoles has its own dedicated data connection," Noah said. "I bet the computing core isn't far from here."

"Reminds me of the archives at Sanctuary, but this setup is more advanced," Lenora said.

The consoles all had a holographic interface, and after a few minutes of accessing the data repositories, they confirmed that the bunker had been home to the Bhatdin.

"There are historical logs that go back hundreds of years," Lenora said. "The earliest entries read as if they knew they'd come on a one-way trip."

Connor stood next to her, reading the same logs. "It doesn't say where they came from. They didn't build a gateway here."

"That could have been due to a lack of resources, but they brought enough to set up this place and study the Ovarrow. I wonder how many years they were here before they left," Lenora said.

Noah laughed. "They may not have built any gateways, but they have data on them. There are also theoretical principles on how they work. We'll need some time to review it to see if there's anything we don't already know. Is it all right if I start the data extraction?"

Connor looked at Lenora and she nodded. "Go ahead."

The consoles were capable of hosting multiple holoscreens for systems access, and he read the earliest entries.

Diaz walked over to him. "Find anything useful?"

Connor nodded. "They were fighting the Krake and had to flee their own world. They sent multiple teams to different universes in an attempt to win the war."

Diaz frowned for a moment. "It didn't work. They were defeated."

Connor considered it for a few moments. "There are survivors. The Mekaal and Konus are here because of what they did, and we definitely benefited from what they were doing. I'm not sure we could have defeated the Krake if not for what was left behind."

It soon became apparent that it was going to take some time to finish exploring the bunker. Connor left Lenora, Noah, and Kara in the command center, and the rest of their team came with him.

Diaz gave him a sidelong look. "Is this the fun part?"

Connor snorted. "You bet."

"At least it's not falling apart," Diaz said.

At that moment, Connor felt the floor vibrate under his feet. The vibrations were small, but unmistakable. He stared at his friend. "You just had to say it."

16

IN THEIR FINAL weeks at the colonial embassy in Shetrian, Isaac and the rest of the interns had begun using some of their downtime on the sectioned-off part of the embassy's rooftop. Some of the areas functioned as landing pads while others held communications equipment, but there were still places for them to gather. Rooftop gardens, along with several seating areas, provided a nice respite for people who worked at the embassy.

"Restricted travel is finally lifting," Julian said.

A Konus diplomatic envoy had arrived a few days ago, looking to improve their relationship with the Mekaal in an effort to try to put the past behind them. There was plenty of mistrust where the Konus were concerned, and Isaac wasn't immune to it.

"I'm ready to go home," Jordan said, and Kanin agreed with a vigorous nod.

Curtis and Ella came through the doors to the rooftop and walked over to them. Curtis had likely been trying to make his latest play for Ella's attentions, and by the looks of it, those attentions had been refused. The edges of Isaacs lips quirked at that.

Ella had been drilling him mercilessly on key concepts for his placement test. Isaac had to admit that her methods, while relentless and frustrating at times, had helped him. The answers came quickly, and he was able to break down the questions much better than when he'd been studying on his own.

Isaac looked away, pretending not to notice Ella as she came over to them. "Please, no more."

Ella grinned. "You're ready. It's better to be well-rested anyway."

Isaac twitched an eyebrow at her and chuckled. "Thanks. I have nightmares about test questions hunting me down."

Julian looked at him and frowned. "How would that work? Are they beating you over the head, or is it something else?"

Isaac shook his head. "No, it's a phalanx of holoscreens chasing me, and there are these shock-sticks zapping me while Ella threatens to add more study time for each question I miss," he said, shivering as if a chill had gone down his spine. "It was terrifying. Don't let her sweet and innocent exterior fool you. She's a harsh taskmaster."

"Oh, stop it," Ella admonished. "I wasn't that bad."

Isaac grinned and most of the others smiled except Curtis, who ignored the whole exchange.

"Do you think you're ready for the test?" Julian asked.

Isaac had done everything he could to prepare for that damn test, but he had no idea if he was ready. "We'll find out in a few days."

"It's two days," Ella reminded him.

He'd planned to wait and take the placement test in Sanctuary, but Dr. Rostova informed him he could take the test here at the embassy. After that, it wouldn't take long to find out if he'd been accepted into Sierra's medical program. Both Curtis and Ella were already in the program and would be going to Sierra right from here.

Julian looked at Jordan. "Did you tell your family yet?"

"Not yet."

"Tell them what?" Ella asked.

"We're staying at Sanctuary. We got our recommendations this morning," Jordan replied.

At least he wouldn't be completely alone when they returned to Sanctuary. He had no idea what he was going to do if things didn't work out at Sierra.

"Did you tell your parents, Isaac?" Ella asked.

Isaac shook his head. "No."

Ella frowned. "Not even your mother?"

He'd only exchanged a few messages with his mother since he'd left. Those exchanges had been strained, at best, and they'd avoided topics like his father. She was probably waiting for him to bring it up, and he didn't want to.

"I will," Isaac said.

Julian knew that Isaac hadn't left Sanctuary on the best of terms with his parents and quickly changed the subject.

"You know what?" Julian said. "I think I'm going to miss this place a little."

"Not me," Curtis said. "I'm ready to be around more people for a change."

"It's time," Ella agreed, and Curtis raised his eyebrows in surprise.

"Yeah?"

Ella nodded. "Can't stay here forever, can we?"

The others voiced their assent, but Isaac didn't. He didn't want his time with Ella to end, especially if she went to Sierra without him. She looked at him and smiled.

An audible chime sounded from all their wrist computers at the same time.

Julian stood up. "We've been summoned!"

The others stood and started heading toward the rooftop exit. Isaac lingered behind, and Ella gave him a questioning look.

"What are you thinking about? Are you worried about the test?" she asked.

Isaac shook his head. "No, I'm actually *not* thinking about the test."

Ella nodded and waited for him to continue.

"I've gotten used to all this," he said, gesturing to their surroundings.

"I know what you mean." She looked away from him toward the cityscape and sighed.

"Do you?"

She turned back toward him.

"I'm going to miss you, too," Isaac said.

He thought about adding the others into that statement but decided to be straight with her. He stepped closer to her, and when she looked up at him, he leaned toward her until they were just inches apart.

"Isaac," she said softly.

Heat filled his chest and he reached for one of her hands. She let him.

"You guys coming?" Curtis asked loudly from the doorway.

Isaac didn't turn toward them. They probably had an audience, but he wasn't going to let Curtis or anyone else take this moment away from him.

"Ella, there's something here between us that's worth exploring."

She gazed up at him and her mouth opened a little. He thought about kissing her, just lay it all on the line. He wanted to, and he thought she wanted to as well, but he didn't want to rush her.

Another chime came from their wrist computers. Ella looked down at hers and acknowledged the alert.

"We have to go," she said almost regretfully and gave his hand a gentle squeeze before she let it go.

They walked toward the others who waited for them in the elevator nearby. Everyone was looking at them, trying to figure out what had happened. Isaac started to feel foolish but dismissed those thoughts immediately. He'd wanted to tell her for a while, but there hadn't been the right time. If he kept waiting for the 'right' time, then he might never get the chance.

The elevator doors closed with Ella standing next to him. She looked up, watching the floor count go down. Julian made some comment and Jordan seized the opportunity to start a conversation.

Isaac glanced at Ella and leaned toward her a little. "Awkward," he said softly.

She snorted a little and her lips quivered. Luminous dark eyes twinkled as she regarded him for a moment with a knowing look. Then the elevator doors opened. She hadn't given him that sympathetic, forever-friend-zone look that women gave as a way to soften rejection. That was something.

They walked through a crowded atrium and Dr. Rostova waved them over.

"Good, you're all here," she said.

Deasira joined them. "Exciting news. Thanks in no small part to your hard work, our presence has been requested to present our findings to the High Commissioner. This is a great honor, and you should be proud of what we've achieved."

Dr. Solomon and Dr. Townsend stood nearby.

"Will they announce our findings to your people?" Dr. Solomon asked.

"Soon. This is the first step," Deasira replied.

"This requires all of us to attend?" Dr. Townsend asked.

"Of course. The entire team was invited," Deasira replied.

Dr. Townsend frowned and glanced at Isaac and the others. The uptight bastard didn't want to share the limelight with lowly interns.

"It's only fair, Gerry," Dr. Rostova said. "This was a team effort."

Dr. Townsend sighed. "Very well."

They walked outside where a long line of black-colored rovers was waiting. Isaac's eyes widened. Not just them, but a full colonial diplomatic envoy would be traveling to the Mekaal capitol building. CDF soldiers were stationed near each of the rovers.

Isaac and the others were guided toward the rovers at the end of the procession. He hadn't expected that this was to be so formal an event. These were the larger N-Class rovers, which had enough seating capacity to accommodate half the team. They walked toward the last rover, and a CDF soldier waved to them.

"Good afternoon, I'm Corporal Reznick, and I'll be with you for the short drive to the Mekaal capitol building. You can go on and get inside. We'll be underway shortly."

Isaac walked toward the nearest door and climbed inside, sliding across the bench seat to the other side. Julian climbed in next to him and Jordan followed.

Julian arched an eyebrow toward him. "Expecting someone else?"

"Just hoping," Isaac replied in kind.

Julian laughed.

Isaac glanced behind and saw that Ella was sitting at the very back with Kanin. They were speaking to each other. Curtis climbed into the middle row with the equipment for the presentation. He gave Isaac a smoldering glare and then looked away.

Isaac turned back around and looked out the window. He thought he'd seen Agent Franklin somewhere close by, but he couldn't find him now. The CIB agent could vanish with the best of them. Over the months, it had become a bit of a competition with them to see if Isaac could spot him.

Julian leaned toward him. "What happened up there?"

Isaac scratched the side of his head. "I told her."

"What did she say?"

Isaac inhaled deeply. "Nothing."

He'd hoped that Ella would sit next to him, but she hadn't. He tried not to read too much into it.

Jordan looked at them and frowned. "Who?"

Julian twitched his head toward the back and whispered, "Ella."

Jordan nodded and smiled. "It's about time. Cutting it kinda close there, weren't you?"

Isaac shook his head. "Did you guys have a betting pool going or something?"

"Oh man, I should have thought of that," Julian said.

Reznick climbed inside and put the rover into gear. Not long after, the colonial diplomatic motorcade left the embassy and began heading toward the Capitol.

Julian and Jordan chatted, and Isaac just looked out the window at the line of rovers in front of them. The scientists were in the rover ahead of them. They appeared to be speaking to each other, and he wondered what they were talking about. Did they talk about anything other than work? The entire time he'd been here, he hadn't seen Dr. Townsend loosen up once. Dr. Solomon was more laid back, and Dr. Rostova was almost like a normal person. Her work was important to her, but she hadn't forgotten how to be human, unlike the wooden board that was Dr. Townsend. A little resentment had built up over the months since Townsend had fired him as his intern, and things had settled into a general dislike between them. Isaac was long past trying to figure out why Townsend didn't like him and had decided to return the irritation in kind. He wasn't disrespectful toward the geneticist, but he didn't go out of his way to be helpful like he did for the other scientists.

Many Mekaal gathered on the side of the street to watch the procession drive by, and Isaac wondered what they thought about all this. Most Mekaal he'd met were friendly toward the colonists, but not all of them. Some kept their distance. Sometimes it was difficult for him to judge what the Mekaal or any Ovarrow was thinking. They weren't quite as alien to him as they had been six months prior, but they were by no means an open book.

He was looking out the window at a Mekaal who stared back at him, when a sudden loud boom made him duck instinctively. The ground shook and a large plume of orange blazed behind them. Isaac twisted in his seat and his mouth hung agape. The explosion had been so close to them.

"Was that the embassy?" Julian asked. "I think that was the embassy."

Reznick stopped the rover and stepped outside. "Stay in the rover."

Another explosion came from their left. Reznick scrambled back into the rover and slammed the door shut.

"Hang on! We're getting out of here!"

17

As Reznick stomped on the accelerator and the rover jerked forward, Isaac was thrown back into his seat. The convoy turned off the main thoroughfare. Mekaal ran down the streets, and some took cover in the buildings. The convoy blew past a side street that led back toward the colonial embassy, which was blocked by a disabled vehicle that was on fire.

Isaac tried to peer down the side street to catch a glimpse of the embassy, but they were going too fast. The rover tilted to the side as Reznick drove around some kind of makeshift barricade.

"Colonial Embassy," Reznick said, "this is Rover 5. All occupants are accounted for. Following the rest of the convoy."

Isaac couldn't hear who the CDF soldier was speaking to. It must be a status check-in.

"Negative, I haven't seen any hostiles," Reznick said.

"Is he talking to someone at the embassy?" Julian asked.

"I don't know. I think so," Isaac replied.

As they drove toward an intersection, Isaac looked toward a

side street they were passing. It was blocked off. He knew in his gut that something wasn't right. There was more going on here.

"Corporal," Isaac said.

Corporal Reznick was driving the rover while on a comlink with someone else, so Isaac waited. The first rover was rapidly approaching the intersection.

"Corporal," Isaac said again.

"Maybe you shouldn't distract him," Curtis said.

Isaac had heard stories of tactical engagements almost his entire life—stories his father told and the soldiers who frequented the family restaurant. To him, everything that was going on seemed to be carefully orchestrated chaos.

Isaac unbuckled his seat belt, leaned forward, and grabbed the soldier's arm. "Corporal, slow down. Something's wrong with that intersection."

Reznick's head jerked toward him in surprise and then he eased off the accelerator. The first two rovers darted past the intersection, and a Mekaal hauler came out of nowhere and plowed into the third. Reznick slammed his foot on the brakes, and the rover in front of them swung to the side.

"Go left!" Isaac shouted.

Reznick spun the wheel to the left, and Isaac was thrown into the door as the rover turned sharply.

"That's the wrong way!" Curtis shouted from the back.

"He's right," Julian said. "This is taking us away from the embassy."

Isaac pulled himself up and looked behind him. Ovarrow were jumping out of the hauler.

"We're being herded. The intersection was an ambush. All the side streets on the way here were blocked by something. That can't be a coincidence," Isaac said.

"Shit. Shit. Shit," Reznick said and glanced at Isaac. "Get up here. What's your name?"

"Isaac."

Reznick frowned and looked at him for a second. "Diaz. Your last name is Diaz?"

Isaac nodded.

Reznick blew out a breath. "Your father is Captain Juan Diaz."

"Yes."

"Good. Good," Reznick said quickly. "Help me keep an eye out for danger. There's a pistol in the storage compartment. Grab it."

Isaac climbed into the front seat, which was much easier said than done because the rover was still speeding down the street.

"What about the others? Shouldn't we go back and help?" Ella asked.

"She's right," Jordan said. "Someone could be hurt. That construction hauler slammed right into them."

"Negative," Reznick replied.

The others started to protest.

"Guys!" Isaac said and turned toward them. "His orders are to get us to safety. There will be response teams dispatched to help the other rover."

"How the hell do you know that?" Curtis asked.

"Because the rovers have trackers on them, and the onboard systems will register the impact."

"Isaac's right," Reznick said. "My orders are to get you to safety. No rescue missions."

The others went quiet for a few moments.

"I saw Mekaal coming out of that hauler," Ella said.

Isaac opened the storage container in front of him and

retrieved a predator pistol. There was a small ammunition block next to it. He loaded the gun and kept the safety on.

Julian leaned forward and looked at the weapon. "Since when do you know how to use military sidearms?"

Isaac swallowed hard. "My father taught me. He taught all of us."

"Are you sure they were Mekaal coming out of that hauler?" Curtis asked.

"Who else would it be?" Ella replied.

"Seriously? The Konus are here. It could have been them," Curtis said.

"That's crazy," Julian said. "They only brought a diplomatic envoy."

Jordan and Kanin agreed.

Isaac looked out the front of the rover, scanning for anything suspicious. He didn't see anything, which made everything look wrong.

"Do you guys have a better explanation," Curtis said. "Anyone?"

Isaac pressed his lips together for a moment. "We don't know who did this, but if the Konus are involved, they must've had help."

The others went quiet for a few moments.

"All right, listen up," Reznick said. "I want everyone to keep their eyes open. Let me know if you see anything suspicious."

"Uh, Corporal Reznick," Julian said, "if Isaac is right and this is some kind of inside job, then couldn't they be tracking the rover?"

"The Konus can't break our encryption," Reznick said.

"That's just it. What if someone else is doing this? Someone with knowledge of how we operate," Julian said.

Isaac felt a wave of panic seize his guts.

Reznick looked at him. "Isaac, can you disable the tracker?"

Isaac accessed the rover's computer systems and began navigating the interface. Each option he selected led him to another subsystem. The rover's designers hadn't made it easy.

"I think we're far enough away that we can start heading back to the embassy," Reznick said.

"Are you sure that's a good idea? I mean, that's where the attack came from—uh, the area that was attacked," Julian said.

Isaac was listening while trying to disable the tracker. "The vehicle's communications systems are disconnected from the embassy."

"What!" Reznick shouted.

"The comlink went down almost ten minutes ago," Isaac said and brought up the timestamp for the loss-of-signal-status message.

"Wouldn't it have warned us? An error message or something?" Reznick asked.

Isaac shrugged. "I don't know."

Curtis groaned.

"I don't know. I didn't design the damn system," Isaac snapped.

Reznick tried to open a comlink to the embassy. "I can't reach anyone. Do your comlinks work?"

Isaac couldn't get his to connect either. None of them could.

A smaller gray rover sped up behind them and then pulled alongside. Isaac recognized the driver.

"I know him," Isaac said. "That's Cohsora. He's been part of our protective detail before. Our local guide."

He waved toward him and Cohsora returned the wave. Then the Mekaal gestured ahead of them.

"He wants us to follow him," Isaac said.

A message appeared on the rover's HUD for a short-range comlink from the other rover.

"Embassy is not safe. Will guide you to secondary safe-house location," Cohsora said.

Some kind of alphanumeric code appeared below the message.

Isaac frowned. "What is that?"

Reznick read it and nodded. "Authentication code. It's part of our security protocols," he said and gestured for Cohsora to take the lead.

The smaller, two-seat rover sped ahead of them.

"Are there any other weapons in here?" Julian asked.

Reznick scanned the area for a few seconds before answering. "Not that I know of, but you could look around."

The others started searching. Isaac checked the storage container and the other compartments in the front, but there wasn't anything for them to use.

"There's nothing back here. What about you guys?" Julian asked.

"The only thing here is the field lab equipment in these containers. Looks like they restocked them for some reason," Ella said.

"What about you, Curtis?" Julian asked.

Curtis didn't reply. He kept looking out the window, his body rigid.

"Curtis, are you okay?" Ella asked. She'd leaned forward. "Hey," she said, calmly.

Curtis blinked several times. "No, I'm not. None of this is okay. Who the hell decides to blow shit up? We're cut off from the embassy. Fuck, we don't even know if there *is* an embassy anymore. What if they blew it up? What if everyone who was left there is dead? What if—"

"Curtis!" Isaac said. "Keep it together."

Curtis glared at him. "Why do you get the gun?"

"Because I told him to take it," Reznick said.

Curtis shook his head and muttered something under his breath.

"This isn't helping," Ella said.

Curtis whirled toward her. "Who the hell cares? Do you think you can help? I saw the Ovarrow that came out of that hauler. They were armed. Dr. Rostova, Solomon, and Townsend were in there. They're all dead."

"You don't know that," Ella replied.

"Don't be so naive. You know, not everyone supported us being here. What if they were right?" Curtis swore again and shook his head. "Stuck here. We don't know what's going on."

"Shut him up," Reznick said.

"Come back here and make me."

"Curtis," Isaac said.

"Oh, what the hell do you want? Are you going to tell me to calm down?" he sneered.

"Think it through. Even if you saw armed Ovarrow, it doesn't mean the others are dead."

"Sure, because you're the expert on everything. You're never getting into the Sierra medical program."

Isaac ignored the jab. "Think about it. Whoever was driving that hauler took out the third rover so they could cut us and the rover ahead of us off. If they wanted to kill us, they wouldn't go through the trouble."

"He's right," Reznick said. "Sounds like a surgical operation if I've ever heard of one."

Curtis inhaled deeply and then seemed more in control of himself. Ella leaned forward and spoke softly to him. He nodded a few times, and Isaac turned back around to face forward.

Reznick glanced at him. "Good job."

It didn't feel good. Curtis was saying what they were all thinking, even if only in part.

"Thanks," Isaac said.

Cohsora led them farther into the city. Isaac tried to reach Dr. Rostova through a short-range comlink but couldn't. He was unable to reach anyone, and he couldn't figure out why. He tried the emergency channels to reach Agent Franklin, and that failed as well. He frowned in thought. No one could block communications over the entire city, so it had to be something else. Something local, but he couldn't think what.

Cohsora turned off the road they were on and took another that began to descend toward a tunnel. Reznick followed. Isaac had no idea where the safe house was or what the protocol was for it. He thought about asking Reznick, but the CDF soldier seemed fine with where they were going, and he didn't want to distract him.

The rover's headlights became brighter, piercing the dark tunnel. Isaac glanced behind them as the light from the entrance faded. The city had an extensive network of tunnels, but Isaac didn't know anything about them. Reznick drove them past construction equipment. There must have been a restoration effort going on. How long had the Mekaal been working down here?

"This has to be some kind of shortcut, but where are they taking us?" Isaac asked.

Reznick shook his head. "I don't know. I was assigned just a few minutes before we left."

They reached a cross-section of tunnels, and Cohsora stopped. There was green lighting that kept the chamber from total darkness. Isaac had seen similar lighting at the Ovarrow archives in Sanctuary. The Mekaal used chemical illumination in emergencies when there was a loss of power. As long as the light casings remained intact, they worked just fine.

Reznick stopped the rover and scanned the area in front of them. There wasn't much to see.

"Isn't there anyone else here?" Julian asked.

"Maybe we're the first ones to arrive," Isaac replied.

Cohsora stepped out of the rover.

"I'm going to go see what's going on," Reznick said.

"Should I come along?" Isaac asked. "Give you some backup?"

Reznick considered it for a second and shook his head. "No, stay here." He looked at the others. "That goes for all of you. Stay in the rover. I'm going to see if I can find out what's going on."

Reznick opened the door and stepped out of the rover. He unholstered his weapon and walked toward Cohsora.

"Isaac," Ella said. He turned toward her. "Can you hear what they're saying?"

"Maybe you should roll down the windows," Julian suggested.

Isaac turned back toward the front. "Let's just wait." He peered ahead. Reznick was speaking with Cohsora.

"I still can't reach anyone on the comlink," Jordan said.

"Neither can I," Julian added.

Isaac checked his again and it was the same. The CDF had ways to suppress communications, but there was always a limit to how far a suppressor worked.

"How could they jam our comlinks here?" Ella asked.

Isaac frowned. They were underground and well away from the attack. "They shouldn't be able to."

"This is bullshit," Curtis said. "What's the matter, Isaac, can't figure out why our comlinks don't work. You've got the military family. How would the CDF do it?"

"I don't know. Some kind of suppression field, but we should be beyond it by now. Especially down here."

"Why wouldn't the field extend down here?" Julian asked.

"It would have to penetrate the ground, which absorbs the signal," Isaac replied, and a thought came to him. "Unless there's something on the rover that's preventing our comlinks from getting out."

"Holy shit! Can they do that?" Julian asked.

"I don't know. I guess they could. It's not like I'm trained in any of this stuff."

"Maybe we should ask Corporal Reznick," Ella said.

"He told us to stay in the rover," Curtis said.

Isaac rubbed his chin for a few moments. "Take a look around inside. Is there anything that looks like it could interfere with our comlinks?"

"Could you be more vague?" Julian said.

"Look for something small. Doesn't need to be big. It would need some kind of power."

Isaac looked around at the vehicle's controls. He didn't see anything. The others didn't either.

Bright lights shone from ahead of them, coming from farther down one of the adjacent tunnels.

"I see something," Ella said.

"Duh, it's the lights from over there," Curtis said.

"No, it's just under the window here."

"What's it look like?" Isaac asked.

Ella knelt on the seat and turned toward the back of the rover. "I can't get a good look at it. It's small."

Isaac puffed out a breath. "I'm going to take a look."

"But Reznick said to stay here," Julian said.

"I'll be quick," he replied.

He opened his door a little and watched to see if Reznick or

Cohsora heard. They didn't. He quickly slipped out of the rover and carefully closed the door, hastening toward the back of the rover. Ella gestured toward where she'd seen the device.

Isaac circled around to the back of the rover and squatted down. A circular mechanism looked as if it had simply been pressed into place with some kind of adhesive. He didn't recognize it. He felt around the smooth edges and pulled. After a few seconds, it came loose. It felt warm in his hand. He lifted it near one of the rover's lights to get a better look at it. There was a seam along the middle. When he twisted it, something clicked inside. All at once, his comlink came to life with a barrage of messages and connection attempts. Flashing lights came from inside the rover as the others' comlinks began working.

Isaac smiled and began walking back toward the front.

"Hey, Reznick," Isaac said.

As the CDF soldier turned toward him, bright lights pierced the darkness all around them and the chamber was awash in it. Isaac squeezed his eyes shut and put his hand on the rover to brace himself. He blinked several times and looked away from the lights.

Reznick began shouting. Isaac held his hand up and tried to see in front of the rover but couldn't.

There was a little *phunt* sound, followed by several others. Reznick screamed and Isaac heard shots being fired from a CDF predator pistol.

Isaac gripped his pistol, but he couldn't see anything, and he wasn't going to fire his weapon blindly. He scrambled to his door and climbed back inside the rover. The windows of the rover were polarized to filter out the bright lights.

"Someone shot him!" Julian said.

Isaac peered ahead and saw Reznick sink to the ground. He

couldn't tell where the shooting was coming from. Small impacts clipped the ground near the fallen CDF soldier.

Isaac scrambled over to the driver's seat and put the vehicle into drive, pulling around Reznick to give him some cover. The others ducked. He looked for Cohsora but couldn't find him.

Reznick had blood leaking from a wound in his middle. Isaac opened the door and squatted down by the CDF soldier. Reznick looked up at him. "Run!" he hissed. "Don't stop. Run!"

Isaac tried to lift him up, but his hands kept slipping. The soldier was too heavy for him to lift alone. He turned toward the rover. "Help me get him inside."

Julian and Curtis opened their doors and came over to him.

Whoever had been shooting at them had stopped. A half-strangled cry came from beyond the rover, and Cohsora landed nearby in a tangled heap. The Mekaal's lifeless eyes stared up at them.

A large figure walked in front of the bright lights, casting an imposing shadow. Isaac heard the foot stomps of others approaching.

He gritted his teeth and picked up Reznick's pistol, aiming it.

"Go ahead, human," the figure said. He was an Ovarrow.

Isaac saw others—a lot of them. There were so many. He froze, unable to think, and the pistol he held sank a little. The Ovarrow came closer, and others surrounded them. They wore green metallic armor.

Konus!

The lead Konus walked up to Reznick and shot him in the head. A bright plasma bolt and there was nothing left above the shoulder.

Isaac's eyes widened and a cry caught in his throat. He started to raise his weapon, but the Konus aimed at Isaac. The other soldiers readied their weapons, aiming them at the rover. Isaac heard someone sobbing from behind him.

"Just put down the pistol, Isaac," Julian said, his voice shaking.

Isaac stared at the pistol in his hand. They'd just killed Reznick right there in front of him. He was dead. The Konus commander stepped toward him and grabbed the pistol from his hand.

"You're no soldier," he said.

"Commander Koukax," a Konus soldier said, "they've disabled the jammer. We have to get them out of here."

Isaac looked at Koukax, but the Konus commander was looking at the others in the vehicle. "Anyone still inside the rover by the time Strovax reaches me will be shot."

The Konus soldier began walking around the rover.

"Come on, we have to get out of here," Ella said.

Isaac looked at his wrist computer and started entering a message, but just as he was about to send it, Koukax struck him with the butt of his long rifle.

Isaac staggered and fell to a knee. He looked up in time to catch a stomping kick to the sternum that knocked him back in a short, brutal arc to the ground. Stars exploded in his vision and something in his head felt loose and hot. The breath was gone from his lungs. He tried to inhale but couldn't. He coughed and someone grabbed him, lifting him up.

"On your feet," Koukax growled.

Isaac watched as the Konus soldiers dragged the others from the rover, pushing them toward the bright lights. He heard Ella cry out and tried to turn toward her, but a strong hand shoved him forward and it took everything he had to keep his feet under him.

18

THE VIBRATIONS SPREADING throughout the bunker were reported by all teams. Lenora looked at Connor, and he gestured for her and Noah to hurry.

"Repeat the last," Connor said into his comlink.

"The seismic activity appears to be concentrated in the vicinity of the bunker," Specialist Weps said. "I've routed sensor data back to the Hercules and the waves are just here. I don't have the equipment to determine whether there's other activity a few kilometers away."

"Understood. Start making your way back to the main entrance," Connor said.

He walked over to Lenora and Noah. "How long is this going to take?"

There were several holoscreens active. "There's a lot of data here," Noah said. "I've tried a few compression algorithms to see if I could speed up the transfer, but it's not helping, so we're just transferring the raw data."

"Why isn't it working?" Connor asked.

"To compress the data, the algorithm needs to manipulate every piece of data before it can be transferred. The Bhatdin's data handling for their repositories already has it in a compressed state for efficient storage."

Connor nodded. "Got it. Double compression gets us nothing. So, we can't save time on the transfer. How long is this going to take?"

"Thirty-six hours. Maybe more." Noah winced.

Connor's gaze darted to Lenora. They might not have that much time. "I know. I know," she said. The ground shuddered. "I'm trying to find the physical storage used for the data. If we can't copy it, then maybe we can take the storage medium with us."

Her voice was tight with frustration.

"Okay, let's slow down a second. What if we left the data uplink running and went back to the Hercules? It's not like we have to watch the data transfer."

"We don't know how long the bunker will have power. Urret couldn't make it to the power station. It's cut off from the rest of the bunker. Do you know what's causing the quakes?"

Connor shook his head. "They're not sure. It might just be in this area."

Noah arched an eyebrow. "That's not suspicious or anything."

"It could just be a coincidence, but I'd rather not get trapped in here."

Lenora shook her head and sighed. "How long can you wait before we evacuate?"

"I've told the other teams to start making their way back to the main entrance. Urret found some equipment they're bringing out. The team exploring the dormitories found what they think are personal log devices. They're collecting them. We have a little time if you want to head to the computing core."

Noah looked at Lenora. "It's worth a shot."

She nodded. "I know, but we could lose it all if we're wrong."

Connor looked at them and waited.

"If we start removing the storage devices, there's a chance it could stop the transfer. I won't know until we go down there and take a look."

"Okay, two questions first for both of you. Is this really the Bhatdin? Is it their bunker?"

Lenora smiled. "It is. The same logo is here, and the earliest log entries are for when they first arrived here."

"Is the data here worth the risk of staying longer?" Connor asked.

"I think so," Noah said.

"If we leave and the bunker sinks, gets crushed, or suffers from some other kind of catastrophe, we could return with salvage teams and retrieve what's left, but we might lose some or all of the data," Lenora said.

Connor had expected as much, but he needed to be sure. The information stored here couldn't be found anywhere else on New Earth. It could give them new insights into the Ovarrow and even the Krake.

"Let's get moving," Connor said.

They left the command center. The recon drone had mapped the area, and a path was highlighted on their personal HUDs showing them how to get to the computing core.

"I tried to run searches to narrow down just the important information, but there's too much here for that," Noah said.

"Too much here and not enough time," Connor replied.

The computing core was a series of circular rooms packed with equipment. The layout reminded Connor of Krake facilities he'd been to. How much had the two species' technology been intertwined? The Krake home universe had contained two habitable planets. One, like New Earth, had been home to the Ovarrow, and the second was home to the Krake. In all the other universes the Krake had explored, their home planet was a lifeless rock while the Ovarrow homeworlds thrived. This revelation had led to war between the two species.

They walked inside the nearest room. There was equipment lining the walls and in the center of a wide metallic column. Green holoscreens were active. Connor circled the room while Noah and Lenora went to the column. Some of the equipment was dark. It must have suffered damage and was now offline.

A comlink chimed on his wrist computer. It was Diaz.

"We're going to start moving what they found to the Hercules."

"Understood, we'll be going back to the main entrance in a little while," Connor replied.

"Don't take too long. I don't want to have to rescue your ass again."

"I thought we were even," Connor replied.

He heard Diaz grin as the comlink severed, and he walked out into the main corridor with an answering grin on his face.

Sergeant Tui came toward him. "The other rooms look similar to that one. Mostly in good shape. Is there anything we can do, General?"

Corporal Eldridge and Private Rhodes watched.

"Let's go see what the experts have for us," Connor said.

He returned to Noah and Lenora. They had several access panels open at the base of the column.

Noah gestured inside. "They look like they come right out."

"Yeah, but we need to attach portable power supplies to them to keep them working. We don't have enough," Lenora said.

"We'll need to guess which ones to take, then transfer as much as we can," Noah replied.

Connor and the CDF soldiers walked over to them. "What have you got?"

Noah gestured inside the access panel. There were glossy, black-colored ovals a half-meter long. A purple glow swirled inside.

"Is that the data module?" Connor asked.

"That's it," Lenora confirmed. "They're similar to the ones we found in the archives at Sanctuary, but these hold way more data."

"How do we extract them?"

"That's what I'm trying to figure out," Noah said.

"If they work like the ones in the archive, you have to put them on standby in the computer system before you can detach them. Once they're detached, we need to connect them to a portable power supply and take them with us," Lenora said.

Noah stood up and began navigating the option on the holoscreen. "Okay, this one should be on standby."

Connor peered at the data module. It didn't look any different. "Are you sure?"

"Yes, that's the one on my screen," Noah said.

Connor took out his portable power supply and connected it to the data module. There was a dimming of the purple light in the module. He looked at Noah.

"It can come out now."

Connor reached in and lifted the data module out of the panel. It was heavier than it looked.

"How many of these are there?" he asked.

"One for each panel at the base here. It's probably the same for each of the rooms in here," Lenora said.

Connor nodded. "All right then. You and Noah put them on

standby, and we'll come around behind you and retrieve the modules."

Noah left the room and Sergeant Tui followed him along.

Lenora put the rest of the data modules on standby, and Connor began retrieving them. He handed them to Corporal Eldridge and Private Rhodes. "Bring those to the main entrance," Connor said.

The two CDF soldiers left.

"We're not going to be able to get them all," Connor said.

Lenora nodded. "I know."

Over the next fifteen minutes as they retrieved the data modules and carried them through the bunker, the seismic activity became more frequent. Connor had hoped they'd be able to come back to retrieve the rest of the modules, but they couldn't. Not with the bunker as unstable as it was.

Noah had set up a data uplink for the rest but wasn't sure if they even had the capacity to take it all on their equipment on the Hercules.

"Once we get back to the ship, you can set up another comlink to relay it back to Sanctuary," Connor said.

"I'll send word to the Research Institute to get a temporary storage array set up for us," Lenora said.

The air inside the bunker became much cooler as they reached the main entrance. With so much foot traffic coming and going, the climate controls were having trouble keeping up with the temperature extremes.

Connor heard shouting coming from outside and quickened his pace. He quickly made it through the access tunnel and into the frigid air. Cloud cover had increased, and although they still had daylight visibility, it was diminishing with a coming storm.

Diaz stood with his tri-barreled shotgun pointed at Shuno and other Konus. Everyone had their weapons drawn. Urret and the Mekaal soldiers flanked Diaz and also had their weapons aimed at the Konus soldiers.

Specialist Weps and the other two CDF soldiers had their weapons ready as well.

Connor put down the data modules he was carrying. "What's going on here?"

"Tell me again how you don't know about the bombs!" Diaz shouted.

Shuno and the other Konus soldiers crouched in defensive positions.

"Diaz!" Connor shouted. "What happened?"

Diaz kept staring at the Konus soldiers. "There was a bombing at the embassy in Shetrian. The Konus did it. I'm finding out whether they know anything."

"General Gates," Specialist Weps said, "we just received an update from COMCENT. It was an alert about the bombing. That's all we know."

Connor walked over to them. "Everyone stand down. We're not going to shoot each other. Lower your weapons," he said and looked at Shuno and the other Konus. "Lower your weapons."

Shuno glared at Connor for a few moments and then lowered his weapon. The other Konus did the same, and the Mekaal soldiers followed suit. Diaz didn't.

"Juan, I need you to lower your weapon. We'll find out what happened, but I can't have you threatening them."

"He knows something. I can tell it by the look on his face. He's not even surprised!"

Connor came over to Diaz but didn't reach out to him. "We'll get to the bottom of this. They've been with us, so they couldn't have been directly involved. I need you to calm down. Let's get some more information and take it from there."

Diaz looked at him. "The alert said the Konus were involved. I told you we couldn't trust them."

"Juan, you know there's always more to it. If it's just an alert, there isn't any information about the survivors. Isaac could be fine. We can't find out from here. Come back to the ship with me and we'll find out what's going on."

Diaz looked away from him, but he lowered his weapon. "If anything has happened to my son, there's gonna be hell to pay, starting with them," he said and began walking toward the rovers.

19

CONNOR CLIMBED inside the nearest rover and opened a priority comlink to COMCENT. The others began loading the rovers, except for the Konus. Shuno stood off to the side and appeared to be speaking quietly with his own people.

Connor reviewed the broadcast alert and then contacted Nathan. A video comlink came to prominence on the holoscreen showing Nathan's head and shoulders.

"Connor, I'm still getting updates, but here's what I know. There was an attack in Shetrian and bombs did go off throughout the city, including the area around our embassy there. There are survivors. Local Mekaal forces are cooperating with us. I've sent several quick-response units to the embassy. Search and rescue efforts are ongoing," Nathan said.

"Are the Konus responsible for this?"

"We don't know for sure. The Konus warlord has denied responsibility, but we do have evidence of Konus involvement. However, it gets worse. There's evidence of Mekaal involvement as well."

Connor's eyebrows pulled into a tight frown. "Mekaal?" His mind began to race. "Is the entire embassy destroyed or—who was the target?"

"We're still working on it. No, the embassy wasn't destroyed. We've got a lot of people working on this. We're still trying to locate all our people in Shetrian," Nathan said.

Connor's lips formed a grim line. "I have a Konus squad with me. I'm going to question them. If I learn anything, I'll contact you."

"Understood. When I learn more, I'll make sure you're informed."

"Have someone there send me a personnel list for everyone at the embassy."

Nathan frowned for a moment.

"Diaz's son was there. I need to know his current status."

Nathan gestured to someone off-screen. "Isaac Diaz," he said to them. After a few moments, he looked back at Connor and shook his head. "I'm sorry, his whereabouts are unknown. They weren't at the embassy during the attack. His last reported location was with a group heading to the capitol building. Some kind of presentation for the High Commissioner. All the scientists were invited."

Connor nodded. "Thanks, Nathan."

"Tell Diaz we'll find his son."

The comlink went dark and Connor stepped out of the rover. Diaz waited a few feet away.

"Isaac is missing. They're looking for him."

Diaz took several breaths. "We need to go."

"We will."

Diaz blinked several times and then nodded. "Was it the Konus?"

"Their warlord denies any involvement, but there were Konus spotted during the attack."

Diaz regarded him for a moment.

"The Mekaal were involved, too. They're still trying to piece everything together."

Diaz turned away from him.

"Isaac wasn't at the embassy when the bombs went off. He's missing."

Connor watched as Diaz squeezed the tri-barrel shotgun in his grasp as if he were choking the life from it.

"Damn it!" Diaz screamed. He spun toward the Ovarrow, and Connor hastened to stand in his way. "I told him not to go, that they couldn't be trusted. I should have stopped him, but no. You, Victoria, told me I had to let him go. I couldn't have stopped him. Well, I could have stopped him! If I had, he'd be safe at home in Sanctuary where he belongs."

Connor stood there watching his friend's anguish. Several of the others looked over at them.

"He's not dead," Connor said.

Diaz glared at the Konus.

"Juan, this isn't going to help."

Diaz swung his gaze toward Connor. "I don't give a fuck about helping anyone. My son is missing. There was an attack on our embassy."

"Not just the embassy. Bombs went off throughout the city."

Diaz shook his head. "Is that supposed to make me feel better?"

"No, it's not. It's to get you to think. There's more going on here than we know right now."

"I told you the Ovarrow were your crusade, not mine," Diaz said and shook his head. "I should never have come on this expedition. They'll never be like us. They'll never be able to live in peace because all they know is war. They're broken. No, you listen to me now. I know what you're going to say. We need to let the CDF and the intelligence bureau and every other damn agency out there do their investigation. Find out who is responsible and stop them. But how many of our people have to die for this? How many have to die for them!"

Diaz stormed away from him, and Connor let him go. This wasn't the first time someone had lashed out at him. He'd done it to others on occasion, but it didn't sting any less. He remembered when Mekaal insurgents had triggered the collapse of several bridges in Shetrian, and Lenora had been trapped. Connor had gone to the city with an army at his back, and he'd threatened and bullied the Mekaal into cooperating. He looked at Lenora. She was speaking to Kara and then turned toward him. If she'd been in Shetrian during another attack, he'd do the same thing again. The colony could banish him, but he'd be lying to himself if he thought he'd do it any differently. The fact that Diaz had reacted the same way wasn't a shock to him.

Connor turned toward Shuno and the Konus soldiers. "Sergeant Tui, you and your squad on me."

The CDF soldiers came to his side and followed him toward the Konus. One of them began to raise his weapon.

"If that barrel comes anywhere within the vicinity of anything but the ground, I'll order my soldiers to kill you where you stand," Connor said.

The Konus soldier lowered his weapon.

Connor continued until he stood in front of Shuno. "First Fist Shuno, I need to ask you a question. Do you know anything about this attack? Are you aware of any military operation being conducted by your people in Shetrian?"

"General Gates," Shuno said, "I need to contact my superiors."

"As soon as you answer my question."

Shuno regarded him for a few moments. "And if I refuse? What then?"

"Don't," Connor replied, putting even more steel into his voice.

Shuno looked at the CDF soldiers and the Mekaal that had come over to them. He threw down his weapon and ordered the others to do the same. Then he looked at Connor. "I am unaware of any military operation in Shetrian. I am unaware of any plans for a military operation that involves Shetrian, the Mekaal, or the human colony."

Connor regarded the Konus soldier for a few moments.

"Are we prisoners?" Shuno asked.

"I will allow you to contact your superiors, and you may advise them of the situation," Connor replied and turned toward Specialist Weps. "Get them a comlink back to Renoya at once. Sergeant Tui, you'll monitor the whole comlink session."

"Yes, General," Sergeant Tui said.

Connor turned to Urret and gestured for the Mekaal soldiers to follow him. He walked a short distance away. Diaz was watching him, and Lenora and Noah stood next to Diaz.

Urret waited for Connor to speak.

"The current intelligence for the attack has both Mekaal and Konus involved," Connor said.

Urret considered this for a few moments. "Soldiers?"

"Unknown."

"There has always been some resistance to our alliance with the colony, but to attack the colonial embassy seems far-fetched," Urret said.

"How so?"

"There is nothing to be gained by attacking the embassy. In fact, we have everything to lose by doing so. Our independence from the Konus is dependent upon our alliance with you. Our militaries have worked together to defeat the Krake and the Konus. I can't believe any of our soldiers would be involved with this."

"I thought so as well. What if the Ovarrow involved weren't soldiers? Current soldiers. There was a Konus diplomatic envoy in Shetrian. How difficult would it be for the Konus to sneak into the city?"

"Not that difficult. We try to emulate the colonial model for our city, and we haven't had security checkpoints in quite some time. The Konus never gave us reason to re-institute those security measures, and our citizens embraced the freer society," Urret said.

Connor had planned and executed enough clandestine operations to know that identifying the primary objective was critical to understanding the reasons for the attack.

Diaz walked over to them. "What did they say?" he asked and inclined his chin toward the Konus soldiers.

"They don't know anything about the attack."

"You believe them?"

Connor inhaled deeply and sighed. "I do." Diaz rolled his eyes. "Now, hear me out. Shuno and the others could be lying, but I don't think so. He's a soldier. His position has been compromised, and he has no hope of changing that. I've allowed him to contact his superiors in the hopes that we might get more information."

"Do you really think they'll cooperate?" Diaz asked.

"We'll find out. In the meantime, we'll pack up and get out of here. Head to Shetrian," Connor said.

Diaz nodded, looking relieved. "Connor, about what I said before. It's not your fault."

"Don't worry about it."

"I'm not. I know you can take it."

"Captain Diaz," Urret said, and Diaz looked at him. "I understand that your son is missing. I want you to know I'll do everything I can to find those responsible."

Diaz stared at the Mekaal for a few moments. "Thank you."

Urret stepped closer to him. "I know your opinion of us. We've all heard it. You're right. Your opinion of us is correct."

Diaz frowned and he glanced at Connor. "What do you mean I'm right?"

"We are not trustworthy. Trust takes time to build. We've improved, but there is still a long way for us to go. Making this right will help us on that path."

Diaz stared at the Mekaal soldier. "Do you have any children? Do you have a son?"

"I have no children."

"I think you're just telling me what you think I want to hear."

"Juan," Connor warned. "He's trying to help."

"I know what he's trying to do," Diaz snapped, and swung his gaze toward Urret. "You mean well, but just so we're clear, I don't care. You can make all the promises in the world. Spout more sentiments about how your people are trying to improve. I don't care! We brought you out of stasis almost fifteen years ago and since then, there have been nothing but empty promises and bloodshed. Now my son is missing. He got caught up in your deranged politics, but I have a promise to make to you. I will dedicate my life to ensuring that the Mekaal or any other Ovarrow are kept as far away from the colony as possible. Do you understand me? I will dedicate my whole life to it. So, you can make all the promises you want about helping and being better, but you're not. You're not better and I just can't bring myself to care about what happens to you or any of your kind."

Diaz turned around and walked away from them.

Urret watched him go, as did the rest of the Mekaal. "I keep my promises," he said.

Connor looked at Urret. "I'm sorry about that."

"Do not apologize."

"He's out of line, but he's worried about his son."

Urret regarded Connor for a few moments. "I envy him. He will do what he must to protect his family. We would do no less to protect our children."

Connor blinked several times and his eyes widened. "Children! That's it! That's what this is about."

"I don't understand."

"There was a group of scientists working at the embassy to help with infertility among the Ovarrow. The attack occurred after they left the embassy. They were going to meet with the High Commissioner. The scientists might have been the target."

"They were to be killed?" Urret asked.

"I don't know. Diaz's son was with the scientists. He's missing and I'm willing to bet the other scientists are missing as well. Come on," Connor said.

20

AT SOME POINT after they'd been shoved into the back of a vehicle and began moving, Isaac lost consciousness. The last thing he remembered was the metallic clang of a door being slammed shut. The blow to his head must have been worse than he'd thought.

He woke with a God-awful pounding in his head, and his stomach attempted to slither out of his mouth, but it was blocked by some kind of gag. He tasted metal in his mouth, and his jaws were forced uncomfortably wide. He couldn't see anything. Their captors had put a shroud over his head.

He exhaled through his nostrils several times until he was able to do it long and steady, and the obnoxious pounding of his headache lessened enough that he was able to think a little clearer. The nausea retreated to the back of his throat, but his mouth was dry from the gag.

The vehicle rocked back and forth as they were taken somewhere. He wasn't sure how much time had passed. He heard a few of the others groan, but they sounded muffled, and he realized they were probably gagged as well. He tried to make himself as comfortable as possible. Doing a quick assessment, he found that his wrists were tied together behind him. The air stank of sweat and possibly urine, but his pants weren't wet. Was it one of the others? The smell wasn't potent. Maybe he was wrong about it. He tried to bite down on the gag, and that attempt was as ineffective as his line of thinking. He needed to figure out what was happening to them. Why had they been kidnapped, and how could they escape?

The vehicle lifted up on a sudden incline and Isaac shifted to the side, making his shoulders ache even more. He slid into someone, who groaned softly. It was one of the girls. Isaac gave her an answering groan, trying his best to make it sound like an apology.

His mouth felt as if all the moisture had been sucked out of it, and he was incredibly thirsty. He pushed on the metallic gag with his tongue, but it wouldn't move. Then, he raised his shoulder to his cheek, trying to move the shroud, but it was too tight. It must have had some elasticity that kept it in place. Their captors weren't taking any chances. What did the Konus want with them? Were they hostages for them to barter with, or was it something else?

The vehicle stopped. A few moments later, there was a loud clang, and a warm puff of clean air blew in. Someone climbed in and roughly dragged Isaac to his feet, after which he was unceremoniously dumped out of the vehicle and the shroud yanked off his head.

He blinked his eyes and looked around. There was a dense forest canopy above them, home to a continuous cadence of forest creatures. They'd obviously been taken out of the city, but how far had they gone? There was nothing around them but an old path and a fallen tree nearby that was as thick as he was tall.

Ella stood next to him, and he looked around to see that the others were being unloaded from a small, dirty delivery vehicle that looked like it had been used to transport livestock. Armed Konus soldiers stood nearby, and their feline gazes tracked them with rigid intensity that burned with surety of purpose. Isaac was in no condition to run. None of them were going anywhere.

Someone came around and removed the gag from his mouth, and the muscles of his jaw and neck immediately began to cramp. Reflexively, he opened and closed his mouth in an effort to stop the spasms, noting the others doing the same.

Their bindings were changed so their wrists were bound in front of them, and a group of soldiers began walking away from them. The soldier who'd removed his binding pointed ahead, and Isaac needed no further direction. He followed the soldiers, and his friends followed him. No one spoke.

Isaac glanced at his wrist computer. It still worked, but one of the soldiers must have been carrying a suppressor because all communications were offline. He heard Curtis try to ask the Konus for water, receiving several harsh blows for his trouble. The message was clear. Don't talk. Just move.

It was still daytime. Isaac didn't think he'd been unconscious for more than a few hours, so they couldn't be far from Shetrian. The Konus must be leading them away from the city, but where? It couldn't be more than a couple hours before nightfall.

The Konus marched them at a relentless pace. The forest was getting darker in the waning light and their captors showed no signs of slowing down. He'd thought they might stop at night, but he was wrong. They didn't slow down at all, marching well into the night without stopping. Isaac saw the light from New Earth's rings above the trees and wondered how far they'd come. Someone must be searching for them by now. Whoever was monitoring their signals must have figured out that they'd been in those tunnels under the city. The CDF would send out search teams for them. There were probably recon drones in the air searching for them as well. It would just be a matter of time until they were found. The comlink suppressor would make them difficult to track, but Isaac knew that wouldn't stop the CDF. The way they were being guarded made it unlikely that they'd have a chance to escape so they needed to cooperate and stay alive until they could be rescued. One of the reasons the Konus set such a strenuous pace was probably to keep them from trying to escape.

Isaac couldn't get an accurate count of their captors. There was always a large group surrounding them, but the Konus commander ordered smaller squads to leave them from time to time—whether to scout the area or lay false trails, Isaac didn't know, and he wasn't sure it mattered. There were too many for them to try to escape, even if they could arm themselves.

He heard Ella stumble behind him and whirled around to help her up. The nearest Konus soldiers scowled at them.

"Keep moving."

The translator did its best to convey vocal inflection, but the growl of their voices was two-toned because Ovarrow had multiple vocal cords. Those sounds became more divergent and menacing the angrier they became.

Ella hastened to her feet, and they kept moving. Before long, the others began to stumble in the darkness. They were exhausted. Each time they stumbled, there was always a Konus soldier there to make sure they didn't stop. Isaac wasn't sure how much longer they could keep going.

"We need water," Curtis said.

The translation came from his wrist computer so the Konus could understand him. He was ignored.

"Give us some water!" Curtis shouted.

Isaac heard Julian try to get him to stop but Curtis wouldn't.

The Konus commander ordered them to stop and strode toward them. Curtis backed up a few steps, but two soldiers grabbed him and held him in place.

"I just want some water. Please, we're so thirsty. Just give us some water," Curtis said.

Koukax stared at them for a moment. His long rifle was strapped to his back. "We have no water. We carry no provisions. The camp has these things. Begin to walk or you will be dragged by my soldiers."

Curtis inhaled deeply and looked as if he was going to make another demand.

"Curtis," Isaac warned and shook his head.

Koukax turned his attention toward Isaac and stared at him for a long moment. Isaac's gaze went to the ground and stayed there, even when the commander approached. As the Konus stepped near him, Isaac winced and retreated a step, but Koukax passed him without slowing. He'd expected the commander to hit him. There was always an angry glint in the leader's gaze.

Isaac followed. There was no use pushing his luck. He'd watched Koukax kill Reznick without a hint of remorse, and the Krake commander regarded them in the same cold, calculating manner. There was no doubt they were being kept alive because Koukax wanted them to live, and their only choice was to keep moving.

An hour later, they reached an encampment. More Konus were there, but there were also other Ovarrow. These were Mekaal, but they weren't soldiers. Why were they helping the Krake?

There were several rugged ground-transport vehicles nearby, and Isaac saw other prisoners in the camp. Dr. Rostova shot to her feet and began to walk toward them, but several Konus aimed their weapons at her, and Dr. Townsend stopped her.

When Isaac's group reached the other prisoners and stumbled to the ground, gasping, Dr. Rostova, Townsend, and Solomon gave them water. Isaac and the others drank as much water as they could, and then they were allowed to rest. Isaac saw that Deasira was lying on a stretcher. The Mekaal scientist had been wounded. He couldn't tell if she was simply asleep or unconscious because of her wounds. Another person lay beside her. Isaac's eyes widened when he recognized Agent Franklin.

"Are you all right?" Dr. Rostova asked him.

Isaac swallowed hard. "They killed him. Both of them."

"Who?" Dr. Rostova asked. "Who did they kill?"

Isaac felt his fear push its way to his chest, and a lump grew in his throat.

"Just breathe. Take your time," she said.

Isaac took several breaths. "Reznick. He just shot him in the head. And... And he killed Cohsora."

Townsend stood nearby, listening. His gaze narrowed.

"I tried to stop them. I tried to contact..." Isaac said and looked toward Agent Franklin.

He needed to calm down and get his thoughts in order, but he couldn't. While they'd been marching, he only worried about keeping himself moving, but now that he'd had a moment to catch his breath, it was all coming back to him. He looked at his wrist computer.

"Don't," Dr. Rostova warned. "Don't try anything. Just cooperate."

Isaac nodded and stared at the ground. He should have done something. If he'd gotten back into the rover and left when Reznick told him to, maybe they wouldn't have been caught. This was his fault. He felt his jaw slacken and his eyes became tight. Why hadn't he listened to Reznick? He'd thought he could save him, but then everything happened so fast that it almost didn't feel real. He glanced at Ella and the others. They were all catching their breath, and the colonial scientists were checking on them.

He kept going over what had happened—reviewing the events and wishing he'd done something different. Why had Cohsora led them to that damn tunnel? It was a trap. Had Cohsora betrayed them?

Isaac lifted his gaze and searched for Koukax. The Konus commander was speaking with several of his soldiers, and Isaac recognized that he was getting a status report. Something reckless took root inside him and he clenched his teeth. His gaze darted around, and he began to weigh his chances of reaching Koukax. A soldier stood nearby, and Isaac thought about ways to tackle him. If he took the soldier by surprise, he could steal his weapon — And then what? Open fire on the other Konus soldiers? They'd kill him and hurt the others. He had to do something but couldn't think what. He felt so powerless. His father wouldn't just sit here, helpless, and neither would Connor, but what could he do? In a moment of sudden calm amid his panic, Isaac realized that they would want him to be smart, keep a level head, and pay attention.

Koukax walked purposefully toward them, each step sounding as if he were crushing the ground beneath his feet. His soldiers followed, keeping a respectful distance until he stopped near where Deasira lay and gestured toward her. Two of his soldiers lifted her stretcher and carried her away.

"She was wounded by your soldiers," Dr. Rostova said.

Koukax turned toward her. "That is unfortunate. Her work is very important."

"She needs medical attention."

"That depends on you," Koukax said, and he looked at Dr. Townsend and Dr. Solomon. "My sources say that you've succeeded."

"That depends on what you're talking about," Dr. Rostova replied.

Koukax stared at her coldly. Then he gestured toward Isaac and the others. Konus soldiers swarmed toward them instantly. It happened so fast that Isaac couldn't keep track. One moment they were watching Dr. Rostova speak with Koukax, and the next, Konus soldiers were charging toward them.

Isaac started to stand, and one of the soldiers dragged him toward Dr. Rostova. A sharp blow with a baton to his hamstrings forced him to kneel. Julian, who'd been right behind Isaac, landed so hard that he slammed into Isaac's side, knocking them both down. The Konus soldier pulled them back up, roughly. Jordan, Kanin, Ella, and Curtis were given the same treatment.

"You seek to mislead me," Koukax said. He pointed one of his long, thick fingers toward Julian. "Bring that one to me."

Isaac's mouth hung open, and he looked at Julian. He saw his friend's wide-eyed gaze change to a painful wince as one of the Konus soldiers grabbed a fistful of hair and shoved him toward Koukax.

Julian cried out in pain.

"Stop!" Dr. Rostova shouted.

"You're right. We did it," Dr. Solomon said.

Dr. Townsend tried to step toward Julian, but one of the Konus soldiers restrained him.

Julian was forced to his knees as tears streamed down his face. The soldier yanked Julian's head back, exposing his neck.

"I didn't do anything!"

Koukax grabbed a rifle from one of his soldiers.

Julian reared back and screamed, but the soldier held him in place.

Isaac gritted his teeth and struggled to rise, but a soldier held him down. He glared up at his captor, who stared down at him without mercy.

A plasma bolt fired, and Isaac swung his gaze back toward Julian. His friend fell backward from the force of the blast and didn't move. Isaac stared at Julian and then screamed himself raw. It took two Konus soldiers to hold him down. He couldn't make himself stop screaming.

Koukax raised his weapon, pointing it toward Isaac.

"Stop!" Dr. Rostova shouted. "Stop it!" She charged toward Koukax, but he didn't move, and his weapon remained pointed at Isaac.

Isaac stared at the orange glow inside the barrel of the plasma rifle. It was primed and ready to unleash its lethal force. His gaze slid toward Julian, and sorrow closed his throat.

"We were successful!" Dr. Rostova said. "We were able to reverse infertility in Ovarrow females. That's why you kidnapped us. That's what you want, isn't it? Stop now, or you'll never get it from us."

Koukax looked at her. "I know."

"You know! Then why did you kill him?" she asked, her voice hitching up at the end.

"Humans are slow to learn. Now you know the price. If there is even the slightest hesitation, this one will die next. It's a promise that you know I will keep, but I wonder if killing one of them is enough," Koukax said.

"We'll cooperate. We'll give you what you want. Just don't hurt them. Please!"

Koukax turned toward Isaac. There it was. Isaac could see it in the Ovarrow's gaze—the certainty of death. Koukax was going to kill him. There was no remorse, only surety of purpose. Koukax wouldn't hesitate to kill them all. Isaac flinched inwardly. He wanted to make himself as small as possible, but he just knelt there, stunned. After a few moments, he lifted his gaze and glared back at the Konus commander. His life was in the hands of another, and there was nothing Isaac could do to stop him from taking it.

"I need him," Dr. Townsend said. "I need him for my work."

Koukax swung his gaze toward him.

"You need us to recreate the vaccine that will cure infertility. I'm a geneticist. You'll get nothing without me, and in order for me to get it done, I need him. The work is too much for any one person. It will go by much faster if they help us," Dr. Townsend said. "All of them."

"He's right," Dr. Rostova said. "You have time constraints."

"You presume to know what my plan is," Koukax said. "You don't. But there is something to be said for working quickly. They will live so long as all of you cooperate and deliver to me what you promised the Mekaal. Is that understood?"

"Yes," Dr. Rostova said. "Now, let them go."

Koukax gestured for the soldiers to release them.

"They'll need their bindings removed," Dr. Rostova said.

Isaac was allowed to stand and a Konus soldier used his knife to cut through the bindings on his wrists. He looked at Dr. Townsend with a thoughtful frown. The scientist had just saved his life. Koukax was going to kill him. Before today he hadn't thought Dr. Townsend would even hold open a door for him, but the scientist had just saved his life. Isaac promised himself that he'd find a way to repay him.

He looked down at Julian and stepped toward his friend, who had rolled onto his side. Blood soaked the back of his shirt, and Isaac pulled him onto his back, wincing. A hole had burned through the middle of his chest. Isaac squeezed his eyes shut and shook his head. He heard Jordan sobbing behind him while Ella spoke quietly to her.

Someone put their hand on Isaac's shoulder. He opened his eyes and saw Dr. Townsend looking at him.

"Help me bury him," Dr. Townsend said.

Isaac wiped the tears from his eyes and stood up.

"There will be no ritual. We are leaving," Koukax said.

"We can't leave him here," Isaac said. "He's not an animal to be left for the scavengers. He deserves to be buried."

He clenched his fists and his shoulders became tight.

A Konus soldier who held an open container walked over to Julian and poured a creamy white liquid onto his body. There was a hiss as a chemical reaction began. Within a minute, Julian's body was just gone. Gone! The ground appeared wet, and a few wisps of vapor rose from the spot.

Isaac swallowed, and in a futile gesture, reached toward where Julian had been. He'd just been alive. A few minutes ago, he'd been with them. They'd lived together for the past six months, and then, in the span of a few moments, his friend was dead. And now there was no body. There was nothing for them to bury. He was sick with rage. His breath became trapped in his chest. He clenched his teeth, and a small growl came from deep in his chest.

From the recesses of his mind, a memory came to him of his father's voice, and it was as if he were talking in a nearby room. He was speaking with Connor about the brutality they'd seen. Isaac blinked several times as the memory became clearer. It was a recounting of what they'd experienced off-world, and Isaac had listened in secret. His father had seen horrible things, and that mission had changed him. He'd hardly left Sanctuary after it. His father had tried to warn him, but Isaac wouldn't listen. The

Ovarrow couldn't be trusted. Isaac glared at the spot on the ground and whispered a prayer for his friend until someone gently pulled him away. They were leaving.

Isaac looked back at the place where his friend had died. No one would know that this was where Julian had been murdered. He'd never be able to find this place again.

Isaac glared at Koukax and made a promise to himself that somehow he was going to find a way to kill him. The molten fury in his gut swirled, but parts of it became cold, freezing away his emotions. He would do it. He was going to find a way to kill Koukax.

21

CONNOR QUESTIONED the other Konus soldiers while Shuno spoke with his superiors. They claimed not to know anything about the attack at the Mekaal city. Nathan had sent him an update in response to his query about the scientists. They were all missing, which confirmed who the targets had been.

The CDF soldiers stayed nearby while Urret and the other Mekaal soldiers helped load the data modules into the rovers.

Shuno closed the comlink and then asked to speak to Connor.

Connor had Urret join them since the attack had occurred in Shetrian.

"Warlord Tritix has spoken with the Mekaal High Commissioner and the colonial leadership. This attack wasn't sanctioned by our government. They've agreed to conduct their own investigation," Shuno said.

Connor regarded him for a few moments. "Would they admit to it if they *were* involved?"

"General Gates, I'm conveying the official message from my

superiors. They've also requested that we be returned to the designated landing zone outside our territory. I'm to send them your reply within one hour."

Connor had to be careful with whatever he was about to do. He wasn't authorized to hold Shuno or any of the other Konus soldiers in custody. Shuno was here of his own volition and was free to leave at any time. They were guests.

"General Gates, I need to know what your actions will be for me and the rest of my squad," Shuno said.

If Connor held Shuno and his squad against their will, he'd be breaking colonial law. He didn't think Shuno knew anything about the attack, but he still might be able to help them.

"First Fist Shuno, I think we need to lay all our cards on the table. Then you can decide what will be the best course of action," Connor said.

"Connor, no," Diaz said.

Connor glared at his friend. Diaz held his hands up in a placating gesture and backed away.

"I don't understand," Shuno said.

"I have no authorization to hold you and your squad."

Shuno considered this but didn't say anything.

"I'm going to share a few things with you before we act. There was a team of colonial scientists that was working with Mekaal scientists to help alleviate infertility among Ovarrow females. I don't know the specifics, but they were ready to begin actual testing among the Mekaal," Connor said.

"I did not know of this," Urret said.

"It was kept secret. The project had the support of the High Commissioner, and the science team was going to the capital to present their findings. Following that, I expect that they would have informed the rest of your people about this."

"That would have given the Mekaal a decisive advantage over us," Shuno said.

The Konus had the largest population of Ovarrow on New Earth, with population numbers approaching a million. The Mekaal only had a population of fifty thousand.

"Eventually," Connor replied. "However, that assumes the cure wasn't shared with your people. Did Warlord Tritix mention any of this to you?"

Shuno regarded Connor for a few seconds. "No."

Diaz sighed explosively. "It doesn't mean anything if he didn't know. That level of intel is way above his rank. What are you trying to do here, Connor?"

"I'm trying," Connor said, looking at Diaz and then back at Shuno. "I'm trying to ask for his help."

"We don't need his help."

Connor snarled toward Diaz. "Do you want to find Isaac?" He stepped closer to him, and Diaz's eyes widened in shock. "Do you want to find him!"

Diaz narrowed his gaze and stared at him.

Connor stared back. "This is how we do it," he said, and flung his arm toward Shuno. "You put your prejudice aside and we get their help." He closed the distance to his friend. Diaz scowled, grabbed Connor, and shoved him back.

The two men grappled.

Diaz screamed in rage.

"Come on. Keep going!" Connor shouted. He pulled Diaz toward him.

His face twisted somewhere between rage and anguish. "My son—"

The ground shuddered violently beneath them, causing them to tumble to the ground. Diaz landed on top of him. Connor twisted out from under his friend and climbed to his feet. The rovers shook as the ground beneath them lurched upward in an explosion of snow. Connor pulled Diaz to his feet and out of the way of the rover as it rolled past them.

Connor watched as the rover landed on its wheels, rocking back and forth. He spun toward the bunker and saw Lenora climbing into the rover that was parked there. Noah was in the driver's seat. He gunned the accelerator and the rover sped away just as something colossal burst from the snowy depth beneath it. A huge, armored claw rose up and smashed into the ground. Then, a snow-covered beast the size of three rovers bawled out an unworldly cry. Its mouth was big enough to chomp them in half, and there were multiple eyeballs along its cranial ridge. The snow beast's massive head swept toward the fleeing rover. Its blue-gray body had rubber-like muscles, and it looked as if it were made of deep-sea ice that had suddenly come to life.

Connor brought up his weapon and fired, aiming for the head. A barrage of supersonic darts pelted the creature's snout, but it didn't slow down. The CDF squad began firing, and plasma bolts from the Ovarrow's weapons also slammed into its chest.

Connor changed the rounds in his rifle to incendiary and ran toward the creature. Diaz ran by his side, pausing to unleash a plasma blast from his tri-barreled shotgun.

The snow beast swung its head toward them.

"Draw it away from the rovers!" Connor shouted.

Two other rovers were parked near the snow beast. As Connor ran, he fired a few bursts and glanced at the fleeing rover with Lenora in it, hoping Noah would drive straight back to the ship.

The snow beast let out another unworldly cry and slithered the rest of the way out of its hole. It used its giant claws to propel itself forward, and its eyes were locked onto him like a predator to prey.

Dark bluish blood streaked behind it from its wounds, but it hadn't slowed down at all.

"What's the plan?" Diaz asked.

An onslaught of plasma bolts fired into the snow beast's belly from the side. The Konus soldiers had retrieved their weapons.

The snow beast pushed itself forward on a giant, fin-like tail. Connor cranked up the power output for his AR-74 and set it to full plasma mode. When a high-pitched whine came from the rifle, Connor aimed at the creature barreling toward them. He squeezed the trigger and a bar of blue-white fire so dense that it was nearly a solid object lashed across the distance to the snow beast and slammed into it like an enormous lance. The beast howled in pain as the plasma lance burned through its thick, rubbery skin and flash-boiled the blood inside. The snow beast rolled to the side and the plasma lance cut through its underbelly. The creature thrashed in its death throes, its howling dying away as it suddenly became still.

A smelly wave of burnt flesh and dead fish washed over them, and Connor clenched his teeth to keep from throwing up. He backed up, trying to escape the stench.

"That's disgusting," Diaz said.

They backed away from the carcass. Sergeant Tui ran over to them, followed by both the Mekaal and Konus soldiers.

"General, what was that beam?" Sergeant Tui asked.

"Plasma lance. It uses the entire ammunition block," Connor replied.

"We can't stay here. We have to leave," Urret said.

A sound came from beneath the ice—a moaning wail that went on and on. Then came an answering call from farther away.

"Holy shit! How many of them are there?" Diaz asked.

The ground began to shake.

"Run!" Connor shouted. "Run to the rovers!"

They turned toward the two rovers parked by the bunker. A large shadow swooped underneath them and broke through the ice, throwing the rovers high into the air. They skidded to a stop.

"There's one over there," Diaz said.

They started running toward the remaining rover, and Connor turned toward Sergeant Tui.

"Head back to the ship, Sergeant," Connor said.

The CDF soldiers wore a light version of the Nexstar combat suits.

"Not a chance, General," Sergeant Tui replied.

"I don't have time to argue with you. Get that ship flight-ready. You and your squad can beat us there."

Sergeant Tui swore and then tossed his rifle toward Connor. "On me!" he shouted to his squad.

The CDF soldiers engaged their combat suits' full capabilities, then went into high-power mode and blazed a path toward the Hercules. Several of the CDF soldiers leaped high into the air, using suit thrusters to hover while they fired their weapons at the snow beast, drawing its attention. The creature slithered out on top of the ice, then slammed its powerful head through the ice and plunged back into the depths.

A comlink came from Lenora. "We made it to the ship. Get your ass over here."

"Working on it," Connor said. "Tui is on his way to you. Tell the flight crew to get ready."

He severed the comlink and ran toward the rover. A misty fog seemed to gather in the area near the vehicle. Connor thought he saw dark shapes moving all around them. The ground shook, and he ran faster.

Connor glanced to the side and saw Shuno running, the

Ovarrow's head bobbing as he took long strides. Diaz sprinted ahead of them. Connor wasn't a slow runner by any means, but Diaz could move when he really had to. He made it to the rover first and climbed into the driver's seat.

The ground lurched up, throwing Connor high into the air. A gaping maw of teeth chased him, and he fired his weapon blindly. Something hard hit his feet and he pushed off from it. The ground raced up to meet him and he tucked his shoulder in, grunting as his body bounced off the ground. Shuno landed next to him, and his long rifle sprang from his grasp.

Connor crawled to his feet and fired his weapon into the fog. He leaned down, offering his hand to Shuno. The Konus soldier grabbed it and pulled himself up.

Fog engulfed them. Connor spun, trying to figure out where the rover was. He heard the snow beast howling nearby, and another answered its call. Several more sounded off. They were surrounded.

Shuno spun around, his eyes wide, and then let out a two-toned screech. The call went on for ten long seconds before he stopped. He then cocked his head to the side, listening. An answering call came from behind them, then another off to the side, and two Konus soldiers ran over to them.

"This way," Shuno said.

Connor followed him, and after a few seconds, he heard Diaz shouting for him.

"We're coming," Connor answered.

"Hurry up, or we'll leave you behind," Diaz replied.

The red glow of the rover's lights grew brighter in front of them as they ran toward it. The ground shuddered and a Konus soldier cried out as something slammed into him and pulled him out of view. A scream came from behind them and then suddenly died. Connor sprinted toward the back of the rover and climbed onto the roof. Urret pulled him up and then lent a hand to Shuno.

The rover sprang forward, all six wheels spinning. The ice exploded behind them as another huge snow beast broke through and slithered toward them, but the rover sped forward, outrunning the creature.

Connor peered ahead through the lessening fog. "Watch out!"

Ahead of them, three snow beasts were attempting to cut them off. Diaz jerked the rover to the side and Connor grabbed onto the rooftop bar, flinging his other hand out to grab whoever was next to him. Urret locked grips with him and Connor held on tight until the rover evened out.

The Hercules rose into the air, and Sergeant Tui opened a comlink to him.

"Couldn't stay, General. Six of those beasts were heading for us. We'll come to you."

Connor patched the comlink into the rover's comms systems. "Stay ahead of them. They're coming to pick us up."

"Roger that," Diaz replied.

The ground exploded next to them as a snow beast burst into the air. The giant creature angled toward them, and Diaz narrowly avoided a collision.

There were three others with Connor on the rover's rooftop. "Suppressing fire!" he shouted.

He brought up his rifle and began firing at the creatures. "Aim for the head."

Urret fired his rifle.

The rover swung to the side, and Shuno grabbed Connor's waist.

Connor fired his weapon into one of the creature's eyes and it spun away from them. As they outran the fog, Connor saw twenty snow beasts slithering across the ice, gaining on them.

"Go faster!" Connor shouted.

"I'm trying," Diaz said.

The rover bounced as it hit rough terrain, and the cohort of snow beasts closed in on them.

Connor twisted the dial on the AR-74, increasing the power to maximum, and set the configuration to plasma lance.

"Where the hell are they?" Diaz asked. "We're running out of ground."

Connor peered ahead. A few hundred meters away, the ground disappeared in a sea of clouds.

"Anytime now, Sergeant," Connor said.

"On your six," Tui replied.

The C-cat flew above the distant fog and began to descend, but the damn snow beasts leaped into the air, trying to grab the ship. The pilot banked to the side, avoiding the thick claws. The Hercules class C-cat wasn't an agile ship. It flew like it was dragging its ass behind it.

The ship closed the distance and flew ahead of them, slowing down and allowing them to catch up as the loading ramp lowered. Connor saw one of the snow beasts slithering ahead. Plasma bolts from Urret's rifle bounced harmlessly off the thick hide. He couldn't get a clear shot at the creature's vulnerable underbelly.

The snow beast increased its speed, moving toward the ship. It carried enough mass to pull the ship out of the sky, and Connor couldn't let that happen.

With Diaz gunning the accelerator, the rover closed in on the loading ramp and lurched forward as the front tires bounced off the ramp.

The snow beast bawled another unworldly howl and leaped

into the air. Connor aimed his weapon and fired a bar of blue-white fire. The plasma lance slammed into the creature with such force that it sloughed off its bottom jaw and then sliced into its neck. The creature went limp like a flying sack of meat.

The ship turned away from the creature and slowed down enough for the rover to get on the ramp. Diaz jerked the wheel to the side to keep them from flying off, and the ramp began to close. The ship rose, and Connor watched as the creatures chased them to the edge and dove beneath the low-lying clouds, disappearing.

22

Connor dropped his rifle. Shuno had his eyes squeezed shut and still clutched Connor's waist.

"It's over," Connor said.

Shuno opened his eyes and let Connor go. Connor sat down to take a few deep breaths and exchanged looks with Urret and Shuno. The rover's doors opened, and Diaz climbed out, along with several Mekaal and Konus soldiers.

Connor looked at Urret. "What the hell were those things?"

"I don't know," Urret replied.

Connor looked at Shuno.

"I don't know what they are either," The Konus soldier said.

Connor puffed out a breath and looked at Diaz. "Nice driving."

Diaz barked out a laugh. "Leave it to us to find some new creature no one has ever heard of before."

Lenora ran over to them, her eyes wide.

"I'm all right," Connor said. He still sat on the roof, not wanting to move.

"Are you sure?" she asked.

Connor looked down at his legs. "I'm pretty sure," he said and looked around. "We're missing some people."

"The pilot is making another pass, but not everyone made it," Lenora said.

Connor climbed down from the roof of the rover, and they were checked for injuries. The survivors had managed to escape with a few bumps and bruises. They'd lost two rovers. Three of Urret's soldiers hadn't made it, and two Konus soldiers also died at the hands of the snow beasts. As quickly as the fog had rolled in, it left, and only small remnants could be seen on the icy plains. The area around the bunker looked as if it had been bombarded.

Sepal confirmed that there were no records of those creatures but said he'd need to search the historical archives in Shetrian to be sure.

"Why did those things attack us?" Noah asked.

"Could be territorial," Lenora replied.

Connor frowned. "They could have been protecting the bunker. It was clear they didn't want us anywhere near there."

The others became quiet.

"That's a long time for any creature to guard something," Noah said.

"They probably made a home there," Lenora said.

Connor looked at Noah. "The two rovers we lost—were they carrying the data modules?"

Noah nodded. "We lost half of them, but the uplink is still working."

Lenora looked at Connor. "Maybe we should see if there's anything to salvage from the wreckage."

The pilot flew the ship over the bunker, making several

passes, but the creatures had dragged the rovers under the ice as if they were erasing all evidence near the bunker.

"That answers that," Connor said.

They separated to get cleaned up and regroup. Connor was alone with Lenora.

He looked at her. "Thanks."

Lenora frowned. "For what?"

"For going back to the ship."

A flicker of annoyance showed in her gaze. "Noah convinced me it was for the best."

"He was right."

Lenora closed her eyes. "I know, but that doesn't mean I have to like it."

Connor hugged her and she squeezed him tightly. A soft moan escaped her lips.

She stepped back. "You'd think I'd be used to it by now."

"Heck, *I'm* not used to it. You think I expected giant snow beasts to break through the ice and attack us?"

Lenora rolled her eyes. "Snow beasts," she said.

Connor chuckled. "Until the biologists come up with a better name, I prefer to keep it simple."

Diaz walked over to them. "We need to talk."

Connor nodded. "All of us."

Diaz looked at Lenora. "Give us a second."

Lenora nodded and patted Diaz's arm as she walked past him.

Diaz smiled a little and then lifted his gaze toward Connor. "I know what you were doing."

Connor arched an eyebrow. "You're going to have to be more specific."

Diaz shook his head and sighed heavily. "I was out of line. I'm sorry."

Connor reached out and squeezed Diaz's shoulder. "We'll find him."

Diaz nodded and his eyes became tight. "We better."

"Come on," Connor said.

They returned to the common area where the surviving members of the expedition had gathered.

"We're cutting the expedition short," Connor said. "There's been an attack on the colonial embassy in Shetrian. The latest intelligence shows that the attack may have been a distraction to kidnap a group of scientists who were working to improve fertility among the Mekaal."

He paused for a moment and looked at the two groups of Ovarrow in the room.

"The Mekaal and CDF are searching for them while investigating how the attack managed to breach so many security measures. The latest update I've just gotten suggests that there was both Konus and Mekaal involvement in the attack. The Konus government is denying responsibility in this matter." He looked at Diaz for a moment before continuing. "If we get wrapped up in blaming people for the attack, we'll never get to what's important. We need to find those scientists. Whoever took them executed a well-planned operation."

"Why would anyone do this?" Noah asked.

"The method for increasing fertility among Ovarrow females requires genetic manipulation that will lead to behavior changes. That's as much as I know about it. It's a controversial topic. Perhaps there were those among the Konus who saw this as an advantage that they wanted for themselves," he said and looked at Shuno. The Konus soldier stared at him. "However, since there was also Mekaal involvement, indications are that maybe there were some who thought this type of solution had gone too far. We'll find out eventually, but what concerns me are the innocent lives who've been caught in the crossfire. Diaz's son is among those who've been kidnapped." Several Mekaal and Konus looked at Diaz for a moment. "On this ship we have representatives from all parties involved. Shuno has been ordered to return home. And Urret, I've just received similar orders for you."

"So, we're heading to Shetrian then?" Noah asked.

Connor inhaled deeply and sighed. "That's what we're here to decide. I'm not going to hold anyone here against their will. However, I am going to do everything I can to rescue those scientists. I think there's help to be had here."

Urret leaned forward. "We will assist in any way we can."

Shuno looked at Connor for a few moments. "You'd let us go?"

Connor nodded. "I would."

"What are you proposing?"

"That we work together to find Diaz's son and the rest of the scientists."

"I don't know how I can help with that," Shuno said.

"We can get to that, but first, are you willing to help us find the scientists?"

Shuno looked at the other Konus soldiers. Then he looked at Connor. "Disobeying orders could lead to exile."

Connor wasn't surprised. Both the Mekaal and Konus lived by a much stricter code, with sometimes harsh repercussions.

"We've had to contend with rogue groups in the colony, which the Mekaal have had to deal with. And I'd be surprised if the Konus were immune to this, whatever the current Warlord says."

"I still don't know what you expect from us," Shuno replied.

"Help us with the search. I don't think they're in the city anymore, but searching the surrounding countryside is going to take too long. If we work together, perhaps we can narrow the search grid."

Shuno considered this for a few moments. "If I agree to this, it must be kept secret. Our cooperation cannot be known to anyone outside of those on this ship."

Connor had hoped to share their findings with the search efforts, but he recognized that Shuno was taking on a significant risk to help him. "Okay, we'll keep this between us. Agreed?"

"Agreed," Shuno said.

"Agreed," Urret said.

Connor looked at Diaz, and his friend gave a single approving nod. Connor brought up a holoscreen with a map of the region where Shetrian was located. "Okay, first I'll take you through how the attack occurred and we can go from there."

23

For days, Koukax had marched them at a relentless pace. Isaac and the other prisoners had hardly been allowed to rest. They eventually made it to another camp where they collapsed from exhaustion. The harrowing days since they'd been kidnapped stretched out in his memory like a nightmare he would never be able to forget. He couldn't figure out how far away from Shetrian they'd gone. He hadn't seen or heard anyone searching for them. Koukax and his soldiers ensured that they kept moving. Anyone who couldn't go on was beaten until they started walking again. If they failed to do that, they would be shot. Isaac had helped Jordan as much as he could. She was devastated by Julian's murder. Even Curtis had helped, lending his shoulder to keep her upright and moving. Their captors didn't care if they helped one another as long as they kept going.

Over time, Isaac caught Curtis staring at him with a scowl and then nodding to himself as if he were having a private conversation. Ella had tried to speak to him, but he just withdrew as though trying to separate himself from the others.

The entire trek was conducted under a forest canopy, and Isaac thought this was done to keep them ignorant of where they were going, as well as hiding them from potential rescuers.

Koukax had brought their lab equipment. After letting the prisoners rest for a few hours, they were ordered to set up the lab to reproduce the cure for Ovarrow infertility. After Koukax's previous demonstrations, no one put up much resistance and began setting up a mobile lab. The message was clear to all of them. The lab assistants would be put to death for any delays by the scientists.

Agent Franklin had regained consciousness during their journey and managed to convince Koukax that he was also a scientist. Dr. Rostova had vouched for his claim. Franklin walked with slumped shoulders, favoring one side. He did this so well that even Isaac believed he'd been defeated.

Isaac threw himself into his duties, helping the scientists with whatever they needed. None of the interns wanted to be seen standing idly by, and the scientists kept them as busy as possible. They needed time for the CDF to find them, but Isaac was losing hope that it was ever going to happen. He was tired and frustrated.

Koukax wanted a working version of the infertility cure, but they only had the equipment they'd taken from the embassy as part of the presentation at the Capitol. They also had a limited amount of time to recreate the compounds that still needed to be tested in an Ovarrow female, but Koukax wasn't concerned with any of that. He wanted what he referred to as 'the serum,' and if they didn't deliver it, they were as good as dead.

Isaac searched through a storage container for empty sample trays. Curtis stood nearby as if in a daze. Isaac looked around to see if the soldiers on duty were watching them, but they weren't.

"Curtis, are you all right?"

Curtis's head twitched to the side.

"Come on, you've got to keep moving."

Curtis turned toward Isaac. His blond hair hung over his eyes in a greasy mess, and he lifted his chin and scowled. "This is your fault," he hissed.

Isaac frowned.

"You could have gotten us out of there, but you had to be a hero," Curtis said, softly.

Isaac gritted his teeth, ignoring Curtis as he retrieved a small bag of sample trays, but Curtis grabbed his arm as he was passing.

"It should have been you."

Isaac tried to pull his arm away, but Curtis wouldn't let go.

"Julian is dead because of you," he said in a deadly soft whisper.

Rage like hot plasma seared through Isaac, and he punched Curtis in the face. Curtis fell backward, letting go of Isaac's arm, and Isaac charged toward him, growling. Blood leaked from Curtis's nose and lips. Isaac hunched over him, fist raised. Curtis glared up at him, and for a moment, all Isaac saw was Julian being shot by Koukax and Julian's lifeless body falling to the ground.

Someone grabbed Isaac from behind and pulled him away. Isaac growled, reaching toward Curtis, but someone else had rushed toward him, blocking Isaac's view.

"That's enough!" Agent Franklin said.

Isaac struggled against the CIB agent, but he was much stronger than he'd been acting. Franklin grabbed Isaac's arms and leaned toward his ear. "They'll kill you. They will *kill* you. Stop now."

Isaac looked toward where the Konus soldiers were standing

guard, watching with their weapons half raised. Isaac raised his hands a little and stopped struggling.

As if summoned by the commotion, Koukax approached the soldiers and swung his cold gaze toward Isaac. Then, he strode over to them.

Agent Franklin released Isaac.

"What is the meaning of this?" Koukax asked.

Isaac stared at the ground for a moment.

"It was just a disagreement about the size of sample trays to be retrieved," Agent Franklin said.

Koukax narrowed his gaze and leaned toward Isaac, peering at him intently. Isaac raised his gaze, and the cold, vertical pupils seemed to freeze Isaac's guts. "Get back to work. Your life is worth little as it is."

Isaac swallowed and his mind went numb. He stood up and retrieved the fallen sample trays.

"We've got it from here," Agent Franklin said.

Koukax stared at him for a few moments. Agent Franklin gestured toward one of the tables with the lab equipment.

"Get those over there, now," he said to Isaac.

Isaac carried two trays over to the table. A few seconds later, Agent Franklin joined him and they began preparing the empty trays. A few minutes passed before Isaac glanced behind him. Koukax had gone, but the soldiers watched him.

"Stay focused," Agent Franklin said quietly. Isaac turned back around. "Don't give them a reason to hurt you."

Isaac nodded.

"Listen to me. Curtis is barely keeping it together. Don't let him get to you."

"Why hasn't anyone come for us yet?" Isaac asked while lining up small containers in the slots on the sample trays.

"They're looking for us, but it takes time."

"We should try to escape."

Agent Franklin picked up one of the test tubes and peered at it. "The ryklars would pick us off before we got very far."

Isaac almost turned to look at him.

"I heard one of the soldiers talking," Agent Franklin said.

"I can't just do nothing and wait to be rescued."

Agent Franklin nodded and placed the clear tube back onto the tray. "If you want to help, then pay attention."

Isaac frowned and waited a few moments. "To what?"

"Everything," Agent Franklin said. "Watch. Listen. Remember. Look for the kink in their armor."

Isaac nodded a little. "I can do that."

"Good. Also, I think there are some old buildings nearby. The suppressor field generator is there."

"How do you know?"

"They're using portable suppressor generators and they have a limited range. I think there's a small comms tower. If they link off of it, they can extend the range without depleting the power supply."

Isaac sighed. All this time, he could have been doing something useful, gathering intelligence like Agent Franklin had.

"Hey," Agent Franklin said. "Stop beating yourself up. I'm trained for this. You're doing fine."

Isaac exhaled through his nose. "If that were true, they never would have kidnapped us."

Agent Franklin looked at him. His shoulders were slumped and he looked as if he were exhausted, but his eyes were alert. "I heard what happened. You can't do anything about it now."

He picked up a tray and started to walk away but stopped. "Remember, you're still here because of what you did. That's gotta count for something," he said and then added in a louder voice, "Those are all wrong. Go back to the storage containers and get the right ones."

Agent Franklin walked over to where Dr. Rostova and Dr. Townsend were hunched over a workstation attached to some lab equipment.

Isaac turned and walked to the storage containers. They were kept away from the work area so their captors could keep track of the equipment they were using. The soldiers eyed him suspiciously.

"I got the wrong thing. I need to put these back and get the right ones," Isaac said.

One of the soldiers stared at him.

"You can go ask them if you don't believe me," Isaac said and nodded his head toward the scientists.

"Move quickly," the soldier said.

Isaac hastened toward the equipment area and started opening various containers. Franklin had told him to pay attention. How was he going to do that with his movements restricted to running errands here or assisting the scientists directly? He shouldn't have let Curtis get to him like that. He'd lost control, and that was stupid. Isaac glanced at his wrist computer and then looked around. Koukax was about twenty meters away, speaking to his second in command. Isaac looked back at his wrist computer and enabled the small microphone hidden inside it. He increased the sensitivity and then had the AI filter out ambient noise.

"I don't trust them either, Strovax," Koukax said.

Isaac started recording the conversation.

"They haven't searched this far, but it's only a matter of time."

"If they reach us, we'll cut our losses and leave."

"Empty-handed? No."

"Of course not," Koukax said. "Mustn't let the others know. The search will be abandoned if they think the hostages are dead."

"What about Deasira?"

"She'll be the first one they test. They'll do as I say."

Strovax lifted his gaze, and Isaac quickly squatted down. He heard one of the soldiers tell him to hurry up.

Isaac scrambled to the other side of a stack of containers and stood up. "Almost got it," he said to the soldier.

He opened another container and angled his wrist computer toward Koukax.

"Don't worry about the factions. When we control this cure, we'll seize power over all the Konus. The colonists won't go to war for this. Warlord Tritix will deny involvement."

"The colonists will require irrefutable proof, but we need to return undetected and then create more of the cure."

"And as our numbers swell, command of all the Konus will be ours," Koukax said.

Isaac heard the soldier stomping toward him so he grabbed a field kit and hastily closed the container, nearly running out of there. The soldier glared at Isaac as he walked by.

He now had proof that Koukax wasn't going to let them go. He was going to kill most of them, and those that he didn't would never go home again. Isaac had known their time was limited, but he had no idea just how quickly it was running out. He needed to tell Agent Franklin, but the soldiers were watching them closely, and he couldn't risk it right then. He needed to wait a bit for them to relax, but he didn't have long. They needed to find a way to escape, or at the very least, send out a signal to the CDF.

"Good, Isaac, the cleaning wipes from the field kits are just what I needed," Dr. Townsend said and gestured toward his work area.

Isaac walked over and began helping the scientist.

24

CONNOR LOOKED AT SHUNO. "Would they call for backup?"

"Doubtful. There would be no communication until the operation was completed," Shuno said.

Connor glanced at Noah, who gave him a small nod. Noah had been accessing the comms logs captured by the monitoring stations secretly deployed around Renoya. All communications from the Konus city were being monitored by the CDF and the Colonial Intelligence Bureau. He'd given Noah access to query the data but didn't tell anyone else about it. Shuno had agreed to help them, but there were limits to how much of their capabilities Connor was willing to share with the soldier.

"So, it's either a rogue operation or some kind of black ops," Diaz said. "Either way, in order to reduce the risk of being discovered, they're not going to communicate with anyone on the outside."

Connor nodded. "Makes sense, and it gives all groups involved deniability until everything shakes out."

Diaz looked up at the ceiling and sighed. "This doesn't narrow down the search at all."

"They wouldn't have traveled east of Shetrian. That would take them toward colonial territory," Connor said. "The tunnels where they found the rover makes it appear they're heading west of the city."

"CDF has been searching that area since the attack," Noah said.

"They wouldn't have gone that way," Shuno said.

"Why not?" Diaz asked.

"Because your soldiers would have tracked them down. They had help from the Mekaal, so they would have sent a few teams to lay false trails."

Diaz placed his hands on his hips and swore.

Connor crossed his arms and stared at the map on the holoscreen. "The search perimeter would extend twenty kilometers beyond the city, and then they'd extend it outward each day they hadn't been found. They might have been able to guess the response time. Either way, they had a significant head start."

"So, where do we search?" Diaz asked.

The Hercules was flying south toward Shetrian, but they hadn't decided on an area to search. Connor didn't want to interfere with the efforts already underway.

"How would they have traveled?" Noah asked. "The method they use for traveling would give us an idea of how far they could have gotten."

"Ground transportation is most likely, but they might have stayed on foot to avoid detection," Connor replied.

"So, no gliders. That does narrow it down some," Noah said.

Shuno peered at the map for a few moments and then looked

at Connor. "If this were my operation, I would take my prisoners in the direction you'd be least likely to search first. This area here," he said and gestured toward a region north of the city.

Diaz frowned. "North? But there isn't anything there. Wouldn't they go south so they could make it back to Renoya as quickly as possible?"

"Not necessarily. They don't need to return to Renoya at all," Connor replied.

"What? They're going to stay out there in the middle of nowhere until we give up?"

Connor frowned. He didn't like what he'd already guessed. He glanced at Lenora, and she could see it on his face.

Diaz inhaled explosively. "They're going to kill the hostages. Once they get what they came for, the hostages are as good as dead. That's what you're afraid to tell me."

Connor clamped down on his anger. It wouldn't help Diaz at all if he didn't remain focused.

"We won't let it come to that," Connor said. "I think Shuno is right. North of the city is our best bet."

Diaz's eyebrows pushed forward, and he stared at the holoscreen intently.

"If they're using suppressors, then finding them by their comlinks is going to be next to impossible. Maybe we should have search and rescue focus their operations north of the city," Noah said.

Connor shook his head. "No, they need to follow standard operating procedures in case we're wrong. But we can search using the equipment on the ship. We've got sensors capable of mapping the ground. A few tweaks and we can adjust those sensors to detect life forms or even groups of life forms."

Noah nodded and his eyes widened in understanding.

"We can have the sensors search for ryklars, in addition to Ovarrow and humans," Lenora said.

"Let's get it ready," Noah said and walked over to Lenora. "We need to define the search patterns to 'alert on.' Otherwise, we'll get a lot of garbage alerts."

Diaz walked away from them.

Shuno looked at Connor. "There aren't a lot of ryklars in the area."

"No, there aren't, but if I wanted to add another layer of security, I'd bring a few of them along to keep anyone from escaping," Connor replied.

Shuno looked at Connor for a few moments. "An effective strategy."

Connor got the impression that Shuno wanted to ask him something. The Konus commander had hinted at the decreasing numbers of the ryklar population. "We're relocating them."

Shuno blinked several times. "Where?"

Urret turned toward Connor. "Relocating what?"

"The ryklars. We've found a world in another universe where the ryklars can live without crossing paths with any of us," Connor said.

Shuno and Urret exchanged glances. "You didn't know about this?" Shuno asked him.

"No, I had no knowledge of this," Urret replied.

The two Ovarrow looked at Connor. "The High Commissioner and Warlord know about it. We've kept the operation secret for the past two years, but as the ryklar population numbers went down, we knew it was a matter of time before others would notice."

"What gives you the right to do this?" Shuno asked.

Connor thought for a few moments. Urret looked as if he

were reserving judgment, but Shuno acted as if he'd been betrayed. "Maybe we *don't* have the right, but we certainly have the ability. The ryklars are apex predators that exhibit many primitive sentient attributes. Our scientists believe they will eventually evolve, but this wouldn't happen for hundreds of thousands of years. Their best chance to achieve their full potential is on a world of their own without any interference from us." Connor paused for a moment. "Including your people."

"You had no right to do this," Shuno said.

"And you have no right to keep them enslaved. They were part of a strategy for a war that you no longer need to worry about. They're a solution from another world, and they have no place here."

"You had our support?" Urret asked.

Connor nodded. "We considered a lot of solutions. We could have kept using the deterrent signals to keep the ryklars at bay, but they would still be under the control of the signals. We also could have culled their numbers, which wasn't a solution we wanted to pursue. The most peaceful solution, and the one that was best for everyone, was to relocate the ryklars to their own world."

"Why reveal this now?" Urret asked.

Shuno simply stared at him.

"Shuno already suspected we were involved in the declining ryklar population."

"So, it's no longer a secret?" Shuno asked.

"You can tell whoever you want. We're still going to proceed with the program because it's the right thing to do. Maybe one day you'll understand that," Connor said.

Shuno considered this for a few moments and then said,

"You've given me much to think about. I appreciate you sharing this information with me."

The Konus commander returned to his squad and sat down. His response had been more than Connor hoped for. Maybe he'd underestimated the Konus. Perhaps there were some who could be more reasonable.

25

Isaac watched as Dr. Rostova spoke with Deasira, who'd regained consciousness a short while ago. She lay on a cot near the work area. Three Konus soldiers stood guard nearby, but Isaac noticed that two more were patrolling past the area. He'd been noting the times to get an idea of when the next patrol would come by. Every thirty minutes, two more soldiers would walk a circuitous route by their work area. He'd nearly panicked when it first started happening. Koukax was going to kill them and leave enough remains to convince colonial search and rescue teams that they'd all died.

Isaac tried to inform Agent Franklin of what he'd learned, but the timing had never been right, not even for a quick conversation. He needed to come up with another way to send the information to the CIB agent. Koukax was periodically pulling scientists aside to question them individually. With so many captors watching them, there was very little Isaac could do. The situation was wearing on his nerves, and he had to do something.

Ella came to stand next to him at one of the folding tables, checking the list of test samples against the list on her personal holoscreen.

"Are you okay?" she asked.

Isaac shook his head a little. "Something is going on. I need to tell Franklin."

"What is it?" Ella asked.

Isaac considered not telling her for about half a second before deciding it would be foolish not to. "We don't have much time. They're going to make it appear as if we've all been killed and then take some of the others with them to wherever they're going from here."

Ella was quiet for a few moments. She inhaled deeply and breathed out slowly. "They'll keep Dr. Rostova and Townsend alive for sure. And Deasira. You heard them say this?"

Isaac nodded. "I think Franklin has a plan, but I can't get near him."

Ella lifted one of the sample trays and tilted her head to the side as if she were having trouble reading the label. "I can tell him."

Isaac hesitated.

"I have to go by where he is anyway." She raised her chin toward the sample trays.

He didn't want to put her in any more danger than she was already in, but he had no other choice.

"Okay," he said quietly.

"What are you going to do?"

"I need to find a way to stall them."

"They're about to create the first batch of serum," Ella said.

Isaac's eyebrows raised. "That's why they brought Deasira here. They're going to test it on her."

The breath hitched in Ella's throat. "I have to go," she said.

Beautiful dark eyes looked into his, and his pulse quickened. "Be careful," she whispered and walked away.

He had to focus, but his mind kept racing. The serum was going to be ready and then tested on Deasira. Proof that it worked could be measured in the hormone levels taken from the test subject—from Deasira. She was the only female Ovarrow here. The increased hormone levels weren't enough to prove that the serum worked, but he doubted Koukax would wait for irrefutable proof. That was why he'd keep some of them alive.

Isaac had to do something. The centrifuges had to spin through multiple cycles, so he pretended to drop something and squatted behind the table out of view. He used his wrist computer to remotely access the centrifuges' control systems and brought up the options. If he did this, he'd delay the serum's completion, but it wasn't enough. They could just make more.

He inserted a cleaning cycle into the job queue, which would heat the inside and destroy the serum. He then increased the priority so that cycle went to the top of the queue. Next, he accessed the computer systems that Dr. Townsend was using to modify the proteins that would affect the hormone levels in female Ovarrow and thought about just deleting all the data. That would buy them some time, but Koukax might execute one of them as a result. He needed to sabotage the cure, and... his eyes widened. Buying them more time wasn't enough. He needed to get a signal out to the CDF, and to do that, he needed to bring down the suppression field that blocked their comlinks. He couldn't sneak away, but he could cause a distraction that would give him some time for a head start. Sabotaging the cure would put them all in danger, but he didn't have a choice. And discussing his plan with everyone else wasn't an option.

Isaac stood up. There were several tables with lab equipment on them and groups of people gathered around. He saw Ella about twenty meters away. She was speaking to Agent Franklin. If Isaac could have found a way to tell the CIB agent what he was going to do, he would have. This would likely get him killed, but Koukax was going to kill them anyway.

A high-pitched whine came from the centrifuges, and then a red ring appeared around the outside to indicate a cleaning cycle had begun.

Isaac copied Dr. Townsend's formula to his wrist computer and then deleted it from the scientist's computer. The centrifuges were already gathering the attention of those nearby.

Agent Franklin looked at Isaac and their eyes locked. Isaac inclined his chin. Then he spun around and ran.

26

CONNOR WATCHED as Diaz set his tri-barreled shotgun back into its case. For what they were going to do, an AR-74 was a better option. Diaz closed the case and stroked his fingertips across the top in an admiring caress.

Sergeant Tui was speaking to his squad. The CDF soldiers were all wearing their combat suits. There wasn't an extra for Connor to wear, so he had to stick with an MPS. He wouldn't be first into a firefight, but at least he wouldn't be without any protection.

Diaz wore an MPS as well. When activated into protect mode, it became dark gray, and the onboard computer systems controlled the reactionary smart fabrics to repel incoming objects. It could give them slightly better than minimal protection from an Ovarrow plasma rifle. But this equipment was all they had, and remaining in the safety of the ship wasn't an option. Connor had gone into battle with less.

Once they'd decided on the search grid, the ship flew south

at a rapid speed. Those who would be deployed on the ground were armed and wore whatever protection they had.

Lenora, Noah, Kara, and the other non-combatants would remain aboard the ship. They had set up multiple workstations where scan data was being routed to their holoscreens.

Connor turned back toward Diaz. Sometimes, the waiting and anticipating could be just as bad as any high-risk operation they'd undertaken together. But this wasn't just another operation. Try as he might, Connor couldn't avoid thinking of how he'd have reacted if it were Lauren or Ethan who'd been kidnapped. He didn't want to think about it, and it wouldn't help his friend if he allowed his own dark fears to distract him.

Diaz checked his AR-74 and then set it down next to him. He shook his head and sighed, peering over at Lenora and the set of holoscreens.

"Damn it," Diaz said quietly. He looked at Connor and shrugged, trying to dismiss what he'd said.

Connor nodded. "We'll find him."

"I know. I know we will," Diaz replied. He shook his head. "Isaac sometimes was one of those kids that just flew under the radar. He didn't upset things and kinda just went along with everything. He was always reliable. Then at around sixteen or seventeen, it all changed. He argued a lot more. Started getting into trouble. I tried to take a firm hand with him. Give him the tough love I thought he needed, but looking back, I'm not sure whether it helped. I might've made it worse."

"You don't know that," Connor said.

"The more I came down on him, the harder he pulled away. We thought it might have been just a phase."

"Those are tough years. He's trying to figure out who he wants to be. They all are."

Diaz nodded and then leaned back in his chair and rested his head against the bulkhead. "He liked the internship at the research institute because he had something for himself. I couldn't see it at the time. All I focused on was all the mistakes. I kept looking for them. Then, the accident with the aircar happened and all those people got hurt. I couldn't let it go. It started tainting everything." He grimaced. "I let it infect my relationship with my son, Connor. If he dies out there, the last thing he'll remember about me is that I told him he was a failure. And I threatened him."

"You were trying to protect him. Isaac is a smart kid. He knows you love him. Sometimes the words we say in anger are just that—words that don't mean anything."

Diaz shook his head. "They mean something. They do. They hurt."

"Fine, if you want to believe that all the stupid stuff that comes out of our mouths when we're mad is going to shatter Isaac's world, then keep telling yourself that. I'm not saying it's okay, but Isaac is resilient. He's a strong kid, just like his father. They lash out at us when they're angry, testing their limits and ours. Make it better with him after we find him. Focus on what you could do better and go from there, but constantly beating yourself up about what happened isn't going to help him at all, or you."

Diaz stared at him and blew out a breath.

An alert flashed on one of the holoscreens. Noah peered at the data. Then after a few moments, he turned toward them and shook his head.

"I'm going to remember all this sage advice when it's your turn," Diaz said.

Connor snorted. "I know you will."

Diaz rubbed the top of his head and remained quiet for a few minutes. Connor sat next to him, and they waited. He hoped they were searching in the right area. He'd gone over the data they'd gotten from the investigation many times, and he stood behind his reasoning. But if he was wrong, he wasn't sure he'd ever forgive himself.

27

THE CAMP WAS SURROUNDED by dense forest. The Konus had selected this place because it gave them some cover, but it also covered Isaac as he ran from the camp, and the soldiers couldn't get a clear shot at him. He darted off the main path and cut through the shrubs, listening to Koukax as he bellowed orders to his men.

Isaac paused, looking for the transmission tower Agent Franklin had told him about earlier. He heard Konus running nearby and started moving again. Keeping his head down to avoid notice, he ran past a grouping of thick trees. Several plasma bolts blazed by him. They'd found him. He darted to the side, trying to use the trees as cover.

He checked his wrist computer to see if his comlink was working. If he'd somehow gone beyond the suppression field, it should come back on, but he'd had no such luck. He spotted some older buildings hidden among the vines that had overtaken them. That had to be it.

In the distance, he heard several loud screeches. There was no mistaking that sound—ryklars were on the hunt. He'd never encountered a ryklar, but all colonists knew what they sounded like, and anyone who went out into the field learned about them.

Isaac ran toward the ruins of a building, looking for any sign of a suppression device. He couldn't find anything, so he moved on, searching the next building by going around the outside. When he rounded the corner, two Konus soldiers spotted him, so he hastened back the way he'd come and slipped behind a bush. His back was up against the wall. Isaac held his breath so he wouldn't give himself away to his pursuers.

Armed with long rifles, the soldiers ran into the area and paused, examining the ground around them.

"Search the bushes," one of the soldiers said.

They split up, and one of them headed toward him. If he moved, the soldier would hear him. Just then, Isaac saw movement among a group of bushes by a building across from him.

The soldier kept getting closer and peered at the bush where Isaac sat. Isaac became still. If the soldier saw him, he would fire his weapon, but he kept coming toward him. A branch snapped across the way, and the other soldier gave a startled cry. The soldier coming toward Isaac spun around, and Isaac watched as Agent Franklin fought the first soldier.

Isaac scrambled out from behind the bush, tackling the soldier, and the long rifle clattered to the ground nearby. Isaac swung his fist, unleashing a barrage of punches to the soldier's head. He grabbed him by the scruff of his neck and banged his head to the ground. Dark greenish blood splattered on the ground. At some point, the soldier stopped struggling.

Someone grabbed Isaac and pulled him off the dying soldier.

"Isaac," Agent Franklin said, "come on. More are coming. Let's go."

Isaac stood up but just stared at the soldier he'd killed. Agent Franklin grabbed him by the shirt and pulled him away with one hand. He carried a long rifle in the other.

Isaac followed him.

"Where's the tower?" he asked.

"It's this way."

"How did you find me?"

"It wasn't hard to figure out where you were going," Agent Franklin said. "Ella told me what you'd learned."

Several ryklar screeches sounded through the forest, and both of them froze. The predators were getting closer. Agent Franklin started running and Isaac followed.

The tower was hardly a tower at all. The metallic supports of a building were exposed, and the Konus were using it to extend the suppressor's effective range. The building was ten meters tall. They started climbing to the top, using thick vines to hoist themselves up. Gaps in the exterior walls gave him enough of a foothold to keep climbing. Once they reached the top, Isaac saw six small disc-shaped devices attached to an exposed metallic rod.

Agent Franklin lifted the long rifle and aimed it at the suppressors. As he was about to shoot, something big scrambled over the roof and sprang toward them, snarling. Franklin knocked Isaac out of the way.

The ryklar shrieked a battle cry and bounded toward them. Agent Franklin fired his weapon, and the plasma bolt scorched the rooftop. He'd missed the ryklar. The creature threw itself at the CIB agent, and they tumbled to the ground below.

Isaac scrambled to the edge of the roof and looked down. He couldn't see anything. There was no sign of Franklin anywhere. The ryklar howled from nearby, and a few others bawled out answering howls. Isaac jerked away from the edge and peered into the forest.

He heard plasma bolts firing and then nothing. Isaac sat there for a few moments, gasping. He wanted to call out, needing to know if Franklin was okay. He squeezed his eyes shut for a moment. There were three ryklars, and they moved so damn fast. Franklin would want him to focus. He turned toward the suppressors and hastened over to them, examining how they were set up. A patchwork of wires connected them to the metallic frame of the building. Isaac recognized the suppressors as the same that were used on the rover when they were captured. He started yanking the wires apart, breaking the connection. After he'd pulled half of them apart, he checked the comlink status on his wrist computer. It was still blocked. Muttering a curse, he kept going until every wire was detached from the rod. Then, he disabled each of the suppressors, but he still couldn't send out a signal.

Several ryklars screeched a hunting call from the ground below. They'd returned and were circling the building. His stomach sank. Agent Franklin must have been killed. He grabbed one of the suppressors and flung it as far as he could off the roof. It bounced off a nearby tree and tumbled to the ground. The ryklars were on it in seconds.

He grabbed another and hurled it even farther. As the suppressor flew through the air, a ryklar leaped up from the ground and caught it. Two powerful outer arms grabbed onto a tree, its claws cutting deep, and it was able to hold itself up. The ryklar turned toward him. It had a face of folded gray skin and a beard of blood-red tentacles. A mouth filled with large teeth opened wide, and the creature howled, making the tentacles flail wildly.

Isaac flinched back, trembling. He had no weapons, and there was no way he could outrun those creatures. They moved too fast. The ryklar dropped to the ground and charged toward the building. Two more joined it, circling around.

Isaac sucked in a deep breath that caught in his throat. They were going to tear him apart. He'd disabled the suppressors, and his comlink should have worked. Why didn't it work? He was broadcasting a distress beacon from his wrist computer, but there was no acknowledgment. The signal wasn't getting out.

He frowned. The ryklars hadn't climbed up.

"You have something that belongs to me," Koukax said.

Isaac leaned toward the edge of the rooftop.

Koukax stood on the ground. There were two soldiers with him, and the ryklars sat on their haunches nearby, waiting.

"It was a good plan. You distract us at the camp and try to disable the suppression field. Where is Dr. Franklin?" Koukax asked.

The Konus commander didn't know that Hunter Franklin was a CIB agent, but it didn't matter now.

"Those things got him," Isaac replied.

Koukax glance at the ryklars. "They're perfect hunters. They would have killed you if we hadn't shown up."

Isaac glared at him. "Didn't want to deprive yourself of the pleasure?"

"Killing you is a necessity, not a pleasure," Koukax said and looked at the ryklars. "There are much better ways to die than to be torn apart by them."

"A plasma bolt to the chest is so much better."

"There is no way for you to escape," Koukax said.

The certainty with which he said it made Isaac want to howl in defiance, but the Konus commander was right. He couldn't escape, and no amount of resistance was going to change that.

"You have something I need. You stole what didn't belong to you," Koukax said.

They'd already figured out that he had Dr. Townsend's formulas.

Isaac looked at Koukax. "Are the others dead?"

"Not yet, but if I have to ask again, they will be."

Isaac was blinded as his vision blurred. He was going to die no matter what he did, but if he resisted, Koukax could make it worse for the others. He clenched his teeth.

"They're hungry," Koukax said.

Isaac's gaze slid toward the ryklars. Their powerful chest muscles heaved, and they appeared to be mere moments from springing into action.

Bile crept up the back of his throat, leaving a bitter taste. He sighed and began to climb down. Once he reached the ground, the Konus soldiers aimed their weapons at him. Koukax stared into his eyes for a few moments and then walked ahead of them. The soldiers shoved him forward, following the Konus commander. The forest around them had settled into a stunned silence, and Isaac could hear the dull thud of his footsteps on the forest floor as he marched toward his own death.

28

ISAAC FOLLOWED Koukax back to camp, glancing behind them a few times in the hopes that Agent Franklin had somehow survived. If he'd been able to contact the CDF, they would have found them, and they would have been rescued. Everything he'd done had been for nothing. Koukax walked a short distance in front of him, secure in the knowledge that Isaac would never attack him. Isaac knew that if he were to try something, the soldiers following them would shoot him. He'd climbed down and surrendered on the vague promise that Koukax would make their deaths less painful.

Isaac shook his head and tried to convince himself that he hadn't given up. He'd surrendered because Koukax was moments from sending the ryklars up to the rooftop to kill him. They'd dragged Agent Franklin off easily enough. What hope did he have of fighting them?

Isaac followed Koukax, and with each step he took, he clenched his teeth harder. His lips lifted, moments from a snarl as he remembered killing the Konus soldier and imagined doing the same thing to Koukax. A small part of his mind quivered. Could he kill again? He'd just reacted before, but was he a killer? Was he like Koukax? He stared at the Konus commander's back, and dark, violent thoughts stirred. He hated him, and he hated the soldiers behind him. Had his father been right? He thought about all the time he'd spent in Shetrian, and all the Mekaal he'd met. They were different than Koukax and his soldiers, but some of the Mekaal had been part of the attack. He'd come to Shetrian determined to keep an open mind about the Mekaal and the Ovarrow in general, but Koukax had shattered that for him. It would be easy to simply hate them, but he knew it was wrong. There were good Ovarrow on New Earth. He hated Koukax and anyone who followed him, but that didn't mean he must hate all Ovarrow. If he did, then Koukax not only controlled whether he lived or died, but would control his mind... his soul, and Isaac wasn't going to give that up.

They entered the camp. Dr. Townsend had a gash on the side of his head, and blood had dried over his swollen eye. Isaac locked eyes with Ella for a few seconds. She looked hopeful, but Isaac shook his head. Dr. Rostova looked at Isaac and then glanced behind him. She was looking for Agent Franklin. When she didn't see him, her gaze sank to the ground, and she began to weep.

Koukax led him to Dr. Townsend's workstation. "Put the formula back and initiate the serum creation protocol."

Isaac stared at the workstation. The amber-colored holoscreen was displaying a data window with several error messages. He lifted his wrist and accessed his own computer. This was it. He would upload it back to the workstation and initiate the protocol, and then Koukax was going to kill them. Isaac raised his gaze to the sky and spotted bright, clear blue above the treetops.

He looked at his wrist computer. He could delete it and deny Koukax what he wanted—just delete the data and contend with whatever horrifying death the Konus commander had waiting for him.

"There it is," Koukax said. "At least there is one fighter among you, but it's a fight you cannot win. Betray me now and I'll make you watch them all die one at a time. You'll witness each agonizing moment of their suffering, and it will be all your fault."

Isaac looked toward the Konus soldiers. "He's going to betray you and use the serum to gain power for himself."

Koukax tilted his head to the side. "Of course, I am. They're loyal to the Konus, and this serum is what's best for us all. It will be ours."

"Will they stay that way once you become the Warlord? You don't plan to bring the cure as a gift for the Konus. You plan to keep it for yourself."

Several of the Konus soldiers shifted their feet, and several exchanged glances.

Isaac played his recording of Koukax loud enough for everyone to hear it. The soldiers listened, and several of them glared at Koukax.

Koukax raised the end of his long rifle and gestured toward the workstation. "Do as I say."

Isaac stepped toward him but kept his wrist raised high. His personal holoscreen was easily visible. "All I have to do is delete it and you'll have to wait for Dr. Townsend to recreate the formulas, but you don't have that kind of time. The CDF is coming. They're closing in on us as we speak, and they're going to catch up to us. They're going to catch up to *you*. Even if you kill all of us—*especially* if you kill all of us—they'll never stop hunting you."

"They have no idea where we are. Now, stop lying and upload the data you stole," Koukax said. After a few seconds, he aimed his weapon toward the others.

Isaac gritted his teeth and moved to comply, but a high-pitched whine echoed above the trees. It was distant but unmistakable, and the soldiers glanced upward.

Koukax's eyes flicked toward the sky and Isaac leaped toward him. When he spun around, Isaac grabbed at the long rifle and they each locked grips on the weapon, but Koukax was stronger than Isaac. The Konus commander used his long, powerful arms to pull Isaac off his feet, swinging him through the air, but Isaac held fast, refusing to let go. When his feet touched the ground, he pushed as hard as he could. Koukax backed up a few steps, off-balance, and plasma bolts shot from the end of the rifle. Konus and humans alike scattered out of the way. There was movement all around them, but Isaac didn't know what was happening.

Koukax twisted the rifle, and Isaac was pulled toward him at an awkward angle. The commander pivoted and drove him to the ground. Pain spread like lightning across his back. Koukax pressed the rifle to Isaac's neck, and Isaac looked up. His eyes widened when he saw an active suppressor at Koukax's hip. That was why he hadn't been able to send out a distress beacon. Koukax had been blocking it.

The Konus commander lifted Isaac up and then slammed him back to the ground. His vision swam, but he was able to see Ella come up behind Koukax and smash something on his head, hard. Isaac kicked the Konus commander's leg and lunged for the suppressor, but Koukax stumbled forward and the rifle tore from Isaac's grasp. Isaac twisted around and scrambled toward Koukax, slamming his fist onto the suppressor. A small electrical arc came from the device, and it started smoking. His wrist computer chimed. The distress beacon was broadcasting! Isaac blinked several times, staring at it. A chorus of chimes could be heard as comlinks heralded an active connection.

Koukax growled and grabbed Isaac by the neck. The powerful Konus lifted him up, and Isaac kicked out with his feet. Koukax dropped him to the ground and staggered backward.

Ella helped pull Isaac to his feet, and he stood up, a little wobbly at first.

"We have to run," Isaac said. "The beacon is up, and the CDF will be coming," he said. He looked at the others. "Run!"

Isaac grabbed Ella's arm and pulled her away. They ran as the Konus soldiers erupted into shouts. Some of them were fighting each other, and Isaac ran past them. They needed to move. With the suppressors down, they had a chance to survive, and he wasn't going to waste it—not this time.

As they ran toward the others, Isaac saw Curtis cowering under a table. He pulled him up. "Go. Go! Help is coming."

Dr. Townsend and Dr. Rostova picked up Deasira and were moving as fast as they could.

Isaac saw a Konus long rifle on the ground. He picked it up and swung it around. Koukax was running toward them. He squeezed the trigger, but the Konus commander dove out of the way.

"Come on!" Ella yelled.

Isaac followed, pausing only to fire the long rifle once more. They had to keep moving, but his feet felt lighter than they had before. Help was coming. They had a chance.

29

"CONTACT!" Noah yelled.

Connor swerved toward the nearest holoscreen. Multiple distress beacons appeared.

"They're not far," Lenora said.

"Have the pilot take us in for a low-altitude drop. Then continue to search the area," Connor said.

He walked over to the CDF squad. Specialist Weps had six recon drones ready to fly. They were lined up at the back of the loading ramp.

"We're connected to the ship's computers," Sergeant Tui said.

Connor peered at the holoscreen. Diaz stood next to him.

"They're running away. They're trying to escape," Diaz said.

The distress beacons disappeared.

"The soldiers are using a suppressor field. Lock onto their last known location," Connor said.

The ship sped forward as the pilot increased its velocity. The loading ramp lowered.

Connor attached a tether to the harness he was wearing.

Urret and the Mekaal soldiers did the same. Then Shuno and the remaining Konus scouts followed suit.

The CDF squad would jump first. Their combat suit jets would allow them to reach the ground faster. Then Connor and others would follow.

"It looks like they were splitting up," Diaz said.

Connor nodded. "We'll need to split up."

Sergeant Tui looked at the holoscreen and then at his squad. "Eldridge, you and Schmiddy will stay with General Gates, and I don't want to have to report in how you let something happen to him."

Diaz arched an eyebrow toward the CDF sergeant.

"Don't forget about Captain Diaz, retired," Tui said and grinned.

"It's about time," Diaz said and looked at Connor. "At least they know who the real troublemaker is. Didn't you almost get eaten by one of those snow creatures?"

"Snow beast. Get it right," Connor replied.

Diaz rolled his eyes and then focused on the end of the loading ramp, almost giddy with hope.

The jump-indicator light flashed green, and the CDF squad leaped from the ship.

Connor counted down, giving them time to get clear. Then, he ran to the end of the loading ramp and jumped.

30

ISAAC FIRED the Konus long rifle blindly, and bright flashes of plasma bolts blazed through the forest. He was hoping to slow down their pursuers. The rifle had a powerful kick every time he fired it. The weapon wasn't designed for rapid fire, and he doubted he'd be anywhere near as accurate with it as he was with the standard hunting rifle he was accustomed to using.

The others were slowing down. Deasira was breathing heavily, even with Dr. Rostova and Dr. Townsend helping her. They were all tired and haggard from days of captivity, being beaten or threatened, and only provided minimal food and water.

"The suppressor field is back," Ella said.

Isaac checked his wrist computer. She was right. "They're coming. Someone knows we're here."

She nodded and looked to the side, slowing down a little. Curtis ran into view and Jordan followed, calling after him.

Several screeches echoed, and it was impossible to tell how far away they were.

"What was that?" Ella asked.

"Ryklars," Isaac replied.

He felt a sharp pain in his side and looked down. His shirt was torn, but he wasn't bleeding. He must've cracked a rib earlier.

"My God!" Ella said. "Curtis! Jordan! Watch out for ryklars!"

Isaac heard someone running towards them. "Go on," he told Ella. "Help the others get away."

Ella looked at him and her mouth twisted into a frown. "I don't think so. I'm not leaving you here."

"I'll hold them off," Isaac said and leaned against the gnarled trunk of a tree.

"Good, I'll stay right here and watch your back," Ella said and positioned herself next to him. "I wish I'd grabbed one of those when I had the chance," she said, gesturing toward the rifle.

Isaac was about to reply when he caught movement near them. He raised the long rifle and waited. A Konus soldier emerged onto the path and Isaac fired. The plasma bolt slammed into the soldier's chest and knocked him back in a short, brutal arc to the ground. He didn't move.

Isaac peered back the way they'd come. No one else showed up, but he knew there were more of them out there. They should keep moving. He looked at Ella and raised his finger to his lips, gesturing for quiet. She nodded.

Isaac stepped away from the tree and headed along the path, moving as quietly as possible. As he approached another group of trees, he glanced behind, trying to see whether anyone else was following them. He then turned back toward the trees and walked around them. Koukax was there, feline gaze blazing.

Isaac halted as his breath caught in his throat.

The commander had several lacerations on his head, and

dark green blood leaked down his neck. He glared at Isaac, snatching the long rifle away and throwing it to the side. Isaac charged forward and grabbed the handle of the combat knife on Koukax's belt. He had just pulled it free when an armored elbow slammed into his face, and he fell backward. Stars exploded across his vision. Something felt loose and hot in his head, and the knife slipped from his grasp.

Strong hands pulled him to his feet.

"Pathetic and weak!" Koukax growled.

Isaac's vision slowly came back into focus. A pair of hate-filled eyes glared into his.

"Look," Koukax said.

Isaac felt his body turned toward something, and he blinked several times. Ella was on her knees, and one of Koukax's soldiers was choking her. Both her hands clawed at the soldier's arms, her mouth open and face turning red. She looked at him, and all he could do was stare at her. He kicked out his leg in a feeble attempt to break free of Koukax's grip.

Isaac watched as Ella slipped her hand into her pocket. She pulled out an empty glass test tube and jerked it back over her shoulder, stabbing the soldier in the eye. The soldier screamed in pain and let her go.

Isaac looked down at Koukax's forearm. Corded and unprotected muscle was right there in front of him. Isaac heaved forward, biting down on the exposed flesh, and the commander's blood gushed into his mouth. Isaac growled and bit down harder. Koukax spun around, flinging Isaac to the ground.

Isaac fell to a knee and seized the combat knife. Twisting to the side, he rammed the knife upward into Koukax's middle, hitting something ropey and hot and slippery. Isaac pushed forward, thrusting the blade deeper and deeper, screaming his throat raw while Koukax howled in pain. The Konus commander staggered backward and fell, pulling Isaac on top of him. Isaac jerked the knife from Koukax's abdomen and stabbed him in the throat, yanking the blade to the side and cutting off Koukax's scream until it was just a gurgling hiss as the Konus commander died.

Isaac let go of the knife and climbed off the body. His hands were slick with blood and stringy pink tissue from Koukax's throat. He rolled onto his back, gasping. Each breath he took sent stabbing pain through his side.

Ella ran to him.

The soldier she'd injured was snatching at the broken tube in his eye as Ella picked up the long rifle and fired. The plasma bolt spun the soldier around and he sank to the ground.

She looked at Isaac. Her eyes flicked to his bloody hands and her lips quivered. "Isaac, are you okay?"

She began to put the rifle down.

"Don't," Isaac said. "There could be more."

Ella held onto the rifle as she knelt by his side and tilted her head, listening.

They heard shouting. Someone was yelling their names!

"Over here!" Ella yelled.

Isaac tried to sit up, but it hurt too much.

He heard someone call his name, and it penetrated the fog his brain was slipping into. Then he saw his father.

"Isaac!" his father said. "Just lay still." He glanced toward Koukax.

"I think he's hurt," Ella said.

His father nodded and gave Isaac a once over. "Who are you?"

"I'm Ella."

"Keep that rifle handy. We're not finished yet."

Isaac gritted his teeth and sat up. "The others are out there, running," he said.

"We'll find them," his father said.

Isaac stood up and winced, his hand coming to his side. "There are ryklar in the area."

His father looked at him and smiled. "Damn, son. Are you a sight for sore eyes."

Isaac's throat became thick, and he smiled a little.

His father pulled out his sidearm and handed the pistol over. Isaac made sure the safety was off.

"Can you broadcast the deterrent signal?" Isaac asked.

"They are, but these ryklars aren't responding," his father replied.

Isaac moved his hand to grip the bottom of the pistol.

"Remember—" his father began.

"Check your fire. I know," Isaac replied and smiled a little.

Several Mekaal soldiers appeared, and Diaz noticed Isaac stiffen.

"They're with us."

31

CONNOR LOOKED at his personal holoscreen as the recon drones quickly mapped the area. They were broadcasting the ryklar deterrent signal, but the predators weren't responding.

A comlink came from Diaz. "I found him and another intern named Ella. They said there are more."

"Good. I have Sergeant Tui sweeping the area. They're ahead of your location," Connor said.

"I'll send Urret to you," Diaz said.

Connor glanced at the video feed from the recon drone. "No, have them hold up with you. The ryklars are heading toward you. We're on our way."

Corporal Eldridge and Private Schmiddy scouted ahead. Connor followed close behind, along with Shuno and the remainder of his scout force. They'd encountered other Konus soldiers. Some were fighting among themselves while others tried to run, but most didn't get far. Shuno and the other scouts didn't hesitate to engage them. Several of the soldiers looked at them in shock before firing their weapons, and a few managed to escape, but saving the hostages was the priority.

"They're using an alternate control signal," Shuno said.

Connor scanned the different frequencies and found the source. It was located near where Diaz was. "I can block it."

"It won't stop them from attacking. We train the ryklars to continue to attack even after the signal stops. It'll be several hours before the effect wears off," Shuno said.

Connor swore and began to run faster. There were at least six ryklars in the area, and they were heading toward Diaz. He considered ordering the two CDF soldiers to run ahead but dismissed the idea. Diaz had Urret and the Mekaal squad of soldiers with him.

He got an idea and slowed down. Recalling one of the recon drones, he uploaded the new high-frequency sound wave the ryklars were obeying. Then he had the drone broadcast the signal with more intensity to drown out the original control signal.

The ryklars screeched in response and altered course, heading toward the recon drone located midway between where Diaz and Connor were located.

Connor glanced at Shuno. "Get ready."

Shuno aimed his weapon.

The ryklars ran into the area and entered the kill box. Plasma bolts and high-density darts fired from the AR-74s, cutting them down. Several ryklars scrambled to avoid being shot, but there were too many opponents. Soon, the ryklars were dead and the forest was quiet.

Shuno looked at Connor. "I'll still need to report your ryklar relocation operation to my superiors."

Connor nodded. "I know."

Shuno considered this for a few moments.

"You thought I'd try to stop you?" Connor asked.

"I thought you might have requested that I didn't report it."

Connor shrugged. The time for secrecy about the mission was over. "I won't. I'd report it if I were you."

"This experience with you has been very insightful," Shuno replied.

Connor nodded. "I can say the same. Maybe we'll find some common ground."

CDF Hellcats flew overhead and Shuno looked up at them. "The prisoners."

"We'll question them. Then, our governments will work something out."

Shuno considered this for a few moments and bobbed his head once.

32

Isaac sat in a medical tent while CDF medics checked him for injuries. Healing packs had been attached to his broken ribs, which numbed the area and sped up the healing. A saline IV drip hung nearby. On top of everything else, he was dehydrated. They all were.

In the hours since their rescue, they'd been debriefed by the investigators who were still piecing together the details of the attack, and Ella sat on a nearby cot, speaking to a CDF officer. She nodded a few times and then said something. Sometimes, he just liked watching her mouth move when she spoke. She'd certainly caught his eye in the past few months.

There was a commotion at the entry to the medical tent, and someone else was carried in on a stretcher.

Isaac's father entered the tent and walked over. "We found him. Agent Franklin is alive."

Isaac's eyes widened and he turned toward where the medics had carried Franklin.

His father sat down and rubbed his forehead. "He's going to need surgery, but he should be fine."

"How did he survive? The ryklars…"

"He managed to wedge himself between some boulders, and the ryklars couldn't finish him off," his father said.

Isaac nodded. "He's a good guy."

"Damn right he is. He looked after you," his father said and smiled a little. He stood up and pulled the curtain around them so they'd have some privacy. "There's some things I want to say."

"Dad, I'm sorry. For everything."

Tears welled up in his father's eyes. "Damn it. Here I am trying to apologize to you," he said and looked away for a few moments, wiping his eyes. "What you've done here, son, is nothing short of a miracle. I couldn't be prouder of you than I am right now. You saved their lives. Had you not disabled the suppressors, we wouldn't have found you in time."

Isaac shook his head. "He killed Julian and a soldier named Reznick. And a Mekaal named Cohsora, not to mention the people who died in the attack. But Julian… He shot him right in front of me, and there was nothing I could do to stop it. I couldn't stop it."

His father leaned forward. "You couldn't have done anything, and that's nothing to be ashamed of, son."

"I just feel like I should've done more, but I couldn't. It wasn't until we were about to be killed that I…"

"It's gonna take time. It's gonna take a lot of time to get this straight in your head, but you're gonna be fine. Look at me. Listen to me. You're going to be fine."

Isaac's vision blurred through his tears, but he nodded and let out a shaky breath.

"You've been through the shit—something few people ever

have to go through. And even fewer people live to walk away. You just need to give yourself some time to heal."

Isaac looked at his father. There was a bedrock of strength in his eyes, but also, there was knowledge. He'd seen things, too. Horrible things.

"Just try to get some sleep. I'll be right here."

Moments before, he hadn't felt tired at all, but speaking with his father seemed to drain his energy. He lay back and closed his eyes.

CONNOR ENTERED the medical tent and found Diaz snoozing on a chair next to Isaac. His lips lifted a little. Father and son were reunited.

Diaz stirred and looked up. Seeing Connor, he stood and they walked a short distance from Isaac.

"How's he doing?" Connor asked.

"You know some of those things we go through that we hope our kids never have to know? It's like that. It was bad, Connor. This Koukax was a real piece of shit. Isaac killed him," Diaz said and shook his head. "He killed him with a knife. He's going to need a lot of time to sort this out. They all will."

Connor inhaled deeply and sighed. There was nothing he could really say. All he could do was help his friend pick up the pieces and make sure Isaac had the help he needed.

Lenora walked over to him. She looked at Isaac and then hugged Diaz.

"I spoke to Victoria, but she wants to hear from you."

Diaz nodded. "I'll contact her," he said and walked away from them.

Lenora went over to the cot where Isaac slept and pulled the blanket up to cover his chest. He had cuts and bruises on his face and arms, and the knuckles of his hands were reddish-purple. Connor knew the telltale signs of a fight. The healing packs would work quickly, but there would still be a toll. They could heal the body, but the mind would take the most time to heal. On the other hand, Isaac was young and resilient. He'd find a way to move on from this.

Lenora sat down in the chair next to Isaac, and Connor pulled up a chair and sat next to her, reaching out to hold her hand. She squeezed his in response. He'd known Isaac since he was born. He'd seen men wounded before and it was never easy, but seeing family hurt was worse. He sank into the chair, letting it support his entire weight.

"I'm glad he's alive," Connor said quietly.

"Me, too," Lenora replied. "I don't even want to imagine it any other way."

Diaz soon returned, and Connor insisted he take his chair while he went to retrieve another one. The three of them sat there while Isaac slept, and it felt like the first time they'd sat down in days.

33

Two WEEKS after Isaac returned to Sanctuary, he'd finally taken his placement tests for Sierra's medical program. He thought he'd done well but didn't know the results yet.

He rode the elevator at the Colonial Research Institute and got out on the seventh floor, walking down the corridor toward Dr. Rostova's office. In order to complete his internship, he had to meet with her for an exit interview. He hadn't seen her since they'd been rescued. They all needed time to sort things out. He had nightmares that woke him, but he found that staying busy helped.

He stopped outside Dr. Rostova's door and knocked. The door opened and he was face-to-face with Dr. Townsend.

"Mr. Diaz, won't you join us?" he said.

Isaac frowned in confusion and walked into the office.

Dr. Rostova gestured toward the chair across from her desk, and Dr. Townsend sat next to Isaac.

"I thought this was my exit interview," Isaac said.

Dr. Townsend arched an eyebrow. "Wondering why I'm here?"

Isaac nodded. "You did kick me out of the program."

Dr. Townsend snorted. "I may have been a little rash in my inclination to adhere to a tight schedule."

Isaac blinked and his lips twitched. "Are you apologizing?"

"Never. I'm merely rectifying a misjudgment on my part, but I will say that you've thrived under Dr. Rostova."

"Uh, thanks, I think," Isaac replied and scratched the back of his head.

Dr. Rostova leaned forward, and her blue eyes crinkled on the edges as she smiled. "Normally, for these types of interviews, we'd have a discussion about your experience and discuss your future. But we can all agree that this whole incident was much more than any of us could have imagined. During our time in Shetrian before the attack, I'd noted some of my thoughts on your performance. They're part of my recommendation for you."

"I've added a few things to your recommendation as well," Dr. Townsend said.

"You did?" Isaac replied and pressed his lips together. "We get along like oil and water."

Dr. Townsend chuckled. "You're right; we do. However, that doesn't preclude me from acting in a professional manner. You're allowed to review your recommendation. I don't think anything I've written would offend you, but given our history, I understand your reticence."

"I won't forget what you did for me," Isaac said to Dr. Townsend. The stuffy professor had inserted himself into one of Isaac's interactions with Koukax. In his own way, Dr. Townsend had looked out for him.

"Don't mention it," Dr. Townsend said and shrugged. "Given

what you did after, one might say you've paid me back in spades."

He stood up, and Isaac did as well. Dr. Townsend extended his hand, and Isaac shook it.

"Good luck, Isaac, with everything you do. I hope you have great success," Dr. Townsend said as he opened the door and left the office.

Isaac stared at the door for a second and then sat back down.

"I've never seen him do that," Dr. Rostova said.

"Agent Franklin did say he could be friendly sometimes," he said.

She frowned a little and then smiled.

"How's he doing?" he asked.

She arched a blonde eyebrow. "Why ask me?"

"Aren't you and him… I don't know… close maybe?"

She grinned. "You're the only person I'd let get away with that. Once," she said and paused for a moment. "Hunter and I are complicated. He has a stubborn knack for getting into things, and that's all I'm willing to say about it."

"Okay," Isaac said with a nod.

"I have your test scores, and they're definitely competitive to gain entry into the medical program at Sierra. Considering that, along with your recommendations, I'd say a slot is yours for the taking," she said and smiled.

Isaac inhaled deeply and sighed. "Thank you. That's great news," he said, and his lack of enthusiasm wasn't lost on Dr. Rostova.

Her eyebrows pushed forward. "I thought that was what you wanted. You certainly earned it with all your hard work."

"I had some help."

She nodded. "You and Ms. Kingston."

Isaac smiled and bobbed his head once.

"Are you having second thoughts about the program?"

He shook his head and then pursed his lips. "I don't know. I mean, with all that's happened, I'm not sure what I'm going to do."

"Oh, that's fine. Believe me, there's no rush. You should take as much time as you need. You can defer enrollment," she said.

"Thanks for that. And thank you so much for giving me this chance. You didn't have to do that. I just want you to know that I really appreciate it."

She smiled again. "You're one of the good ones, Isaac. It was a genuine pleasure, and if you ever need anything, you know where to reach me."

Isaac left her office and walked down the empty corridor, stopping by one of the wide windows to look out at the campus. A text message chimed on his wrist computer.

Are you coming? Ella asked.

On my way, he wrote back.

Isaac summoned the elevator and took it down to the main floor. He walked out of the building and saw Ella waiting for him by the fountain, but when he saw a man standing off to the side, his eyes widened. The man wore a hat and a tan Field Ops uniform.

"Agent Franklin," Isaac said and then winced, glancing around. "Did I just give away your disguise?"

Agent Franklin grinned. "You outed me. Come over here for a second."

Isaac walked over to him.

"You can call me Hunter, you know. I figure we're friends now."

"All right."

"How have you been?"

"Me? You're the one who had ryklars trying to fillet your skin. How are *you* doing?"

Hunter smiled. "I'm fine. Healing treatments are going well. It isn't the first time I've been hurt like that."

"I'm almost afraid to ask."

"You'd be smart not to," Hunter said and smiled. "I won't keep you long, not with her waiting," he said and inclined his chin toward Ella. "I heard you got accepted into Sierra's medical program. Congratulations."

Isaac frowned. "I just got my placement scores a few minutes ago. I haven't even submitted my application yet."

The CIB agent shrugged. "Isaac, they're going to take you. You could say your spot is assured."

"Did you—"

He shook his head. "No. Are you kidding? I didn't have to. A lot of people are aware of what you did."

"Oh," Isaac said. "I don't know what to think about that."

"Don't worry about it. When you go there, I'd like to check in on you sometime."

Isaac smiled. "That would be great."

"What happened can have a way of weighing down on a person. Being around friends helps. It'll just take time, all right?"

"My father says the same thing."

Hunter smiled. "That's because it's true."

Isaac pressed his lips together for a moment. "Do the nightmares stop?"

Hunter regarded him somberly. "Yes, they will, mostly."

Isaac inhaled and nodded.

"I think the medical program would be good for you. You can certainly handle yourself under pressure."

"Thanks."

"Another option for you to consider is the CIB."

Isaac blinked at him in surprise. "An agent? Me?"

"Yeah, why not? You've got the right instincts for it. Sometimes people freeze up when they're in danger. It happens to most people, but others are different. They can still take action, and sometimes waiting to act is just as important. You've got what it takes. Look, it's just something to think about."

"I will," Isaac replied and meant it.

Hunter leaned toward him. "It doesn't have to be the bureau *or* the medical program. Both work."

He gave Isaac a playful shot in the arm. "Enough future talk for one day." He twitched his head toward Ella waiting for him by the fountain. "Don't keep her waiting."

Isaac grinned. "Dr. Rostova's upstairs, you know."

Hunter waggled his eyebrows once. "Why do you think I'm here?" He tossed a wave in Ella's direction as he headed inside the building.

Isaac walked to the nearby fountain. It had five stone tiers carved in a floral relief at the edges and a golden replica of New Earth on top. Water cascaded down from the globe to a large reservoir at the bottom.

The afternoon sunlight gleamed off the water sending eddies of light on Ella's long dark hair. She'd dipped one of her hands into the cool water for a moment, and smiled at him.

"Who was that?" she asked, and stood up.

"That was Agent Franklin."

"Oh, I didn't recognize him," she said and shrugged. "Well, are you going to tell me?"

"About what?"

She punched him lightly in the arm. "Your scores, silly."

Isaac smiled with half his mouth.

She stared at him for a moment and then her eyebrows lifted. "You got in. You did it."

Isaac chuckled and then nodded. "Well, not officially, but yeah, I did. Thanks to you."

"I just helped at the end. You did the hard part. I'm so happy for you. We'll be study partners," Ella said, her eyes twinkling.

"We'll be more than that," he said and grabbed her hand, pulling her closer to him.

Ella smiled, lifted her mouth toward his, and kissed him.

It was a good kiss. Her lips were soft and gentle and explored his in gentle surges.

"It took you long enough," she said, her dark eyes twinkling.

"But worth the wait, right?"

She pursed her lips for a moment, and kissed him again.

34

CONNOR WALKED out of his home office and headed outside. Noah, Kara, and Lenora stood in front of a holoscreen that displayed a couple of data windows.

Diaz walked over to him. "They're still talking about the data they retrieved from that bunker. What did Nathan say about the investigation?"

"The Mekaal are still holding the prisoners. Their joint investigation indicates that this was a rogue group acting without any authorization from the Konus government."

Diaz puffed out a breath. "Either they're all extremely dedicated, or they're telling the truth. I don't like it."

"Me either. This was well planned and executed. Koukax was high up in the Konus military. He had connections, and we can't get around the fact that he had help from a faction of Mekaal. They're still chasing those leads."

"So, the Konus just get away with it?"

"What do you suggest? We just start dropping bombs on them?"

Diaz shook his head. "No, but there needs to be some accountability."

"I agree, but it's going to take time," Connor replied.

The others stopped speaking and looked at Connor expectantly. They knew who he'd been meeting with.

"They're still investigating. There are rogue factions at work in both the Konus and Mekaal cities. Our security measures are being addressed. The explosion didn't destroy the embassy, but it did cause some damage."

"What about the infertility cure?" Lenora asked.

"They're moving forward with testing it and making information about it available to the Mekaal. The Konus are interested in it as well, but they'll need to give a few concessions before those discussions occur," Connor said.

"What kind of concessions?" Noah asked.

"Open travel between the Konus and Mekaal, and a colonial embassy established in Renoya, as well as Mekaal and Konus embassies in Sierra."

"At least they're not in Sanctuary," Diaz said.

"The only way things will improve is if we keep the lines of communication open," Noah said.

"That's fine and good, but it also gives us a foothold to keep an eye on them," Diaz replied.

Noah looked at Connor.

"He's right. That's all part of it," Connor replied. "This infertility cure isn't without its risks or drawbacks. They have strong feelings about it. There's no easy solution, but I do think it's interesting that the Ovarrow pushing for it are mostly female."

"That *is* interesting. I wonder why that is," Noah said.

"You're not a woman, sweetheart," Kara said.

"Thanks for noticing," Noah replied and smiled.

"Do you want to be a father?" Kara asked.

"Of course, just not right now."

Kara's lips twitched. "I feel the same way, but we do have urges. It's hardwired into us." She looked at Lenora.

"Oh yeah," Lenora agreed. "It also doesn't hurt that babies are cute. I can just eat them right up."

Noah nodded. "All right, I understand and given that they're worried about their survival it all makes a little more sense. I just hope we're not helping them to create more problems in the long run."

"It's not up to us," Connor said. "They're going to do it regardless."

Lenora nodded. "At least if we help them now, it might help them avoid any major pitfalls."

"The other thing that's being talked about is allowing Ovarrow to defect, to become a member of the opposing nation-state," Connor said.

"I thought that was frowned upon," Noah said.

"It is, but given what's happened, there are groups of Ovarrow that prefer to live differently. There are Konus who wish to join the Mekaal and the same the other way around."

Diaz shook his head.

Noah grinned. "Don't worry, this will all be normal in another twenty or thirty years."

"You're probably right about that. So, how's the data analysis going?" Connor asked.

"We're still piecing things together. The storage modules we recovered held a lot of information, and we were able to transfer a large amount before the data connection to the bunker went offline. That reminds me. There's a team of biologists that wants to study the snow beasts," Noah said.

Connor chuckled. "They're welcome to it. I've gotten as close as I want."

Diaz grinned. "You were almost a snack for one of them."

Noah grinned.

"Sure, we can laugh about it now, but at the time it wasn't so funny," Connor replied.

"We need a better name for them," Lenora said. "They're aquatic but seemed adapted for the ice."

"I wonder if they're native to this world," Noah said.

Connor eyed him.

Noah shrugged. "The Bhatdin could have brought them as protectors. They didn't attack until we started poking around in the bunker."

"What about the technical data? Anything useful there?" Connor asked.

Noah nodded. "There are some things worth reviewing and understanding. Some theoretical principles for how the gateways work."

Diaz gave Noah a sidelong glance. "Still trying to become the fastest man alive?"

Kara laughed. "I was thinking the fastest couple. 'Husband and wife achieve FTL dream.'"

Diaz smiled.

"I'm sure you'll figure it out," Connor said, and they looked at him. "I mean that. I expect to hear all about it one day."

Noah smiled. "Still insisting on staying here when we do?"

Connor looked at Lenora. She smiled and shrugged.

"I guess we'll just have to wait and see what happens. Anyway, at the rate you're going, I might be an old man when you finally figure it out," Connor said.

Noah grinned. "Well, I'll get right to work on it then."

AUTHOR NOTE

Thank you so much for reading. *Impulse* is the 12th book in the First Colony series. New Earth has been home to my imagination for a long time. Helping me to stay motivated to write these stories has been the enthusiasm of the readers who've reached out to me and the people who took the time to review my books. I hope you enjoyed this latest book in the First Colony series. Almost inevitably, I get the question about whether this will be the last book in the First Colony series. No, it won't. I think there are more stories to tell in this series and more characters to explore. I don't believe Noah is going to give up on unlocking FTL travel.

Impulse marks a new beginning for the series. I hope you enjoyed reconnecting with the more familiar characters as well as getting to know some of the new ones. To answer the question about how many books will be in the series, I turn it back to you, dear reader. I think there are many stories to tell in this series and generations of colonists to get to know, but this will only be possible with your help. As an author who earns a living by writing these stories, I can't ask for anything more from this series. I continue to write stories in the First Colony series because I enjoy it, and you do as well. It seems like as good a reason as any to keep writing a particular series. The best way for me to gauge whether people want more First Colony stories is by them reading the book and perhaps leaving a review, or recommending it to a friend or a group. Word of mouth is crucial. I take a lot of pride in my work because I think the quality of the story matters, as well as your experience in reading it.

Thanks again for reading my books. Please consider leaving a review for *Impulse*.

If you're looking for another series to read consider reading the Federation Chronicles. Learn more by visiting:

https://kenlozito.com/federation-chronicles/

I do have a Facebook group called **Ken Lozito's SF readers**. If you're on Facebook and you'd like to stop by, please search for it on Facebook.

Not everyone is on Facebook. I get it, but I also have a blog if you'd like to stop by there. My blog is more of a monthly check-in as to the status of what I'm working on. Please stop by and say hello, I'd love to hear from you.

Visit www.kenlozito.com

THANK YOU FOR READING IMPULSE - FIRST COLONY - BOOK TWELVE.

If you loved this book, please consider leaving a review. Comments and reviews allow readers to discover authors, so if you want others to enjoy *Impulse* as you have, please leave a short note.

If you're looking for something else to read, consider checking out the following series by visiting:

https://kenlozito.com/federation-chronicles/

https://kenlozito.com/ascension-series/

If you would like to be notified when my next book is released please visit kenlozito.com and sign up to get a heads up.

I've created a special **Facebook Group** specifically for readers to come together and share their interests, especially regarding my books. Check it out and join the discussion by searching for **Ken Lozito's SF Worlds.**

To join the group, login to Facebook and search for **Ken Lozito's SF Worlds.** Answer two easy questions and you're in.

ABOUT THE AUTHOR

I've written multiple science fiction and fantasy series. Books have been my way to escape everyday life since I was a teenager to my current ripe old(?) age. What started out as a love of stories has turned into a full-blown passion for writing them.

Overall, I'm just a fan of really good stories regardless of genre. I love the heroic tales, redemption stories, the last stand, or just a good old fashion adventure. Those are the types of stories I like to write. Stories with rich and interesting characters and then I put them into dangerous and sometimes morally gray situations.

My ultimate intent for writing stories is to provide fun escapism for readers. I write stories that I would like to read, and I hope you enjoy them as well.

If you have questions or comments about any of my works I would love to hear from you, even if it's only to drop by to say hello at KenLozito.com

Thanks again for reading *First Colony - Impulse*

Don't be shy about emails, I love getting them, and try to respond to everyone.

Infinity's Edge

Rising Force

Ascension

Safanarion Order Series

Road to Shandara

Echoes of a Gloried Past

Amidst the Rising Shadows

Heir of Shandara

Broken Crown Series

Haven of Shadows

If you would like to be notified when my next book is released visit kenlozito.com

ALSO BY KEN LOZITO

FIRST COLONY SERIES

GENESIS

NEMESIS

LEGACY

SANCTUARY

DISCOVERY

EMERGENCE

VIGILANCE

FRACTURE

HARBINGER

INSURGENT

INVASION

IMPULSE

FEDERATION CHRONICLES

ACHERON INHERITANCE

ACHERON SALVATION

ACHERON RISING (PREQUEL NOVELLA)

ASCENSION SERIES

STAR SHROUD

STAR DIVIDE

STAR ALLIANCE

Made in the USA
Monee, IL
03 August 2021

74866258R00187